Steve Martini, a former trial attorney, has worked as a journalist and capital correspondent in the California State House in Sacramento. He has been engaged in both public and private practice of law. He lives on the US West Coast with his wife and daughter. Steve Martini is the author of the highly acclaimed thrillers *Compelling Evidence*, *The Simeon Chamber*, *Prime Witness*, *Undue Influence*, *The Judge*, *The List*, *Critical Mass* and *The Attorney*, all of which are available from Headline.

Praise for Steve Martini's electrifying bestsellers:

'Fascinating trial scenes and legal insights' *Washington Times*

'Thoroughly absorbing' *Literary Review*

'The exchanges between the opposing lawyers and their witnesses are often riveting and the eventual exposure of the guilty party comes as a genuine surprise' *Sunday Telegraph*

'A fine courtroom drama . . . with a believable plot, a sympathetic hero . . . and a little bit of downbeat humour stirred into the pot' *Irish News Belfast*

'Crisp dialogue and tart observations' *Publishers Weekly*

'A dazzling climax . . . Martini has written the courtroom novel of the year' *Kirkus Reviews*

*Also by Steve Martini*

Compelling Evidence
The Simeon Chamber
Prime Witness
Undue Influence
The Judge
The List
Critical Mass
The Attorney

# The Jury

Steve Martini

First published in Great Britain in 2001
by HEADLINE BOOK PUBLISHING

First published in paperback in 2001
by HEADLINE BOOK PUBLISHING

A HEADLINE FEATURE paperback

10 9 8 7 6 5 4 3 2 1



This is a work of fiction. The events described here are imaginary, and the characters are fictitious and not intended to represent specific living persons. Even when settings are referred to by their true names, the incidents portrayed as taking place there are entirely fictitious; the reader should not infer that the events set there ever happened.

ISBN 0 7472 6609 3

Typeset by Avon Dataset Ltd, Bidford-on-Avon, Warks

Printed and bound in Great Britain by
Mackays of Chatham plc, Chatham, Kent

HEADLINE BOOK PUBLISHING
A division of Hodder Headline
338 Euston Road
London NW1 3BH

www.headline.co.uk
www.hodderheadline.com

To Leah & Meg

# *ACKNOWLEDGMENTS*


As always I owe a debt of gratitude to the people at Penguin Putnam for their tireless efforts and patience, and in particular to Phyllis Grann, my publisher, and to Stacy Creamer, my editor, without whose help Paul Madriani would be but a fleeting image in this author's mind.

I also wish to thank Esther Newberg at ICM and the agents of that firm who have worked diligently to market my works in languages around the world. And to my lawyer Mike Rudell, without whose steady hand and careful judgment I would have lost endless nights of sleep, I owe my life for having lifted the anxieties of business from my shoulders.

Finally and most important, to my wife, Leah, and my daughter, Megan, I owe love and undying devotion for their help and support through difficult times. They have lived with the unending insecurities of a writing husband and father, and for that alone they deserve a place in heaven.

To all of these I owe a debt of gratitude.

SPM
Bellingham, WA
2001

# *PROLOGUE*

Her head rested against the concrete coving at the edge of the pool as she gazed up at the stars under a moonless sky. Her eyes were exotic brown ovals with a hint of mystery in the sculpted arch of the brows. They were always the first aspect anyone noticed when talking to her. Men seemed to get lost in them.

Her wet hair cascaded like liquid velvet and floated around her shoulders, tawny skin and slender neck. Her body had an air of athleticism that made Kalista Jordan a kind of magnet to men. Everything about her was perfectly proportioned, except perhaps her ambition.

Tall and slender, she fit the desired body style of the age. Without half trying, she paid her way through college doing inside spreads for fashion magazines. According to people at the agency, she could have had an annual seven-figure future in modeling. She had been offered some covers but passed them up, refusing to move to New York.

The arc of fame for models was too short. Kalista would rather waste her body than her brain, though she wasn't into giving up either easily. She wanted a career that would span more than a few fashion seasons and end up in a pile of used newsprint.

She finished her undergraduate degree at the University of Chicago and quit the catwalks. An African-American woman with a straight A average in engineering and science, she was heavily recruited by graduate schools. She ended up taking a full scholarship at Stanford.

It took Kalista six years, but when she was finished she held a doctorate in molecular electronics, one of only two women in the field on the West Coast. It was cutting edge, the latest science for a new millennium.

Lying in the warm waters of the hot tub, she marked the guidepost of the dark night sky – something she had learned from her mother as a child.

She located Ursa Major, the 'Big Dipper'. Then, extending her right arm to full length, Kalista formed a loose fist with the thumb and little finger pointed out, like a telephone receiver. Using this to sight, she spanned twenty-eight degrees from the tip of the thumb to the tip of the little finger, the distance from Debhe, the last star on the lip of the

Big Dipper, and found Polaris, the North Star.

She cocked her head a little for a better angle. Floating at the edge of the pool, she slowly mapped the visible Cosmos: Leo Minor and Bootes, Antares, and Scorpius. Off to the left she found Sagittarius. She averted her vision just a little, using the more sensitive cones of peripheral vision to overcome the light pollution of the San Diego skyline. She scanned the myriad beads streaming overhead, the veil of the Milky Way.

She lost it for a moment, her attention distracted, something in the bushes behind her. She sat up, turned and looked: nothing, shadows. Perhaps a bird or the wind, though the night air seemed still.

She slid back down into the water; her head against the concrete coving at the edge of the pool anchored her body. Her bottom bobbed off the underwater bench, lifted by the silky warmth of the jetted bubbles. The billion shimmering stars drifted in and out of focus as the rising plume of steam wafted above the churning pool. Slowly the tight muscles of her back relaxed, tensions born in the rancor of a hostile workplace. It was becoming more difficult to get up and go to work each day.

This evening she'd had another argument with David. This time he'd actually put his hands on her, in front of witnesses. He'd never done that before. It was a sign of his frustration. She was winning, and she knew it. She would call the lawyer and tell him in the morning. Physical touching was one of the legal litmus tests of harassment. While she was sure she was more than a match for David when it came to academic politics, the tension took its toll. The hot tub helped to ease it. Enveloped in the indolent warmth of the foaming waters, she thought about her next move.

The pool was a large, elegant affair – free-form in design. It was located at the center of the complex. Tonight it was empty. The jacuzzi was at the far end. On rowdy nights he had seen it fill with a party of a dozen, pressing flesh and skimpy bathing suits, giggling girls and single guys all looking for a good time. He had been here every night for a week and he had not seen her. Tonight he got lucky.

The only light around the pool came from underwater, dancing blue reflections on the wall of the building nearby. This was the exercise room, though at this hour it was closed, locked and dark. He had carefully checked the facility, knew the terrain and the schedules for security, the locked gates and how to get through them if he had to.

They made it easy. There was an unmanned security kiosk out front, and a rolling iron gate that was automated. Tenants opened it from their car windows with the swipe of a card key. The gate was slow to close. Two or three cars routinely passed through on a single cycle and nobody checked to see if they were all tenants.

The complex was maybe twenty years old, one- and two-bedroom condos with a few studios. There was a sales office next to the exercise room. This closed at six, on the dot. The only security was a hired company that came by and patrolled from a vehicle every three hours. He had timed them. The guard would do the rounds on the roads inside the complex, then sit in his car and smoke a cigarette in the parking lot out near the front gate. It took him between twelve and fourteen minutes to do the rounds and finish his cigarette. He operated like a night watchman, only without using a clock at checkpoints. Then the little white sedan with the blue private patrol emblem on the door would head out toward Genesee, for the next complex.

The area was condo city, graduate students and undergrads from the university, along with faculty and support staff. Some of the condos were rented, others owned outright.

The windows in most of the units at this hour were dark, though a few insomniacs quenched their need for companionship in the flickering eerie glow from television screens reflecting through closed drapes and drawn blinds.

The parking lot was quiet, and for the most part

dark, with only a couple of vapor lamps and some low-voltage garden lights to worry about.

He checked his watch. He had more than an hour before security would do its rounds again.

Alone with her thoughts, Kalista knew she was on the cusp of success. Within months if all went well she would be the director, with a twenty-million-dollar annual budget and control of all research. It was why she had sacrificed and worked so hard all those years. Her first move was to undercut his authority on part of the funding. This she had done. She then developed allies in the chancellor's office.

David lacked tact and had a tin ear when it came to academic politics. He lived in a world of his own making, and believed success should be based solely on one's merit as a scientist. He made enemies daily. In fact she wondered how he'd survived so long. All she had to do was push him into contact with other people. David did the rest, like a nuclear reaction. If anything, he'd become more volatile and careless since she'd made her first overt moves. The man had an academic death wish. Kalista could have that effect on people.

Unable to sleep, she had a knot like a goose egg high in the center of her back. Whether it was tension or anticipation she couldn't be sure. It was why people got married, for the mutual back rubs.

She considered this for a moment, then dismissed the thought. The heated waters of the pool didn't require a commitment or ask for compromises in your career.

She sat up on the bench seat and leaned forward arching her back, trying to stretch herself out. She reached behind and started to untie the top to her bikini.

There was nothing as relaxing as floating listlessly in the state of nature. She struggled with the knot for a moment, then stopped, her hands up behind her back. She heard it again, something in the bushes. It wasn't much, the faintest click, like someone winding a child's toy. Perhaps a small animal or a bird hitting the chain-link fence around the pool. It stopped.

She gave up on the knot in her bathing suit. The complex was a hive of single males, some of whom stumbled home after the bars closed. A glimpse of shoulder-length hair and a tiny pile of lycra at the edge of the pool would be like waving red underwear at a bull.

Instead she picked up her watch that lay on top of the towel at the edge of the pool. It was just after two in the morning.

She heard it again. This time there was no mistake.

* * *

The tip of the nylon cable tie was now locked in the metal teeth of the tool. The pistol grip offered control, leverage if it was needed. A narrow band of white nylon formed a loop more than a foot in diameter and was sufficiently rigid to reach out and snag something. It was designed to bundle large electrical cables and fasten them to an overhead beam or a wall. When tightened it could produce more than two hundred pounds of pressure. Once the loop was pulled closed and tightened with the long trigger grip, only a sharp knife could break it.

He looked up at her apartment window. A single dim lamp lit, probably in her bedroom, marked the unit. He knew because he'd followed her home after work on two occasions and watched from the parking lot as she entered and went up the elevator. He had waited a few seconds, and lights went on in the windows. He then counted from the end of the building, using the outside balconies to distinguish each apartment. She was five in from the end of the building.

Birds sometimes did strange things. Kalista looked out into the darkness, but couldn't see a thing. The bushes were like a jungle around the pool, knifelike long leaves and deep shadows. It was probably a sparrow in the chain-link fence. She had seen them chase insects through the diamond-shaped openings, pecking like a machine gun. The noise had that kind of metallic rhythm, very quick, and then it was over.

She looped the band of her watch around her wrist and fastened it, grabbed her towel, stood, adjusted her bathing suit, skimpy cloth bottom and knotted top, then made her way up the steps and out of the water as she dried her face and toweled her hair.

The quick evaporation from the night air chilled her so that she wrapped the large towel around her shoulders. It only reached to just above her knees, but it cut the breeze as she walked. She headed for the gate. From the inside she didn't need a key, though she would to get into the unit and her apartment. She exited the gate and closed it behind her. Then before leaving the area with its muted light, she fished for her key. She had fastened it with a safety pin to the inside of the halter top of her bathing suit just under the string that looped around her neck. Looking down she flipped the material over and found the pin, started to squeeze it with her fingers; and then she heard it, a rustling in the bushes, movement behind her. This was no bird. Whoever it was was moving quickly through the bushes, thrashing brush, coming around the outer fence to the pool, twenty yards away.

Her fingers fumbled with the pin. The key dropped. It bounced off one of the stone pavers under her feet and caromed into the ground cover around the steps. Kalista turned to look. There was no time. She remembered she had left the door to the inside stairs ajar. If no one had used it after her, she could get in without her key. She ran barefoot down the stairs, headed for the building and her apartment.

She sprinted across the parking lot and down the paved walkway, long legs like a gazelle. She prayed that she might see someone coming the other way. Anyone. But at this hour, the paths were deserted. She ran for the entrance to her building, and reached the covered alcove. She pulled on the heavy metal door with its little slit window that led to the inside stairway. It opened. Relief was palpable in her breathing. Kalista issued a huge sigh, quickly stepped inside and slammed the door closed. It locked behind her with the thud of a bank vault.

She stood inside catching her breath, leaning against the wall for what seemed like minutes, but were in fact seconds. Her heart pounded. Her wet bathing suit dripped on the concrete floor until water puddled around her feet. She turned her head to the left, hugging the wall and the edge of the door with her back, and inched toward the small wire-reinforced window. Outside she could see the path leading to the front door. There was no one on it for as far as she could see.

She stooped down and slipped under the window

coming up on the other side. Now she could see the front door, two double plate-glass doors and inside, beyond them, the elevator doors. There was no one there, and the front doors were closed, locked. Whoever it was had given up.

She caught her breath, and slowly trudged up the stairs, holding the towel around her damp body. She scaled the two flights and came out just across from the elevator doors. When she got to the intersection in the hallway she went to the right, away from her apartment. She went almost to the end of the hall, near another set of stairs, and stopped outside of a door with the numbers 312 on it. Hanging in the center of the door was a decorative flower arrangement, silk roses in a basket that hung flat against the door.

Kalista reached up under the basket and found it, an extra key to her apartment. It wasn't stamped with a number. She'd made the arrangement with a neighbor, another young woman who lived alone. They each left spare keys hidden under ornaments on the other's apartment door.

If a stranger found the key, his first instinct would be to try it in the door. It wouldn't work, and to find the right door he might have to try every one in the complex. There were more than a hundred units in this building alone.

She walked slowly down the carpeted floor,

passed the EXIT sign leading to the elevator and the stairs. The rush of adrenaline had exhausted her. Ten doors down on the left she stopped, inserted the key in the lock of the door, opened it and stepped inside.

She turned and locked the door behind her, flipping the double bolt, then allowed the beach towel to slip from her shoulders. She reached for the light switch next to the door. Her fingers never got there. Like a whisper something moved past her eyes in the darkness, and suddenly like a vise it closed around her throat. Her eyes bulging, she reached up, grasped at her throat. Whatever it was cut into her skin. She tried to scream but couldn't get a breath. Her fingers scratched at the wall. They found the light switch, and suddenly the entry glowed with light. Both hands were back to her throat, she thrashed about, tearing at her own flesh, struggling to get her fingers under whatever it was. She tried to whip her body around, but whoever it was stayed with her. With the sweep of a foot from behind, her legs went out from under her and she landed on the hard-wood floor, first on her side, then facedown. She turned her head to one side, and something cut into her throat. She could feel it as it sliced the flesh. A warm trickle ran down her neck. Her vision blurred. She lost control of her hands. No longer able to command them, she watched as the long nails of her own fingers lay listless in the widening red pool that seemed to spread from under her head across the wooden floor, the side of her face warmed by the flow.

Vague sensations moved through her body, as if it belonged to someone else. The last sharp note, metal banging on the hardwood floor, as a shiny piece of brass bounced coming from somewhere high over her. It came to rest a few inches from her nose. Each of her pupils opened like the aperture of a camera moving toward full dilation; the last image of focused memory was of her own key lying on the floor.

# CHAPTER ONE

I notice one of the jurors, a middle-aged guy, taking his time, carefully studying one of the photographs of the victim. The message from the prosecutors is clear – Kalista Jordan was an African-American beauty, a woman with a lifetime of opportunities ahead of her. But she was not just some pretty face. She was a professional woman with a Ph.D. in an exotic field of modern science.

In the photo she is smiling with two girlfriends on a sunny beach. Jordan is wearing a two-piece bathing suit, a sky-blue sarong wrapped low over curving hips, dipping into a V beneath her navel where it is tucked. A sculpted bronze thigh escapes through a slit in the sarong on the right side. Someone out of the photograph, a shadow on the sand, is taking the picture.

It is in stark contrast to the medical examiner's postmortem shots. As these make their way through the jury box, they leave a wake of increasingly nauseated expressions like a contagion spreading through the panel. Several of the jurors cast their gazes alternately between the photographs and my client, as if trying to put him in the picture.

In the autopsy photos Jordan's face is swollen almost beyond recognition. The dark purple of asphyxiation is trapped beneath the skin by the thin nylon ligature that is still buried in the flesh around her neck. What is left of the body, only the torso and head, is bloated after nearly a week in salt water. The arms and legs are gone. We could argue sharks, but the medical examiner's report is clear on that point; the victim was surgically dismembered, the legs and arms severed cleanly at the joints, '*with apparent skill and medical precision*.' The prosecutor took pains to dwell on the word *medical*.

We have argued for two days in chambers over these photographs, which should be admitted and which ones excluded. For the most part the state got what it wanted, images of enough violence to support their theory that this was a crime of rage.

Harry Hinds and I are relative newcomers to the legal scene in San Diego, though the firm of Madriani & Hinds has made a name for itself in a short period. We still hold forth in Capital City on occasion, Harry and I traveling north for a trial or a hearing. Two younger associates hold down the fort at that end while Harry and I dig to carve out a presence here. The change in scenery was occasioned by a number of factors, not the least of which was the passing of Nikki, my wife, who died four years ago of cancer.

It was that experience, a long brush with illness fearing the worst and living in its grip, that caused me to take this case, for my client is a man of science who offered help to another. It is how I got drawn into this thing.

Dr. David Crone is beefy, broad from the shoulders down, built like a retired NFL linebacker past his prime. He is a big man, only an inch or so shorter than I, and fit. At fifty-six, he does not look his age. In shirtsleeves he shows more hair on his arms and chest than the average chimpanzee. Around a pool some might ask who opened the gate and let in the gorilla. The only place devoid of hair is the tonsure at the top of his head where he is beginning to bald. His brows are heavy, and seem to be perpetually migrating to the center of his head as he studies the direction and nuance of the state's arguments. He makes copious notes at counsel table, as if this entire affair were an academic exercise on which he will be tested for a grade at the end. The softest aspect of his face is the two disarming brown eyes, deep set as they are under brows that keep moving like ledges of rock in a quake.

Evan Tannery is a career prosecutor, twenty

years with the D.A.'s office, and no man's fool. His case is made up of bits and pieces any one of which might be dismissed as mere coincidence. But taken together, they add up to trouble for Crone.

Kalista Jordan had filed a sexual harassment claim against our client. From all appearances this had nothing to do with sex and everything to do with constant friction in the office. He may have been harassing her, but it was because she was moving in on his position as Director at the center. From all indications, Kalista Jordan knew how to play the game of office politics and she played for keeps.

There were months of acrimony, arguments in the office, a few screaming matches between the two of them. Kalista had made a move on funding for some of Crone's pet projects. What is worse, she succeeded. He had made statements to other colleagues in fits of anger, all of them aimed at Jordan, none of them quite making it to the level of a death threat.

The surgical precision of her dismemberment has been trotted out. The inference is that this was done by someone with experience. Crone in his medical training had taken surgical courses. The lack of any alibi, while not pivotal, cuts both ways. The state cannot fix with precision the time of death. For that reason, we cannot provide evidence that our client was unavailable. Worse than that, he has been more than a little vague with Harry and me regarding his whereabouts on the night Jordan was last seen. And finally, there is always the clincher. In this case a damning piece of physical evidence, the nylon cable ties found in his pocket. The problem is that every day is a new surprise.

Tannery is moving at a glacial pace, leaving neither stone nor pebble unturned as he scrapes the ground pushing everything in front of him. Crone is being presented to the jury as if he were the Aristotle Onassis of genetic science. The theory is, Jordan was dazzled by his brain. A woman seduced by gray matter, the power of intellect, and a burning ambition to succeed in her career. To this end they have presented my client's world-class academic credentials as if he were an expert at his own trial.

David Crone is a research physician at the university. He heads up a team of scientists and plays a significant role in the human genome project. Some might call it science by press release. The specter of some new medical treatment and the hoopla surrounding it have become the golden pathway to public funding and private grants. Isolating a gene, and linking it to a specific disease coupled with a timely press release can produce a blip in stock values with an upward curve like

Madonna's tits, and can lead a board at a biotech firm to the euphoric equivalent of a corporate climax.

It is here on this field of play that Crone met Kalista Jordan. A recent Ph.D., she held advanced degrees in an exotic area of science I do not profess to understand, molecular electronics. Crone, like a miser guarding information in the Information Age, has grudgingly explained just bits and pieces of their work. Apparently Jordan was not his pick of candidates. She came as part of a sizeable corporate grant that allowed him to continue his work in genetics. According to him, Jordan's background made her particularly well suited to computer applications in the study of genetics. Beyond that he says nothing, claiming that patent rights and commercially protected trade secrets are at issue. According to Crone, if we press him too hard in these areas, an entire new level of litigation may spring open in our case. He warns of a wave of trade-secret and patent-infringement suits with business lawyers washing over us, companies that provided grant money and seed financing for his research, and who expect a return on their investment. To them the murder of Kalista Jordan and the fate of my client are mere incidentals to the bottom line in what is shaping up to be a genetic gold rush.

Apparently Jordan showed sufficient promise in

her field to attract the attention of several other universities and a handful of corporations, all of which were vigorously recruiting her at the time of her death. Crone attributes this largely to the combination of her minority status and the fact that she was highly qualified in her field. According to Crone, Jordan would have been a major affirmative-action catch for any of these employers. He had to stay on his toes to keep her, and particularly to keep the grant money that seemed to come with her. He was constantly granting her perks, pay increases and promotions. Crone doesn't complain, but others in the lab have told us that Jordan's demands were frequent and increasingly unreasonable.

The last witness of the day is Carol Hodges. She has begun to light a little fire around the edges of their case.

Hodges came out of the blue, a surprise I suspect that Tannery could not wait to spring for fear that sooner or later we might discover the facts from our own client. He needn't have worried.

'You knew the victim?' says Tannery.

'Yes.'

'How?'

'We roomed together for a period.'

'And you remained at the university on faculty. Is that correct?'

'A teaching assistant. Graduate fellow,' she says.

'Now I draw your attention to the evening of the third of April. This year,' he says. 'Do you recall that date?'

She nods.

'You have to speak up for the record.'

'Yes.'

'Do you remember what you were doing about six o'clock that evening?'

'Having dinner,' she says. 'In the faculty dining room at the university.'

'And did you have occasion to see the victim, Kalista Jordan, on that evening.'

'Yes.'

'What was she doing?'

'Having dinner.'

'Were you eating together?'

'No. Separate tables.'

'And what happened that evening?'

'There was an argument.'

'With who?'

'With him.' She points to our table.

'You mean the defendant, David Crone?'

'Yes.'

'Who was he arguing with?'

'Kalista.'

'Kalista Jordan?'

'Yes.'

'What was this argument about?'

'I couldn't hear,' she says.

Harry and I are clearly shaken, though we try not to show it. Harry actually manages a yawn that he covers with the back of his hand as this revelation spills out in front of the jury.

The state has managed to shield much of their testimony. There are few witness statements in their files, and most of the victim's friends have been told by the cops that they don't have to talk to us. Accordingly, they have chosen not to.

'Was this a loud argument?'

'Parts of it.'

'Who started it?'

'He did.'

'Dr. Crone?'

She nods. The witness is clearly not comfortable taking on a tenured professor, the academic pecking order being what it is, though Crone's credentials have long since been tarnished.

'Did Dr. Crone shout at her?'

'He did.'

'Did he threaten her?'

'I'm not sure what you mean.'

'Did you hear him make any threatening statements toward the victim?'

'As I said, I couldn't hear what they were saying.'

'But you did hear shouting?'

She nods. A tangle of hair droops down across her forehead, and she whips it to the side with the back of her hand. 'Yes.'

'Did he touch her?' asks Tannery. This is clearly the high point for this witness.

'Yes. He put his hands on her.'

'How?'

'He grabbed her by the arm when she tried to walk away.'

'She tried to get away from him?'

'Yes. Then he shook her.'

'At any point did the defendant, David Crone, look as if he might strike the victim?'

'Objection.'

'Goes to the witness's perceptions,' says Tannery.

'Overruled. I allow the witness to answer.'

'Yes. At one point I thought he would hit her.'

'Did he strike the victim?' Tannery is not going to leave that one for me to ask.

'No.'

'When Dr. Crone grabbed her, did the victim appear to be frightened?'

'Objection.'

'Overruled,' says the judge.

'She wasn't happy,' says the witness.

'Did she appear to be scared?'

'I would have been,' says Hodges.

'Objection – move to strike.'

Before the judge can rule, Hodges says: 'I believe she was frightened.'

The judge strikes her earlier response, but the last one works for Tannery. He has done his damage.

Within three minutes we are beyond the earshot of guards, safely ensconced in the small conference room near the holding cells, with the door closed.

'Why the hell didn't you tell us?' Harry is bearing down, red out to the tips of his ears. To Harry a client may be a lying sack of shit to the rest of the world, but he is *our* lying sack of shit – that is, until he lies to us.

'I forgot about it. I'm sorry.'

'How do you forget something like that?' Harry is looking at me for answers. 'You tell me?'

'We had a conversation,' says Crone. 'We talked. It slipped my mind.'

'You didn't tell us you saw her that night.'

'Does it matter? Is it that important?'

'Damn right,' says Harry.

'It doesn't prove I killed her.'

'No. But it does show that you lied to the police,' I say. By now I have the file open on the table in front of me, flipping through papers until I find the one I want: Crone's initial statement to the cops.

Crone hasn't thought about this until now.

'They asked you when you saw her last. You told

them you hadn't seen Jordan for at least a week prior to the time she disappeared.'

Those bushy eyebrows now migrate to the middle of his forehead in thought. He scratches his head with the eraser end of a pencil as if this were some math problem for which an equation can be worked out.

'Can't we simply tell them I made a mistake, that I forgot?'

'Convenient that you should be reminded by the testimony of their witness,' says Harry. 'That is the way lies are usually exposed in a courtroom.'

'You're saying they may not believe me.'

Harry nods and rolls his eyes as if to say, *Now he understands*.

'And you want to take the stand?' says Harry. 'In which case they're gonna make you eat your statement to the cops like it was a crow and all the feathers were attached.'

Crone actually smiles at the mental image this conjures up. There are times when he seems amused by Harry's anger and the verbal heat that drips from my colleague's tongue. I get the feeling that to Crone expressions of anger are novelties, like animals at the zoo, something with little use other than to amuse in his world of proteins, enzymes and the mathematical equations of life.

He looks at Harry as if he doesn't understand. So I explain.

'If you testify, they can use your statement in the police report to show that you were lying. A prior inconsistent statement. You did see her that night?' I ask him, simply to make sure of the point.

'Oh, yes.'

'You argued with her?'

'Well, I don't know if I would go so far . . .'

'Was it an argument or not?' Harry is tired of the hairsplitting.

'We had a discussion.'

'A loud discussion?' asks Harry.

'Perhaps.'

'Then your statement to the cops in their report is a prior inconsistent statement.'

'Is that the same as a lie?' asks Crone.

'Only in the eyes of the jury,' says Harry. Harry rolls his big brown ones toward the ceiling and turns away.

'I'm sure the two of you can deal with it. I have utmost confidence,' says Crone.

'I'm glad to hear it,' says Harry. 'Just as long as I don't have to take the needle for you, or do the time.'

Crone actually smiles at this. 'You know, Harry . . . You don't mind if I call you Harry?'

He has spent three months calling him Mr. Hinds, to Harry's continual consternation. Harry's been telling the professor from the beginning that his name is Harry, that his father was Mr. Hinds, and then only to relatives he didn't like.

'You have a very colorful manner,' says Crone. 'Very original.'

Harry shakes his head as if the man hasn't heard a word he's been saying.

'No, I mean it. *"Take the needle . . . or do the time."*' Crone repeats it using his fingers like a metronome. 'It's wonderful stuff. You could put it in a song. Gilbert and Sullivan,' he says. 'Have you ever thought about writing lyrics?'

'Only when I'm drunk,' says Harry.

'They're going to wonder where I've been when I get back to the center spouting all the wonderful new vernacular.'

'Trust me,' says Harry. 'Unless they live on Mars, they'll know where you've been.'

'You mean the TV?'

Harry nods. 'You're a celebrity. Notorious. On your way to becoming Charlie Manson, and you haven't even been convicted.' Harry turns and walks the few feet allowed to him away from the table in the small holding cell.

'Yes. I am sure,' says Crone. On the news every night, being led to and from the courtroom with a guard on each arm. It can't be a pretty picture. 'I don't watch television,' he says. 'That would be too depressing.' His manner of speech is didactic – I suspect from years spent in the academic pit, lecturing.

Harry gives me a look, the kind of expression that makes me think he suspects we might have a mental case on our hands.

'Just to keep the record straight,' says Crone, 'I wasn't lying to them. No matter what you think, Harry. I honestly forgot. It's the simple truth and that's all we can say about it.'

'It's simple, all right.' Harry isn't buying, but in the straightforward tones in which Crone delivers, the jury just might.

Crone is a bag of surprises. It is the second time our client has either forgotten details, or forgotten to tell us about them.

Kalista Jordan attempted to obtain a restraining order against Crone three months before she was killed. That she failed was not for want of effort. She claimed that he was stalking her. Crone admits that he was after her, but insists that it had nothing to do with unwarranted advances. Jordan had taken working papers from his office, and he wanted them back.

Ultimately Jordan's claim became grounds for a sexual harassment complaint that was pending when she died. The claim died with her. Since there was no investigation and no findings, Dr. Crone made the bold assumption that this was not relevant. He viewed the entire episode as personally distasteful, and since it was untrue in his eyes, he declined to inform us.

We managed to ferret out the harassment claim as part of our investigation. The fact that the jury might see this as a motive for murder still has not dented that great brain.

Crone tells us that people do not kill other human beings over such matters. The fact is, people do and have killed for much less. When we remind him that his career is at stake, he offers only a sobering nod and a grudging admission that this might be true.

I get back to the argument he had with her that evening in the faculty dining room. 'Did you put your hands on her in any way?'

'I might have touched her arm.'

'Did you grab her?' asks Harry.

'Maybe I held her arm.' This is not something coming from the deep recesses of his memory. 'She tried to walk away from me. We weren't finished talking.'

'You mean *you* weren't finished,' says Harry.

'Perhaps.'

'So she wanted to end this conversation?' I ask.

'Yes.'

'And you stopped her?'

'She refused to return the documents. The working papers I told you about.'

We're back to the mysterious working papers, documents that Crone manifestly refuses to describe in any detail, saying only that they pertained to the project on which he and Jordan were working before their falling out.

'And you wanted these papers badly enough to get physical with her?' asks Harry.

'I wasn't getting physical.'

'Show me how you grabbed her,' says Harry.

Crone gets out of the chair and Harry plays Jordan, turning his back and feigning a step as if walking away. Crone takes his arm, and Harry pulls away.

'If that's all you did, the argument would have ended pretty quickly,' says Harry.

'Maybe I was a little more forceful,' says Crone.

'Did you grab one arm or both?'

'I don't remember. It happened so quickly.'

'Did you forcibly turn her around?'

'Probably. I think I held both arms above the elbows, like this,' he says. He takes Harry at both biceps.

'Did you shake her? The witness says you shook her.'

'I don't remember that.'

'You can't remember, or it didn't happen?'

'I don't know. I don't remember it.'

'How long did this conversation last?'

'A minute, maybe two.'

'And what did you say?'

'I told her I wanted the documents back.'

'And what did she say?'

'She became abusive. She told me to screw myself.'

'In those words?'

'As I recall. Yes.'

'Did she say anything more?'

'I don't remember. It was a long time ago. I think she called me a control freak, something like that.'

'What did she mean?'

'She had a problem with authority. It was one of Kali's least endearing qualities. She wouldn't follow directions. If you disagreed with her, you became a control freak. She wanted things her way.'

'But she worked for you. You were her boss,' says Harry.

'Perhaps you should have been around to remind her of that. She was a difficult person to manage. She was often doing things you didn't know about. Things relating to work.'

'That's why you canceled her trip. The one to Geneva.'

'That's correct.'

'Still you call her Kali,' I say. 'Not Dr. Jordan, or Kalista.'

'We worked together for almost two years, on a first-name basis.'

'What did she call you?'

'I don't remember.'

'Dave?'

'No.'

'David?'

'I don't think so. She usually referred to me as Dr. Crone.'

'So why didn't you call her Dr. Jordan?' says Harry.

'Why? Is it important?'

'The D.A.'s likely to make it sound important.'

'Did you ever show any favoritism toward her over other employees?' I ask. Office jealousies could present a lot of problems for us, and add fuel to the issue of harassment.

'No. I told you, our disagreement had nothing to do with personal relations. It had to do with differences over professional matters. Matters of judgment relating to the project.'

The fact that Crone won't tell us anything more about their falling out is a continuing theme. He says it relates to the documents that Jordan took from his office, documents that Crone insists contain highly confidential information pertaining to the study they were working on. To my knowledge these documents have never been found. They were not among the items inventoried by the cops when they searched the victim's office at the center. Nor did they find the missing papers among Crone's documents when they searched.

Trying to sort out what a jury will do with all of this is like rolling dice – a kind of sidewalk crap game in which we may end up throwing snake eyes while the judge holds the stakes: Crone's life.

'During the argument in the dining room that night did you yell at Jordan? The witness says you yelled in the victim's face several times.' Harry is now leaning on the table.

'I don't know. I may have raised my voice.'

'Opera singers raise their voices,' says Harry. 'People in an argument yell. Sometimes other people hear what they say.'

'Nobody heard what was said except Kali and myself. Ms. Jordan.' He catches himself. 'Dr. Jordan, if you like.' He's now becoming self-conscious. If we put him on the stand, it's going to take a month to prep him.

'For a man who couldn't remember the event an hour ago you seem pretty sure that nobody heard you,' says Harry. 'Let me ask you, did you threaten her?'

According to the witness she could not hear what was being said, only voices raised in anger. What others might have heard we can't be sure.

'It's an important point,' I tell him. 'If you threatened her, if you said anything that could even be misconstrued as a threat, we need to know that now.'

'I didn't threaten her. I would never do that.'

The problem is that we are hearing all this for the first time from their witness. The prosecution has blindsided us with this.

Crone apologizes for what he calls an 'oversight.' He's been under a lot of stress. According to him, this explains why he can't remember every detail.

'The damage is done,' I tell him. 'But make no mistake, it is damage. Maybe it's time we talked about other matters, so that there are no more surprises.'

He looks at me quizzically.

'I know we've talked about this before. It's the question of these documents, the ones you say Jordan took from your office. I think it's time you told us what these papers were. Specifically what they deal with.'

Crone looks pained, exasperated. 'We've been over all that,' he says.

This has been taboo from the start. The specifics of his work have been placed out-of-bounds since we took the case.

'If I told you the details of what I was working on, I might as well tender my resignation from the university. They would fire me, in a minute, in a heartbeat. Even with tenure I would not survive,' he tells us. 'I'm sorry. You'll just have to trust me.'

'That's becoming difficult,' says Harry.

'If you want me to get another lawyer . . .' says Crone.

'That's not necessary.' I cut him off.

'You don't think they're gonna fire you if you're convicted of murder?' asks Harry.

'I'll have to take my chances.'

'And if we put you on the stand? What are you going to tell the prosecutor when he asks you about these papers?' I ask.

'We'll have to cross that bridge when we get to it.'

I was afraid of that.

# CHAPTER TWO

Monday, and Crone's case is off-calendar for the day. The court has scheduled downtime so that the judge can clear some other matters from his docket.

Harry is at his desk working on a motion in a civil case, trying to save a client from bankruptcy. It is a small manufacturer in San Diego, a third-generation company that employs thirty-two people. For almost fifty years Hammond Ltd. has made custom hunting rifles – elephant guns, for want of a better term. These are rare big-bore double-barreled rifles, pieces of art engraved and tooled, some of them inlaid with precious metals by skilled artisans who mastered their craft in Europe.

Hammond's cheapest rifle runs twelve grand, with models ranging up to eighty-five-thousand dollars. They are not your average Saturday-night special. Only a fool would fire one. They are collectors' pieces out of the box, works of art, fashioned to be polished and displayed in cases on a wall against a background of green felt like a finely crafted clock.

Despite this, the company has been caught up in a class-action lawsuit inspired by politicians mining for antigun votes. The high priests of polling have told them that with just a little more flailing, the hysteria among soccer moms will put women on the liberal plantation permanently. It is now easy to believe there are politicians who go to bed each night praying for just one more good school shooting to put them over the top.

Harry is no lover of guns or those who make them. He is an old-line Democrat, a believer in the working man and the underdog. He has never cared much for the tyranny of any majority, whether silent or otherwise. And when it is coupled with a scent of hypocrisy, it tends to get his attention.

He has taken a loser of a case and is now financing it out of our pocket. The price you pay for Harry as a partner is his tilting at a few windmills. It's well worth the cost.

Twenty states and an equal number of municipalities have now joined the feds in the firearms litigation. A score of small companies around the country whose guns have never been used in a crime are now being driven from business by the cost of government litigation.

He puts his pencil down. 'I think maybe I should

come with you,' he says. Harry is looking up from the pile of papers spread on the desk in front of him.

I have a meeting with the prosecutor in the Crone case. We may be in trial, but Harry smells an offer in the making.

'Even if they do make it,' I tell him, 'you'll never sell it to Crone. He won't cop a plea to anything. Besides, are you sure you can take the time?'

'I'll make the time.' He turns off the lamp on his desk and grabs his coat.

'You know he could do worse than voluntary manslaughter,' says Harry.

'Tannery wasn't saying much on the phone,' I tell him, 'only that it would be worth my while to come over and talk.' Tannery called this morning out of the blue and invited me to his office, said it would be wise if we had a conversation before things went any further. You could read anything into that. Harry is ever the optimist.

I remind him that Crone has already turned down even the hint of such a deal. And it has never been formally offered.

'That was before he saw some of the evidence play out,' says Harry.

'He didn't seem particularly rattled by Hodges and her revelations.'

'They're just getting warmed up,' says Harry. 'I can smell it. I've got a bad feeling on this one.'

'Like what?'

'Like there's a lot we haven't been told by our own client.'

Tannery had dangled a deal before the trial opened, though it was never formally offered. He hinted at a single count of voluntary manslaughter on condition that Crone could provide credible evidence that the murder was committed in sudden rage or heat of passion. He said he would have to sell it to his boss. At the time, he was not able to do that. Crone exploded when I ran even the hint of an offer by him. Harry tried a hard sell. It ended up with Crone questioning Harry's manhood and his willingness to go to trial. Since then, relations have not been smooth between the two of them.

'If they actually make the offer,' says Harry, 'I hope this time you'll lay heavy hands on him. Last time, as I recall, you did a lot of listening while I got my butt kicked around the cell.'

'I told him the risks. That he could do life if convicted. What more can I say?'

'You might remind him they don't do a lot of genetics research at the infirmary up in Folsom. Not on any life forms he'd recognize, anyway. The man may be a Phi Beta Kappa, but he's not too bright,' says Harry. 'With voluntary man, he could be out in six years, maybe less.'

'I don't think he'll budge.'

'Why not?'

'Maybe he didn't do it.'

'Then there'll be one more innocent lifer in the joint,' says Harry. 'Whether you think he did it or not, we'd be remiss not to tell him the facts. His chances in front of that jury are not good. The demographics are all wrong. We tried for college educated and missed.'

Harry is right. We have three secretaries and a receptionist, a lineman for the electric company who probably wants to know why the state's not using 'Old Sparky' to do our client. The jury foreman never finished high school and probably thinks a geneticist is somebody who performs genocide. These are people who are likely to be more confused than dazzled by Crone's credentials.

'I've looked at their faces, studied their eyes while you were cross-examining witnesses,' says Harry. 'Screw the evidence. They're ready to convict Crone based on first-degree arrogance.'

We head for the door, Harry right behind me. 'I've got a bad feeling about this one.' He says it again like he's scratching an itch he can't quite reach, not exactly sure why, but to Harry something is out of place.

It takes us twenty minutes to bounce over the bridge in my Jeep. With the window panels pulled open, the wind keeps me from hearing Harry's homilies all the way to Tannery's office near the courthouse. We park in one of the lots behind the building and enter through the courthouse. We take the escalator and cross over to the D.A.'s office on the fourth-story bridge. Tannery's office is upstairs, executive heaven where the floors are carpeted, space is abundant, and the desks and chairs are mahogany. Evan Tannery is on his way to becoming chief deputy, in charge of all felonies. He has been dubbed successor-in-waiting and groomed by Dan Edelstein, the outgoing chief who is scheduled to retire in September. For this reason, the Crone case is taking on added visibility in terms of Tannery's career, at least within the inner sanctum of the office. Everybody is watching to see if he drops the ball. Harry thinks this is why Evan may be anxious to deal on the case. Why take chances when you can get a guarantee?

We wait in the outer office, a vast reception area with two flat desks the size of aircraft carriers in opposite corners. A secretary behind each guards her boss's office door like a Roman sentry. Behind one of these, in the large corner office, sits the big kahuna, Jim Tate. Tate has been D.A. in this county since before God chiseled the Ten Commandments in stone with a hot finger and gave them to Moses. For those willing to listen, Tate will tell you that he was master of ceremonies for the event. A blustery

Irishman with a shocking bush of white hair and a ruddy complexion, Tate spends more time on his boat fishing and on the links playing golf than he does in his office. If they sublet the place, Tate would be last to notice. No one can remember the last time he tried a case. But he is a fixture among the county's political set. His name shows up at the top of everybody's list of the usual endorsers when elections roll around.

For all intents the office is run by Tate's number two, his chief deputy for the last twenty years, Daniel Edelstein. Stein, as he is called by those who know him (Edsel by those who don't like him), is a steely-eyed survivor of the bureaucracy. He is a man who doesn't say much at meetings. Instead, he watches the ebb and flow, and has a keen knack of always ending up on the winning side of any controversy. He is master of the subtle illusion of influence. Everybody in town wants his ear, even if one often senses that speaking into it has the same effect as talking to a brick. Anyone seeking success in the prosecutor's office can never stand too close to Edelstein.

At the moment, Tannery is right in his shadow. In fact, I am surprised when the two men come out of Edelstein's office together. We get the once-over from Stein, who smiles the kind of simpering grin that tells me we and our case have been the subject of recent conversation. Tannery peels off and comes our way.

'Mr. Madriani . . .'

'Make it Paul,' I tell him. 'And you know Harry Hinds.'

'Oh, sure.' They shake hands. He is a felicitous soul, particularly for a prosecutor. Tannery doesn't seem to bear grudges or take himself too seriously, a rare quality for someone in his position.

'I think it is important that we have this conversation,' he says. 'In order to clear the air, before we go too much further.'

'Trust you'll make it worth our while.' Harry's smiling, as much as to suggest that Tannery owes us something for crossing town and meeting on his turf.

The D.A. smiles but doesn't reply. We follow him out of the reception area and down the wide corridor outside, away from the bank of elevators. He stops at a set of double doors just a little way away and works a key from his pocket in a shiny lock that looks as if it's just been fitted in the door.

'One of the conference rooms,' he says. 'They put me in here until Dan, Mr. Edelstein, clears his office.'

Inside is a large conference table that Tannery has turned into a desk-cum-storage-area. On one end is his office computer, and a large desk blotter and telephone that he has commandeered from a side table against the wall. On the other is a stack of cardboard boxes, filled with mementos, files and books, stuff from his old cubicle downstairs. The conference chairs have been bunched up around the middle of the long table. Harry and I sit on this side while Tannery goes around, stepping over the telephone cord, to the far side. There's another stack of boxes, three in all, against the wall. He fishes in one of these and comes up with a black-covered three-ring binder. I recognize this as one of the state's trial binders from the case. He sits at the table opposite us and opens it and studies the contents for a moment, then raises his eyes.

'We talked about reduction of the charges some time ago.'

'Manslaughter,' says Harry. 'One count, voluntary man.'

'That's right.'

I nod but don't say anything.

'It would have been a good resolution of the case, at least I felt at the time that it might have been a fair disposition,' says Tannery.

'Our client is a hard sell,' says Harry.

'Yes. My boss is that way, too. He wasn't happy, but he allowed me to inquire. Since then, however, things may have changed.'

I can feel the breath go out of Harry.

'In what way?' I ask.

'Information that we are now investigating. Which may come to nothing, but if it pans out there will be no further offer of settlement. In fact, we may have severely undercharged the case in light of this information.'

'What kind of information?'

'We're not at liberty to disclose right now,' he says. 'Not until we've had an opportunity to check it out more thoroughly. But if it's accurate, there's a side to this case that none of us may have been aware of.'

'What are you talking about? If you have evidence, you've got to disclose,' says Harry. 'There's court policy, standing order in this county. If you have relevant information, any evidence, you have to turn it over.'

'It may not be relevant,' says Tannery. 'In which case you would accuse us of sending you off on some wild-goose chase to waste your time in the midst of trial. That's why we intend to check it out first. If there's anything to it, we'll get it to you immediately.'

'I see,' says Harry. 'Right before we open our case in chief.' Harry is afraid Tannery will blindside us just before we put on our first witness, leaving us no time to prepare.

'I'm telling you now so that this does not come as a complete surprise later.'

'Telling us what?' I ask him.

'That you should be prepared for the possibility of a new element in the case.'

'Is this further incriminating evidence?' I ask him. We are now playing lawyers' dozen.

'Could be. Goes more to the theory of the case,' says Tannery.

'It's not documents?' Harry's thinking the same thing I am. The cops have found the papers Crone claims Kalista Jordan took from his office.

'You're thinking something specific?' Tannery is now fishing.

'Is it documents?'

'No.'

I could try to get an order from the judge to compel Tannery to turn over whatever he has. It would take me a day, maybe two. By then the cops would no doubt have checked it out. If it's damaging, they will drop it on us, and the motion or the order would be moot. If whatever Tannery has doesn't pan out, the entire matter is irrelevant. Tannery would simply have made our blood pressure rise for a couple of days.

Harry will want to go back to the jail and rack Crone, to find out what it is he hasn't told us this time.

'When did you discover this information?' I ask him.

'Friday.'

'This last Friday?'

'That's right.'

'Little late in the game, isn't it?'

'We had no way of discovering this. Witness came to us. Out of the blue,' he says.

'A new witness? Someone not on your witness list?'

He nods.

'We'll probably object to your putting whoever it is on.'

'We'll have to thrash that out in court,' he says.

'How credible is this witness?'

He makes a face, shopkeeper assessing the value of goods, looking at the binder propped up against his chest so that I can't see it. 'One of the things we have to check out,' he says. 'But I will tell you that we know enough that the witness was in a position to know some of the details that have been given to us. It should not take long to obtain confirmation. I feel bad about this,' says Tannery.

'You should,' says Harry.

'No, I mean it. You guys have been straight shooters,' he says. 'I really did want to do a deal. Thought we could. I did believe that it was an impulsive act. That your guy got in over his head, lost his temper. Workplace rage,' he says. 'It does happen. I mean even with the mutilation. We don't usually make an offer in such a case. You know the public sentiment,' he says.

'That was all done after she was dead,' says Harry.

'Soon after,' says Tannery. 'We know that. All part of a single act.'

'So what are you saying?' I ask.

'What I'm saying is that if this information pans out, it could still be a crime involving a good deal of rage. But perhaps with a different motive.'

Harry and I are looking at each other, totally lost.

'What? The motive is less socially acceptable?' asks Harry.

'I think I've said all I can for the moment.'

Tannery is still studying the binder in front of him. I am wondering if he's run into some stone wall, so that he is trying to reinvent his case, coming up with a new theory as to why Crone was angry with Kalista Jordan.

'We are not prepared to wait for long,' I tell him. 'I am compelled to tell the court about our conversation here today.'

'I understand,' says Tannery. 'We've already taken steps to do that.' He opens the binder in front of him, pulls out a single sheet of paper, letter sized, and hands it to me. 'You'll be getting a copy of this in the mail for your files.'

It is a letter to the trial judge advising that the

state has exercised due diligence in discovering new evidence, that they have notified the defense of the nature, but not the details, of this information until the D.A. can assess its accuracy and relevance. Tannery has headed me off. It would be difficult to complain to the court when a disclosure has been made, even if it is only a partial one. His letter removes a lot of the wind from our sails were we to file a motion arguing that we've been sandbagged. Tannery is covering all his bases.

# CHAPTER THREE

Through years of practice in Capital City I had come to observe the disparate forms of evidence in criminal cases, everything from scholarly court lectures by experts to furtive undercover videos of politicians lapping up bribes while making crude jokes about 'servicing the people.'

As entertaining as some of these might be, they could never match the chilling content of a schooled medical examiner reciting the details of a sudden and violent death.

Max Schwimmer's speech still retains hints of an Austrian accent, a remnant of his childhood. 'Of course' comes out '*af coss.*'

He is the county's chief medical examiner, and today Tannery has him on the stand outlining the case of murder against my client.

At the heart of the case is the infamous cable tie, a thin piece of white nylon. This one was nearly forty inches long, though one end had been cut. It is ratcheted on one side by tiny teeth molded into a nylon strip. When slipped into the yoke at the other end making a loop and pulled through, these teeth make a sound like a zipper as the tie is tightened. The tie locks in place and can be moved in only one direction, to tighten it. When pulled fast, it can hold tremendous tension. Cable ties may be purchased in any hardware store and are used by everyone from electricians to bundle mazes of wire, to cops who sometimes use them as temporary handcuffs to collar rioters. In this case, a cable tie was used to strangle Kalista Jordan.

'Doctor, can you state with certainty the cause of death?'

'Asphyxia. Technically, it was mechanical asphyxia.'

'You're not saying that some machine did this?' Tannery is holding up one of the photos of the victim, her head looking like a purple blister about to burst.

'Mechanical asphyxia is a technical term. She was strangled, by the application of a ligature, in this case a nylon cable tie that was fastened and pulled tight around her throat.'

'I believe you stated earlier that the victim was rendered unconscious at some point prior to death. Do you know how long after the ligature was applied the victim would have become unconscious?'

Schwimmer thinks for a moment. 'Perhaps a minute, maybe two after the ligature was tightened. Up here. Up high,' he says. The pathologist motions with both hands, front and back around his throat. 'All movement by the victim would cease within three or four minutes.'

'So she might still be moving even though she was unconscious?'

'Some involuntary reflexes,' says the doctor.

'Would she feel pain during this period?'

'Oh, yes.'

'And how long before death took place?'

'The heart would stop beating within another five minutes.'

'So if my calculations are correct, from the time the ligature was applied to the point of death might have been anywhere from nine to eleven minutes?'

'That's right.'

'So there is nothing quick, instantaneous or particularly humane about this kind of death?'

'Absolutely not.'

'Would you call it a lingering death in that it is slow?'

'Yah. Several minutes.'

'Would you call it a painful death?' asks Tannery.

'Objection. The witness has already testified that the victim was unconscious at the time of death.'

'Your Honor, I'm talking about the period before she became completely unconscious.'

'Overruled. The witness can answer the question.' Judge Harvey Coats is himself a former prosecutor. He was elected to the bench six years ago, knocking off an incumbent appointed by the governor, who failed to heed the warnings of local law enforcement that his man did not have their blessing.

'I would say that strangulation is a painful way to die,' says Schwimmer. 'I would not choose it if I had a choice.'

'Would you call it an agonizing death, Doctor?'

'Objection.'

'I think you've made your point,' says Coats. 'Move on.'

If Tannery wanted to drive this sword in deeper he would now take out his watch, turn to the jury, stare at them, and time it. Two minutes of silence would seem like a year. Nine to eleven minutes, assuming some tepid judge would allow it, would be an eternity. I have had it done to me, and I have done it to others. Fortunately for us, Tannery doesn't think of this.

Instead he takes a different course.

'Can you describe for the jury the physical effects suffered by the victim as the cable tie was applied and tightened around her throat?'

'The tie is very strong. The one in question used here has a tensile strength of two hundred and fifty pounds.'

'What does that mean?'

'You could apply that much tension to the tie before it would fail, stretch or break. And it was thin. It produced a severe cutting edge when tightened. In this case it cut partially into the victim's jugular vein.'

'Can you be sure that the victim died of asphyxiation? Is it possible that she could have bled to death?'

What the significance of this is I am not sure, but Schwimmer quickly puts it to rest.

'Asphyxiation. Due to ligature strangulation,' he says.

'Wouldn't she tend to bleed to death if the jugular were cut?'

'If it were severed cleanly, completely, perhaps. But in this case the cable tie merely cut a deep ligature furrow that abraded a small portion of the surface of the vein. The orientation of this furrow was horizontal with just a little upward deviation at the posterior of the neck. There was some bleeding, including soft-tissue hemorrhage and abrasion, just below the ligature furrow. This groove, the ligature furrow, crosses the anterior midline of the neck, the front just below the laryngeal prominence. Here,' he says, 'around the Adam's apple. And fracture of the hyoid bone.'

'In layman's terms?' says Tannery.

'The voice box was crushed. The breathing

passage collapsed. There is no doubt. She died of asphyxia.'

'In nine to eleven minutes?' asks Tannery.

'Approximately.'

'Can you describe for the jury the physiological changes, what the victim would feel or experience as a result of asphyxiation by strangulation?'

'Yes. The pressure in the head would build as a result of constricted blood vessels, and the inability of the brain to obtain oxygen. There would be panic, a good deal of fear. The back of the tongue would be lifted and pulled into the posterior of the throat. This would block the airway. In a few seconds, the tongue would begin to swell. The head would turn a reddish purple. The lips would ultimately become cyanotic . . .'

'What does that mean?'

'They would take on a pale blue to black color. Death would result from a lack of oxygen in the tissues of the brain.'

'How can you be sure this particular case was not suicide or an accident?' asks Tannery.

Schwimmer actually smiles at this. He looks at the D.A. as if perhaps Tannery is joking. 'You mean apart from the fact that the body was dismembered after death?' asks Schwimmer.

'Yes. Apart from that. I'm talking about a possible hanging, suicide or accident as the cause of death, leaving aside what happened to the body afterward.'

Tannery is covering his bases, on the long shot that we try to defend on the theory that she killed herself, and Crone merely panicked for fear that he would be blamed, and disposed of the body.

Schwimmer considers for a moment. 'Well, the ligature marks. The bruising on the neck was not consistent with hanging, if that's what you mean. When a person hangs herself, assuming she could use this thing – this nylon cable tie – to do this you would get a V pattern of bruising on the neck.'

'A V?'

'Yes. The result of gravity on the body, pulling it downward, and sagging of the ligature. Here you have a straight line, a ligature mark – in fact, in places it is so deep as to be an incision. It takes a straight line, almost level all the way around the neck. This is consistent with asphyxia by strangulation from behind.'

'And how do you know it was from behind, Doctor?'

'Because when the body was recovered, the ligature was still tightened around the neck, embedded in the outer flesh. The yoke, where the cable tie is joined together in a continuous loop, was at the midline here.' He reaches around to the back of his neck. 'It was notched just slightly above the first cervical vertebra at the posterior midline of the neck.'

'And what did you conclude from this?'

'That the victim died as a result of a criminal agency,' says Schwimmer.

'So the jury can understand, Doctor?'

'She was killed by someone else.'

'You're saying this was a homicide? A murder? The intentional killing of another person?'

'That's correct.'

Tannery turns away from the witness for a moment as if to regroup for the next assault.

'Doctor, would you say that the physical evidence as you observed it, the way the ligature was applied, indicated that some thought and preparation had been given to this act?'

'Objection, counsel is leading.'

'Sustained. Rephrase the question,' says Coats.

Tannery does so and gets the answer he wants, that some thought and preparation went into the act. Schwimmer has brought some cable ties with him for purposes of demonstration. Tannery has him take several from a bag. One he gives to the judge, who studies it briefly and lays it on the bench. Another is delivered to our counsel table by the bailiff. Two others, with the court's approval, start filtering through the jury box.

'These are identical to the cable tie used to kill the victim, Kalista Jordan,' says Schwimmer. 'I believe they are made by the same manufacturer.

They are designed as heavy-duty cable ties, thirty-four point eight inches long, three-eighths of an inch wide, made of white industrial nylon. They have a tensile strength of two hundred and fifty pounds.'

One of the male jurors has actually snapped the open end of one of the ties into the yoke and is pulling on the closed loop as if to test its strength. It doesn't budge.

'In order to apply the tie to the victim in the manner in which I believe it was done in this case, it would be necessary first to make a loop by inserting the open end into the yoke.'

Schwimmer demonstrates. The tie is now a large white nylon loop in his hand like a buckled belt, only much thinner, with the tip sticking through the yoke like a tail a couple of inches at one end.

'Why would that be necessary?' asks Tannery.

'If the loop were not started in this fashion, and if the victim were to struggle, it would be very difficult if not impossible for the killer to insert the end into the small opening of the yoke. Like threading a needle,' he says. 'Very difficult to do if someone is jostling you, resisting. No, I believe it is clear that the cable tie was prepared in this fashion prior to the attack.'

'And this would indicate some thought and preparation by the killer?' Tannery is getting at the elements of premeditation and deliberation.

'Yes. Also there is evidence that the killer used a tensioning tool for leverage,' says Schwimmer.

'A tensioning tool?'

The coroner reaches into the bag again and comes up with a device that looks like a pistol with a long trigger. He holds it up for the jury and the judge to see, and we all examine this, though we have seen it before.

'This is specifically designed for tightening cable ties. The open end fits in here.' He feeds the open end of the tie into what would be the barrel of the gun until it hits bottom, then works the trigger. The tool grips the tie, and with each pull of the trigger more than two hundred pounds of pressure can be applied to the tie. The physics of leverage.

'Do you think the killer attached a tool like this to the tie used to kill Kalista Jordan . . .'

'Yes.'

'Let me finish the question, Doctor. Do you think the killer used a tool like this, and that he or she did this in preparation for the murder?'

'I do,' says Schwimmer. 'We found small impressions on the nylon tie used to kill the victim. These marks are consistent with a tool of this type, which is commonly used and sold with the cable ties.

'Also,' says Schwimmer, 'such a tool would give the killer great leverage. The assailant would not have to pull the thin nylon with the hands.'

'Is that important?'

'Yes. Given the pressure applied, the nylon could easily have cut the hands.'

Tannery takes all this in, nodding as he paces a few feet away from the jury box.

Now he moves toward the witness. 'Doctor, can you demonstrate how you believe the killer in this case applied the cable tie around the neck of Kalista Jordan?'

'Sure. I can do that.' Schwimmer gets up from the witness chair and comes out of the box into the well just beyond the clerk's desk. There before the judge and jury, with Tannery playing victim, the coroner approaches from behind. Deftly he slips the looped cable tie over the D.A.'s head and swiftly pulls on the gun-handled tool to tighten it just short of full tension. There is the sound of an audible zip as the nylon teeth slip through the tiny locking yoke.

'Once it is snug,' says Schwimmer, 'the killer would work the trigger on the tensioning device to tighten it. Two or three pulls would do it.'

'Thank you. I think that's enough, Doctor.' Tannery tries to remove the tie by lifting it over his head, but it has been closed too far. It is clear to me, perhaps not to the jury, that the witness and Tannery have rehearsed this. The clerk has to lend Schwimmer a pair of good-sized scissors in order to cut the loop and remove it from around Tannery's neck. The witness steps back up into the witness box and takes a seat.

The D.A. is left feeling with one hand around his throat, a not so subtle gesture for the benefit of the jury. 'All things considered, and assuming the element of surprise,' he says, 'this would be a very effective weapon, would it not, Doctor?'

'Oh, yes. And silent. It makes very little noise.'

'Once it's locked in place and tightened, it can't be removed except by cutting the nylon tie. Is that right?' As if Tannery had not just proved the point.

'Yes. That is correct.'

Tannery heads back toward his counsel table, begs the court's indulgence and looks over a few notes, flipping pages as if to find his place, then comes back toward the box.

'Let me ask you, Doctor. You had an opportunity to observe the ligature that was used in this case before it was removed from Kalista Jordan's throat. Is that correct?'

'Yes.'

'Did you remove that ligature yourself?'

'I did.'

'And where did you do this?'

'In the examination room at the coroner's office. As part of the preautopsy examination. We also took photographs at that time.'

'And as part of that examination, were you able to determine anything else regarding possible identification of the perpetrator of this crime?'

'I was able to make certain determinations.'

'For example?'

'Based on the placement of the ligature around the victim's throat, it is my opinion that the killer was left-handed.'

As he says this, Crone, who has been copiously taking notes at the table next to me, suddenly stops and lays his pen down. Unfortunately, he isn't quick enough. Several of the jurors are looking at the ballpoint pen resting on the table, angled like an arrow toward his left hand, which just laid it down.

'Can you tell the jury how you came to this conclusion?'

'Ordinarily with a garrotte, or a piece of rope, it might be difficult to tell,' says Schwimmer, 'although the dominant hand usually leaves some telltale bruising where the hands cross over. The ligature is twisted as the assailant applies pressure. But in this case it is fairly easy, and certain. The reason,' he says, 'is the design of the cable tie itself.'

He picks up a fresh one from the bag as if to emphasize.

'The assailant would insert the end of the tie into the yoke, making a loop.' Schwimmer does this with the tie.

'From the tool marks on the nylon tail it is clear that the assailant used a tensioning tool to gain leverage. This would give him a solid grip on the thin nylon. In doing this, in using the tool to pull the loop closed, it is natural that the killer would use the dominant hand to pull the handle of the tool, and the weak hand to position the loop in place at the posterior of the victim's neck. That means that when the act was completed, when the cable tie was fully tightened, the tail of the tie passing through the yoke would pass from right to left behind the victim's neck as it exited the yoke. The tail would be in the direction of the killer's dominant hand. In this case, the left hand. This was in fact what I observed before removing the cable tie from around the victim's neck.'

'Thank you, Doctor.' Tannery has some close-up photographs of this, which the witness quickly identifies. These are marked for identification and placed into evidence without objection. He then identifies the cable tie used to kill Kalista Jordan sealed in its plastic evidence bag, still coiled in its deadly loop even though cut. This, too, is lettered for identification and moved into evidence.

'Just as a point of information, Doctor, do you have any scientific basis or knowledge as to what proportion of the general population is left-handed?' asks Tannery.

'About ten percent,' says Schwimmer.

'A distinct minority,' says Tannery.

'Correct.'

I can feel Crone as he bristles at this.

'Were you able to determine anything else from your observations during or before the autopsy?'

'Yes. It was apparent that the killer was taller than the victim. I would estimate, approximately six feet in height.'

'And how did you determine this?'

'The ligature, while being applied nearly on a level, was pulled up slightly higher at the back of the neck. As I said, above the first cervical vertebra. That would indicate that as the killer applied pressure, the ligature was being pulled just slightly upward, accounting for a difference in height. I determined the assailant to be approximately six feet tall by taking the height of the victim and the slight angle of the ligature and making some calculations.'

'I see.' Tannery then takes the witness through the process of dismemberment, the fact that Kalista Jordan's arms and legs were severed neatly at the joints. Three of these were never found when her torso floated up on the beach along the strand.

'Could you tell how long she had been in the water?'

'At least three days.'

'Could sharks or other predators have accounted for the missing limbs?'

'Not unless they had medical training,' says Schwimmer. Several of the jurors laugh at the dark humor.

'Objection.'

'Sustained.'

'Could sharks have accounted for this?' Tannery holds up one of the photographs toward the jury.

'No. There were no teeth marks, no broken bones. Whoever dismembered the body after death knew what he or she was doing.'

'Is it likely that this person had medical or surgical training?'

'Objection.'

'I'm asking the witness for his expert opinion,' says Tannery.

'I'll allow it,' says the judge.

'It's possible,' says Schwimmer. 'The incisions at the joints were made by a very sharp instrument.'

'Like a scalpel?'

'Possibly.'

'Thank you, Doctor. No further questions.'

Coats looks down at me. 'Your witness, Mr. Madriani.'

The tactic here is always the same, playing the game of the possible. Securing little wedges of concession from the expert, issues on which he cannot be absolutely certain, and to maneuver for openings that can be exploited.

'Dr. Schwimmer. Am I pronouncing your name correctly?'

He nods and smiles.

'In your autopsy report you stated that the victim suffered several severe lacerations and contusions to the head.'

'That's true.'

'Were you able to determine what caused these?'

'No.'

'Do you know whether these contusions and lacerations were suffered before death or after the victim was killed?'

'No. It was not possible. The body was in the water too long.'

This was a point covered in his report. Ordinarily bleeding into the tissues surrounding a contusion or laceration might indicate that it was an injury sustained before death, before the heart stopped beating. In this case, immersion in salt water for a few days destroyed many of the forensic signs that the state might have followed.

'So it's possible that these bruises, the contusions and lacerations on Kalista Jordan's head, were inflicted before death.'

'It's possible.'

'As I recall from your report, there were three distinct contusions, one on the left side in the parietal area, and two to the back of the head near the right temporal region. Is that correct?'

'I believe so.'

'Would you care to consult your report?'

'No. That's correct.'

'Were any of these contusions, particularly the two to the back of the head, consistent with blunt-force trauma?'

He thinks for a moment, evaluates the issue, theologian splitting hairs.

'You understand what I mean by blunt-force trauma, Doctor? The application by force of a blunt instrument used to strike the head of the victim.'

'I understand.' He looks at me sternly as if I'm questioning his credentials. 'It's possible,' he says. 'She could also have fallen, striking her head. Or the injuries could have occurred after she was in the water. Wave action, being thrown into rocks. It's not possible to tell,' he says.

'But it's possible that these contusions were the result of blunt-force trauma, before the victim died, is it not?'

'Yes.'

'It's possible, is it not, that they could be the result of the assailant or assailants striking the victim, Kalista Jordan, with a blunt instrument in order to render her unconscious?'

'It's possible.'

The opening I'm looking for.

'So if one or more of these contusions to the head were the result of blunt-force trauma, isn't it possible that the victim was not only unconscious at the time of death, but that she may have been unconscious at the time the cable tie was applied over her head, or around her neck, and tightened?'

He thinks about this for a moment, and then finally says: 'I don't know.'

'Isn't it possible that blows to the head, blows sufficient to cause these contusions, could have rendered the victim unconscious, Doctor?'

The problem for Schwimmer is that he cannot know. A concussion, one sufficient to knock a person unconscious, is virtually impossible to detect, even from tissue slides of the brain following an autopsy. It is difficult to argue with what he cannot know.

He begins to nod in concession. 'It's possible,' he says.

'And if these blows did render the victim unconscious, then there would have been no struggle. No need to slip up behind the victim. No need to prepare the cable tie in advance and no need to attach the tensioning tool before the killer actually used it. Isn't that true, Doctor?'

'I suppose. If the blows, as you say, rendered her unconscious. We do not know that.'

'But we know that she suffered these contusions.'

'Yes.'

'And we know that they could have been caused, that it's possible they were caused by blunt-force trauma and that this could have occurred before death?'

'It's possible.'

I take a long breath. He has opened the door just a crack.

'Let's assume, for a moment, that the victim was knocked unconscious by blunt-force trauma before the cable tie was applied. Is it not fair then to assume that she would be lying down on the ground or the floor, or at least not standing on her own two feet, when the cable tie was applied?'

'I suppose. It's possible.' He is now slipping behind the curve in the game of possibilities.

'Possible? If she were unconscious, how could she be standing?'

'She couldn't. She would be on the ground.'

'Lying down. In fact, collapsed. Isn't that true?'

'Yes.' Schwimmer can see where I am going, but he can't avoid it.

'And if this were the case, if she were lying down, then the cable tie could easily have been placed around her neck and the end slipped into the yoke afterward?'

'I suppose.'

'And in that case the assailant would not have worried about which hand was dominant in order to pull the cable tie tight, would he?'

'Oh, I think he would still use his dominant hand.'

'Yes, but if the victim were lying down, we don't know whether the assailant was standing over her head facing her feet when he pulled the tie closed, do we?'

He sees the problem.

'In that case, the killer would be pulling the cable tie closed with his right hand in order to have the tail of the tie pass from right to left through the yoke. He could be kneeling on her shoulder, reaching across his body and pulling it like he was starting a chain saw. Isn't that a fact, Doctor?'

'Well, if the relative position of the parties is changed . . .'

'What's changed is that the victim is down and unconscious,' I tell him. 'And if that's the case, then your opinion as to the killer's dominant hand is no longer relevant, is it?'

'No. Assuming those facts.'

It wasn't hard for the cops to determine that David Crone was left-handed, and to tailor their case accordingly.

'So that we're clear, if the victim were lying down, since she could have been approached from any angle, is there any way to be certain which hand was used to tighten the cable tie?'

He thinks for a moment, looking for some way

out, then concedes the point. 'No.'

'Nor is there any way to determine the height of the assailant, is there? If the victim were on the ground.'

'No.'

'So the killer could have been a right-handed midget for all we know.'

I don't get a response from Schwimmer, at least not a verbal one.

'Not to make light of the victim and what she lost,' I say, 'but the fact is that all your testimony about the pain and suffering, the fear and agony brought out by Mr. Tannery in his direct, all that would be similarly in error if the victim had been rendered unconscious by one or more sharp blows to the head. Isn't that a fact?'

'Yes. But we don't know if she was rendered unconscious.'

'We don't know that she was not, do we?'

'No.'

'All we know is that someone killed her. We don't know how tall he or she was, or which hand he or she used.' I don't make a question of this, something he can argue with.

'That's all, Your Honor.'

# CHAPTER FOUR

She sits on her mom's lap and looks at me with big brown eyes under a mop of shaggy hair that hasn't been clipped in months. Penny Boyd doesn't like having her hair cut and, given her condition, her mother no longer makes her do things she doesn't like. Penny is nine. She will be lucky if she sees her next birthday.

I first met her with her mom and dad at a PTA function almost a year ago. Her parents, Doris and Frank Boyd, have two other children: twelve-year-old Jennifer, my daughter Sarah's best friend, and a boy, Donald, who is seven. But Doris and Frank harbor a terrible secret. The family lives under a dark cloud that Penny and her siblings still do not comprehend. I have had to keep the specifics from Sarah and develop codes when talking to other parents when she is around.

Eighteen months before I met them, Penny had a problem. The Boyds were at an amusement park.

The kids were watching the orcas do their thing, when a wave overshot the side and splashed the front rows. Children went screaming and giggling up into the stands looking for cover, all except Penny, who lay on the concrete floor in convulsions. She had suffered a seizure of some kind. Doris and Frank raced her to the hospital, where doctors conducted a series of tests and held her for observation. After no further recurrences, the doctors were at a loss. They released her, but told her parents it was possible that Penny had epilepsy. They were wrong.

Over the next few months, Penny began to show disturbing signs of withdrawal. She had always been an outgoing child with strong social skills and quick to learn. Now she began to regress, to turn inward. She stopped playing with other children and began having difficulties with her studies. Teachers identified her as having what they termed learning disabilities. The family tried a private tutor, but the problem got worse. They took her to the family doctor, a pediatrician who had cared for all three of the Boyd children since birth. He was stumped.

Penny ended up at the university medical center for a battery of tests. A specialist finally found the answer. Penny Boyd had Huntington's chorea, a hereditary disease that strikes the brain and central nervous system. In time, it results in loss of brain tissue, an inability to control muscles, and ultimately death. The only positive aspect of the disease is that it rarely strikes children. Penny was the exception.

It is likely that she might never have been diagnosed, except for the fact that recent advances in genetic medicine had resulted in a diagnostic test for Huntington's disease.

In the last year I have learned more about the genetics of Huntington's disease than I ever wanted to know. The mutation of the gene that causes the disease resides on chromosome 4. A total absence of the gene results not in Huntington's disease, but another deadly ailment, Wolf-Hirschhorn syndrome. This kills its victims at an even younger age.

Life is an alphabet soup made up of only four letters: A,C,G and T. You would think this could get boring. Instead it has led to a code of life more complex than any cipher crafted by supercomputers at the National Security Agency.

The four molecules, adenine, cytosine, guanine and thymine, produce amino acids. These in turn give rise to proteins, which lead to enzymes. The enzymes carry out the necessary functions of chemistry to sustain life on the planet.

When the intricacies of chromosome 4 were finally untangled, what scientists found was that C, A, G, three of the four letters of life, were repeated in a kind of chemical poetry on the chromosome. It is the number of repetitions in that sonata that determined the fate of Penny Boyd.

If the word *CAG* were repeated ten times or twenty times or even thirty times, she would be fine. But spin the wheel and come up thirty-nine times or more, and Nature cleans the table in life's bet – you lose.

It gets worse. In a kind of bizarre formula that is both precise and unforgiving, geneticists can now determine with near precision exactly when you will get the disease. We may now learn things we don't want to know. Get fifty repetitions and at age twenty-seven you will grow unsteady on your feet, begin to lose your intellectual abilities, be confronted by uncontrollable palsy of your limbs and slowly lose your mind. In Penny's case, she has more than seventy repetitions.

Until recently, all this, who got Huntington's disease and who escaped, had been viewed as some unfathomable mystery, an accident of fate. Now we know what causes the problem, but can't fix it. Perhaps ignorance *is* bliss.

The Boyds are now faced with the question of whether it is better to live in ignorance, or to have the other children tested. So far, they have declined to do this.

This afternoon I greet Penny with a smile and

touch her cheek. She doesn't recognize me. Sitting on her mother's lap, gangly legs, her feet dragging on the carpeted floor of the living room, she puts one finger in her mouth. A string of saliva quickly forms between finger and tongue. The girl seems mesmerized by this. She now has the mental abilities of a four-year-old, her growing body belying the regression of her brain.

I have only known Doris Boyd for about a year, and in that time she has aged a decade. A manager for a temporary personnel firm, she no longer goes to work, uncertain how much time she has left with her middle daughter, or for that matter any of her children. This is now taking a toll on her marriage.

'Is Frank home?'

She shakes her head. 'He comes home later every night. Can you blame him?'

I have come to pick up my daughter, Sarah, who is working on a school project with Jennifer, the Boyds' oldest child. We talk a little, pass the time of day, avoid the obvious, the dying child in her lap.

She asks me how the case is going. For the parents of most of Sarah's friends, what I do for a living is a novelty. The appearance of my name in the local paper on occasion in association with someone charged in a murder case has given me an unwanted notoriety. She has watched the news on TV. Doris Boyd has a personal interest in the outcome. Strangely enough, she is how I met David Crone.

'We have good days and bad days. Sort of like Penny,' I tell her. This she understands. 'Ask me in a week.'

'They don't make it look good on television,' she says.

'I've seen some of the coverage,' I tell her. I've also grown weary of seeing the same worn images in other cases, some lawyer in a crowded corridor with a microphone stuck up his nose telling the world that when the evidence comes in his client will be exonerated, acquitted. They always use the same words. 'I have every confidence.' The same tired denials broadcast to an increasingly cynical public, followed by the same shopworn analysis from media types whose idea of gathering news is to hang out on the courthouse steps with boom mikes and cameras waiting for a public confession. One day, some freaked-out lawyer will blow his fuse and tell them – 'My fucking client did it. So what?'

Fortunately for us, the judge has seen fit to bar cameras from the courtroom. Even so, the trial is a growing media circus. The press has dubbed it the 'Jigsaw Jane Trial,' a tag line placed on the case by the gallows humor of the coroner's people before they identified the victim from her body parts.

The city's leading television station, a local network affiliate, airs the same image every night, projected on a blue screen over the shoulder of their anchor: a rip-off of the fifties jacket from *Anatomy of a Murder*. This shows an anatomical stick figure with disconnected body parts with jagged cuts and splotches of blood. Give them any story and they can come up with a logo in twenty seconds.

Crone's trial leads the six-o'clock news every night unless there is a mass killing, a nuclear meltdown or some other carnage that can be quickly packaged and labeled. It invariably opens with the same words: 'And today in the Jigsaw Jane murder case of Dr. David Crone . . .' Whether he realizes it or not, and regardless of the trial's outcome, Crone will wear this scarlet letter for life. If he is convicted, he will no doubt become the Jigsaw Jane Killer.

'I suppose they have to do something to keep people watching,' says Doris. Her interest is more than casual. There are fewer than fifty cases of juvenile-onset Huntington's disease in the country. Because of that, there are no clinical tests researching cures for children. I could not believe this when they first told me. We were having coffee one night, and Frank Boyd explained the problems they were having.

They were worn to a nub, fighting with insurance

companies and creditors. Trying to pay mounting medical bills had become a battle of attrition, and they were losing. Their only real hope was to enroll Penny in new clinical trials that held the prospect, no matter how remote, of a cure. Trials were planned at the university medical center. Battles were ongoing for funding, federal and private money. But even if they got the money, these programs were not available to Penny Boyd. She didn't fit the protocol. She was too young. The studies were only taking patients between the ages of thirty-six and fifty-six.

We spend our lives pursuing aspirations, career, family, money, always postponing those silent promises to ourselves that someday we will make a difference, we will reach out and get involved, lend a hand simply because it is the right thing to do. That evening, something spurred me to action, something I do not normally do. I am not by nature altruistic, but the Boyds were drowning.

The next day I stepped into a world I didn't understand, one that was populated by physicians and laboratory technicians, most of whom turned a deaf ear if not a hardened heart as soon as they read the title on my business card: Attorney at Law. This conjured up things they did not want to think about: the perennial enemy of all in the healing arts, the bloodsucking lawyer.

They were not anxious to help, or even to talk. I got enough doors slammed in my face to become an expert on hinges and knobs. I was the pariah. I started leaving my briefcase at home, wearing polo shirts and slacks instead of a suit, just to get through the door. Several times I was mistaken for a patient, and owned up to the truth only after they produced a sharp needle and were getting ready to draw blood. I would have gone all the way, but I knew that as soon as the little glass vial turned blue, the jig would be up – lawyer's type O. I could be transfused only with the blood of a shark.

As I was being led out I always offered the same spiel, that I wasn't suing anybody, just trying to get help for a sick child, while I left claw marks on the frame of their door. This went on for weeks. It included letter writing and phone calls to state lawmakers, one of whom was an old friend, a member of the Senate Health Committee. He finally put me in touch with some hospital administrators, and after eating my way up the food chain I found myself in the office of Doctor David Crone.

I am imbued with all the law school notions about doctors. That they subscribe to a different view of social stratification than the rest of us. In their eyes they are at the top of any pecking order. Don their white smocks, and the waters must part for them. Underlying all this is the notion that since medicine is grounded on good intentions, bad results should be ignored. This starts with the scrub nurse and ends with the hospital administrator, for whom the fudging of a few medical records is considered a virtue.

In my first meeting with Crone, I sensed that he was different. He was canny in the way that most successful people are. He did not want to offend the politicians who had put me in touch with him, but wanted to ease me to the door without wasting too much of his valuable time. I sensed that he had seen enough death in his time that the passing of one more child wasn't going to keep him up at night. It wasn't that he was hard-hearted, only that he was a creature of statistics, and Penny Boyd's chances on the scale of probabilities were dismal. On that point he had me.

He was a man of research science, which meant that if the issue didn't fit into a statistical standard deviation his mind began to wander. Yes, the child was condemned to death. It happened all the time, all over the world. The fact remained that there were not enough children afflicted with Huntington's chorea to justify statistical inclusion of children in the current therapeutic studies.

As the director of clinical studies for genetic research, he'd make the call on whether Penny would be admitted. Crone explained that the protocols had already been written. These were tied to grants, private and federal money that was rigorously monitored by auditors. Then there was the question of liability. If he were to look the other way and allow Penny to slip through the gate and something went wrong, the university, and Crone himself, could be on the hook.

He was a man with a history of controversy. In the early seventies he came under fire for research that led him into the political minefield of racial genetics. He had published two scholarly papers on the subject and found himself the target of student demonstrations and stern rebukes from administrators who didn't need that kind of attention.

So when I approached him regarding Penny, Crone had a veritable bookful of arguments, none of them the kind of answers I could take back to the Boyds. Increasingly their concern was for the other two children. Though I got the sense that Frank never really accepted this, I could tell that in Doris's mind Penny was already gone. She loved the child, but was losing her, and there was nothing she could do. She saw Penny dying by the inch. Frank and Doris hoped that Penny could be admitted to the study. No matter how slim, it was her only chance. If she didn't make it, at least she was of the same genetic strain as the other two Boyd children.

Anything the researchers learned might be used to help them – that is, if they tested positive for the disease.

Crone had a zillion arguments why he shouldn't do it at all, a veritable boatload of downsides, not the least of which was the fact that it might untrack the studies that were soon to start and were already funded. It would require a major infusion of new research money. I stopped arguing. There was nothing I could say. In my own mind, I was headed for the door. I started making small talk, changing the subject, when he looked at me, smiled and said: 'You give up too easily.'

I was dumbfounded.

'Have you ever written a grant proposal?' he asked.

I said no.

'Actually, it would take an amendment. Would you like to learn?'

I smiled, almost laughed out loud, and for six weeks through the fall and early winter we spent evenings and weekends hunched over a computer in my office, typing. I was useless. Crone did it all. Dictated the language, showed me the pitfalls, and finally sent the bundle to the gods of funding in the university administration. In the end it was all for naught, but not for want of trying.

Harry and I have had our problems with Crone,

but for me it always comes back to the same issue: How do you question a man who has done this? Put his body on the blocks for a child he didn't even know. It may be stupid, but it is the reason I cannot believe he killed Kalista Jordan.

Our efforts went up in smoke. Competing applications for grant money on other research dried up the funds that might have been available for the children's portion of the Huntington's study. A few weeks later, Crone was arrested for Jordan's murder and the rest is history.

'Never thought I'd be pulling for a man accused of murder,' says Doris. Then she thinks of what she's just said to the man who is defending him.

'No offense. It's just that I've never been involved with anyone arrested before. How long could this last?'

'It could go on for weeks, perhaps months. And if he's convicted . . .'

'You don't think that'll happen?'

'I don't think he did it, but I can't predict what a jury will do.'

'Maybe he could talk to somebody at the university? Get them to take another look at the funding request?' she says.

'Unfortunately he lost whatever pull he had within the university when they arrested him.'

'Oh.' Her expression sags in a way that tells me

she has been harboring this hope for a few days.

'He's been placed on unpaid leave pending the outcome of his trial.'

Fortunately Crone is financially independent, able to pay my fees without strain. I am told he has family wealth, eastern roots. His great-grandfather was one of the railroad barons of the mid-Atlantic states. All I know is that my bill, computed on an hourly basis, is paid every month without question by an accounting firm in the Big Apple, and the checks don't bounce.

'Maybe if he was out on bail the university would see it differently?' she says.

I explain to her that the court has already denied bail. And even if they did let him out pending trial, the university would never reinstate him as project director. Not while the case is pending. Crone is charged with killing a fellow employee of the university. This has implications. A possible lawsuit for damages.

'Oh.'

I can't get into the details, but the fact that Kalista Jordan filed a sexual-harassment claim before she was killed places the employer on thin ice. Their lawyers are already conjuring thoughts of civil liability, wrongful death, with the university as a party on grounds that they permitted a hostile work environment.

This leaves only one thought in Doris's mind: that I must win the case, and do it quickly.

I'm not even sure this will change the landscape. 'You should steel yourself to the possibility that none of this may help,' I tell her. 'The funds are probably gone. The study may be too far along for them to change it at this stage.'

'I don't want to think about that.' Doris is in denial.

'We may not be able to get her in, and even if we do, effective gene therapies may be a long way off.'

'I know. But I can't think about that.'

'There's something else,' I tell her. 'The possibility that even if Dr. Crone is acquitted, the university may not reinstate him.'

This is something she hasn't considered.

'Why not? Why wouldn't they?' Her eyes are now large and round with indignation. Crone is the only person in a position to help her child, and I am now telling her that even this may be an illusion.

'Embarrassment. Public humiliation. The university may want to stay clear of the scandal even if the jury is not convinced that Crone killed the woman.' It's a fact that reasonable doubt is not the same thing as a social seal of approval. Crone is going to be carrying a lot of baggage when this is over, no matter what happens.

'So what do we do?' she says.

'We may have invested too much hope,' I tell her.

'What else can I do?' Parent hanging from a frayed thread.

I have no answer.

# CHAPTER FIVE

'He was wrong,' says Crone.

'Who?' Harry is sitting at the table, the one bolted to the floor of the small conference room near Judge Coats's courtroom.

Crone is busy readying himself for court, running a comb through long wisps of thinning dark hair so that he doesn't look like the mad professor. He peers into a stainless-steel mirror on the wall to make sure his tie is straight, this despite the fact that the ends are uneven. He is not what you would call a natty dresser. Even with these final acts of preening there is a certain professorial slouch in his stance, and a slept-in appearance to his clothing. He doesn't wear a suit. Instead he opts for the less formal appearance of a corduroy sport coat over a plaid shirt, and gray Dockers, none of which he has allowed to be pressed. It is as if seamless trousers and wrinkled cloth are a badge of academic honor, a message to the world, and the jury, that he flies by some other convention. A generation ago this might have been a problem. Today half the jury pool shows up in T-shirts and jeans and has to be scanned for weapons before they are admitted to the jury commissioner's waiting area.

'The coroner, Max Schwimmer,' says Crone. 'If he's going to testify under oath, then he should get it right. And it's not ten percent.'

'What are you talking about?' says Harry.

'The percentage of left-handed people in the population. It's more like fifteen, not ten.'

'I'll be sure and make a note,' says Harry. He gives me a look out of the corner of one eye as if to say, *That's gonna save us*. Harry has not warmed to Crone. There is something in the air between them, like ozone following lightning. Neither of them will bend to make the first gesture toward the other in order to dispel this miasma of ill will.

Crone is into the little things, meticulous about details, and religious when it comes to numbers. In Crone's eye, mathematics governs the universe. To get an equation wrong is a mortal sin.

He is a man always in charge, brimming with confidence. Except for the orange jumper, on the days we don't go to court you would swear he was running the jail. He strides the dayroom jostling and bumping shoulders with career cons whose sole concern with science is whether some street vendor stepped on their crack too many times to get high. David Crone shrinks for no one, and seems to mingle with everyone as if there is something to be learned from each new experience in life.

I have seen him in animated conversations with droopy-eyed losers, men whose arms were covered with tattooed messages punctuated by needle tracks. Crone always seems to leave them smiling. As strange as it might seem, he has found a home here. There is no family to miss, since he's never been married.

They call him the professor. 'Professor's buffin' himself up again.'

Crone does a session with the weight machine every morning, and is beginning to look fit, having lost that stodgy pudginess with which he started the trial. Jail has provided him with an element of discipline that his life lacked, and Crone, efficient in every aspect, has made the most of it.

He plays cards, mostly blackjack, with other prisoners in the dayroom each evening. I have interrupted some of these games to meet with him. They play for cigarettes, the cons' currency, even though Crone doesn't smoke. They have cheated on him, resorted to elaborate signals and even used shills on the tiers above the tables to read and telegraph his hand. Still they cannot figure out how he keeps winning, the man with the gray-celled supercomputer between his ears. They could shuffle in four more decks and it might slow his counting of the cards to light speed.

This morning Aaron Tash has accompanied Harry and me to the courthouse to talk to Crone. Tash has been trying to see him for days, but I have left strict instructions that the two are not to talk except in my presence. Tash works with Crone at the university, his number two on the genetics project until Crone was placed on leave following his arrest.

Why he continues to report to Crone, who is suspended from his job, I am not sure, but I'm not anxious to have them talking through glass at the county jail on a phone that is monitored by deputies. The possibility of Crone saying something that could be construed as incriminating is too great, particularly if the issue of Kalista Jordan's employment came up.

Tash is in his mid-forties, tall, six four, even with his knees bent and his back hunched a little, which appears to be his normal posture. He is a wiry, sinuous man, with a graying fringe of hair surrounding a bald dome. He is the antithesis of Crone: a man whose personality, if he has one, is cool and reserved to the point of being glacial.

He appears entirely committed to Crone and his cause. Still, he is a university employee, and I assume anxious to retain favor with the powers that be. For all I know, he could be eyeing Crone's job. There is no telling what he might be induced to do if the regents sensed they could be on the hook financially for Jordan's death. After all, they were on notice of her complaint for harassment.

Tash is carrying a thin leather briefcase under one arm. Whatever its contents, it took the guard less than three seconds to check and clear it on entering the jail.

This morning they don't take us into the small consultation chamber with its inch-thick acrylic partition, but into a larger meeting room with a stainless-steel table bolted to the floor and plastic garden chairs. The smaller room isn't large enough for the three of us.

Crone is not there, but I can see him through the windows down below in the dayroom, talking to some inmate, the guard waiting for them. The other man, some behemoth, has just come off the weight machine, covered with sweat and looking like some Nordic bad dream, cheekbones from a horror flick, a blond ponytail, with tattoos on both arms from the pits to the wrists. It could be worse; at least he is laughing with my client. I begin to wonder if Crone has been carrying out fiendish experiments here – Dr. Vikingstein, I presume.

He breaks it up and, followed by the guard, Crone climbs the stairs. A couple of seconds later they unlock the door for him to enter from the jail side.

As soon as he sees us all there, Crone is filled with bonhomie.

'Aaron, I see you've met Mr. Madriani, and Harry Hinds. Harry's an interesting man. Personally, I think he has a way with words.'

'Oh, really. In what way?' asks Tash.

'I think Harry should be writing lyrics for music.'

This gets a snarl from my partner.

'Oh, you've written songs?'

'No.'

'Oh.' Tash looks sorry that he asked.

Crone is looking back into the mirror at the other end of the room. I can see him laughing in the glass.

'You have to watch what you say in here, Aaron. I am told they can read lips.' He nods toward the mirror. 'How's everything at the center?'

'People are pulling for you,' says Tash. 'They know you didn't do it.'

'Gee. Maybe they should all talk to Harry.'

Crone is misjudging Harry badly. The man has a boiling point in the vicinity of liquid oxygen and can be just as explosive.

'I'm glad for the support. It means a lot to me. Please tell them that.' Perhaps Crone has a place to return to after all.

'I will.'

'But you didn't come all this way to tell me that?'

'No. You need to see these numbers,' says Tash. He gestures with a finger, tapping the briefcase under his arm.

Crone holds out a hand.

Tash pulls a letter-sized folder from the briefcase, and from this he draws a single sheet of paper. It appears to be the entire contents of the briefcase. He hands the page to Crone, and the two men study it, Tash looking over his shoulder. Little musings under their breath, nothing said outright as they pore over the page.

Why Crone was doing this, volunteering his time on a project from which he has been suspended without pay, no one could say. But I suspect it is a labor of love, and the fact that he is the ultimate optimist. In his mind at least, he is going back.

Crone traces the page with one finger, his eyes following. He is two-thirds of the way down when he backtracks to the middle. 'Here's the problem.' He looks at Tash. 'You see it?'

Tash shakes his head, and Crone smiles, still master of the universe.

'Give me your pencil,' says Crone.

Tash reaches into the inside pocket of his coat and comes out with a mechanical pencil.

Crone takes it and presses the button on the end twice with his thumb to get some fresh lead. He places the sheet of paper against the wall and starts to write. From this distance it looks like he is scrawling numbers, computing in his head faster than his hand can commit the figures to paper. He scratches over some of the printed numbers, formulas from what I can make out, then writes in the margin, making large scrawled arrows pointing back to the printed text.

'You see it?' Crone shoots a glance at Tash, who has a perplexed expression as he follows the pencil scratching on paper.

Tash's eyes suddenly light up like some kid's who's just been given an electric train set for Christmas. 'Oh. Of course.' He slaps his forehead with one hand. 'Then that means that down here we were off.' He borrows the pencil back and makes his own contribution in the margin.

'You got it,' says Crone.

'That's held us up for almost a week,' says Tash.

'Why didn't you come to me earlier?'

'Ask him.' Tash gestures toward me.

'Mr. Madriani, I thought I made it clear. You cannot interfere with my work.'

'No, what you made clear is that you won't co-operate in your own defense,' says Harry. 'In my book, that's grounds for counsel to pitch the court for an order to withdraw from the case.'

'Go ahead,' says Crone. 'I won't object.'

'Harry, please.' I give him a forced smile, a signal to back off.

'I must have access to Dr. Tash,' says Crone. 'I want you to instruct the jail personnel that he is entitled to meet with me whenever.'

'Only your lawyers meet with you whenever,' I tell him. 'Dr. Tash is a visitor. No matter what I say, he would be limited to visitors' hours. I should also remind you that he's on the state's witness list as well as our own. That creates a problem. I cannot allow you to talk out of my presence.'

'Besides,' says Harry, 'if you do, the conversations can be monitored.'

'Let them listen,' says Crone. 'They wouldn't understand a thing. I would challenge them to make heads or tails of these numbers.' He holds up the piece of paper.

'Then you wouldn't object if they copied it?' I ask.

'I certainly would.'

'That's what they may do if he comes here alone.' The fact is they could do so now. Because Tash arrived with us, Crone's lawyers, the guards in the jail have simply assumed that he is part of the defense team. We did not vouch for him. We merely told them he was with us.

'The guards may not be able to interpret those numbers, but an expert, another geneticist might,' I tell him. 'He or she might also be able to tell prosecutors whether what you're working on has any relevance to the state's case.'

This produces sobering expressions from Crone and Tash.

'Even with us here,' says Harry, 'the D.A. could always put Dr. Tash there on the stand and ask him what the two of you talked about.'

'Is that true?' Crone looks at me.

I nod.

'I could tell them anything I wanted,' says Tash. 'How would they know?'

'Then you'd be committing perjury,' says Harry.

He looks as if this wouldn't bother him much.

'Well, we'll just have to take that chance,' says Crone. 'I must have access to Dr. Tash. You have to understand, we're at a critical stage. Everything we've done for the last five years is coming to a head. You see what's happened? The delays.'

'Then counsel's going to have to be present whenever these meetings occur, and we're going to have to keep them to a minimum. I'm sorry, but that's the way it is.'

Crone looks at me, considers for a moment, then nods. 'Very well.'

'No telephone conversations. No meetings,' I tell him. 'Unless they are approved by me in advance and either Mr. Hinds or myself is present.'

Crone nods. 'Right.'

Tash doesn't. He just looks at me, steely-eyed, down his long, imperious nose, all the while showering me with his benevolent smile. He turns back to scratch a few more numbers on the sheet of paper with Crone looking on. As he writes I realize that Tash is himself part of the fifteen percent that Crone was talking about. He is writing with his left hand.

# *CHAPTER* *SIX*

Jimmy de Angelo is forty-seven, a former street cop turned detective. He has the dour expression and heavy-hooded eyes of a man whose business is death. De Angelo has spent a decade and a half working homicide, and finds refuge in physical conditioning so that the man's body does not look as if it should belong to the furrowed face and sad eyes that rest upon its shoulders.

He has the upper body of an NFL linebacker with a waist that tapers to thirty-four inches, and biceps that move like a boa constrictor under the arms of his tight sport coat.

De Angelo worked his way up to lieutenant through Vice and did undercover with the narcs before that. He has more than two hundred homicide cases under his belt, everything from winos clubbed in alleys to the abduction and murder of a local software magnate. He has held hands with snitches to get rollover benefits in murder-for-hire cases and has served on the local violent-crimes task force with state and federal agents. He has instincts and can feel his way around the hairy underbelly of crime even when it is not possible to see very well. De Angelo has driven much of the case against my client based on feelings; call it a cop's intuition.

This morning Tannery has him on the stand, fleshing out the grisly details of Kalista Jordan's murder and the discovery of body parts on the Silver Strand, the closest thing they have to the scene of the crime.

'We figure the killer used a plastic bag to dump the body, but it didn't stay together,' says de Angelo. 'Either the surf opened it up, or maybe rocks, or sharks. We can't be sure.'

'Did you find evidence that the victim's torso had been mauled by sharks?'

'No. But there were some ragged pieces of black plastic caught under a cord that was wrapped around her neck. The one used to tie the plastic around the body.'

'So that we don't confuse the jury, you're not talking about the nylon cable tie used to strangle the victim?'

'No. That was underneath the plastic we think was wrapped around the body. We believe that plastic of some kind had been tied around the body, probably to conceal it until it went into the water, and something ripped it off.'

'And all that was ever recovered was the victim's torso and head?'

'And one arm,' says de Angelo. He has an advantage over most of the other witnesses. He has a permanent seat at the prosecution counsel's table as the authorized representative of the state, and has heard all the earlier testimony to this point.

'Lieutenant de Angelo, have you ever had occasion to investigate any other homicides in which the victim has been dismembered in this way?'

'If you mean arms and legs severed, the answer is yes. If you mean cut up in the way that this victim was, the answer's no.'

'There was something unique about this case?'

'Objection. The witness is not a medical doctor.'

'But he has experience investigating similar cases,' says Tannery. 'How many cases involving dismemberment have you done, Lieutenant?' He doesn't wait for the judge to make a ruling, and Coats lets him get away with it.

'Eight.'

'In fact your department has seen enough of these kinds of cases, dismemberment and disposal in the ocean or the harbor, that they have a name for them, don't they?'

'Yeah.'

'And what is that name, Lieutenant?'

'Jigsaw Jane, or John, depending on gender,' says de Angelo. 'Usually you find heads bobbing in the water.'

One of the older guys on the jury, a retired Navy demolition expert, sniggers, and covers his mouth with his hand. His forearm under the hair is a mosaic of tattoos. The women on the panel do not smile; instead, they are looking at my client for a reaction. Crone offers none. He is busy as always taking notes.

'I believe, Mr. Tannery, that there was an objection. I'll overrule it, allow the witness to answer the question.' Coats has not even lost his place.

But de Angelo has. 'What was the question?'

'Was there something unique about the dismemberment of Kalista Jordan, say from the other cases you've seen?' asks Tannery.

'Oh, yeah. That's right. Yeah, there was.'

'And what was that?'

'Two things, really. The legs and arms were severed cleanly at the joints. And the head was still connected to the torso.'

'Let's take the legs and arms first,' says Tannery. 'Did you draw any conclusions from the manner in which these were severed?'

'We did. There was a kind of surgical nature to the dismemberment. We concluded that the person or persons who did it knew what they were doing. We believe that they probably had some special training.'

'Objection.'

'Overruled,' says Coats.

'What kind of training?' asks Tannery.

'They knew something about medical science, particularly anatomy. Might have had at least minimal experience dissecting or performing surgery on the human body.'

'Are you saying that it is likely that the perpetrator was a medical doctor?'

'It's possible,' says de Angelo.

Tannery looks toward our table and Dr. Crone, who doesn't even suspend his note-taking to lift his gaze.

'You said there was something else unusual about this case, something having to do with the victim's head?'

'Yeah. It was still attached to the body,' says de Angelo. 'We wondered why. Usually if a perpetrator goes to all the trouble to cut off arms and legs, he's . . .'

'Objection. Assumes facts not in evidence.' I'm into it before he can finish.

'Restate your answer,' says the judge.

De Angelo gives the D.A. a blank stare. He doesn't understand the problem.

'It assumes a male perpetrator,' says Tannery.

'Oh.' He thinks for a second. 'We assume they go to all that trouble, whoever it is' – he looks directly at me for emphasis – 'is gonna take the head off too. But here they don't. You have to wonder why?'

'Why would you assume they'd cut off the head?'

'Why do they go to all the trouble to cut up the body in the first place?' says de Angelo. 'Because they're trying to make it difficult to identify. You take off the hands, there's no fingerprints assuming the hands aren't found. You take off the head, it makes it that much harder. But they didn't here.'

'I see. And you don't have an answer as to why?'

De Angelo shakes his head. 'It's just unusual. Doesn't fit the normal pattern. If anything like this can be called normal,' he says. 'So we thought whoever killed Kalista Jordan was trying to do a copycat.'

'Can you explain for the jury?' asks Tannery.

De Angelo turns toward the box. 'There were two murders almost three years ago now. The bodies of two women were dumped in the harbor. We found the torsos with the heads attached. Arms and legs had been cut off. It was in all the papers. Those cases got a lot of publicity because it looked like a serial murder. Papers always pick up on that,' he says.

'Unfortunately, sometimes it becomes an invitation for somebody who's looking for an opportunity. You get a person, wants to kill his wife, or his girlfriend. He sees the article. So he tries to make it look like the same M.O. They copycat it. Usually they don't succeed.'

'And why is that?'

'Little details,' says de Angelo. 'Things we never disclose to the media. For example, in this case, the earlier jigsaws, out in the harbor. They were in fact done with saws. Bones cut right through like a butcher would do it with a saw. We found tool marks from the teeth of a saw blade. Probably a hacksaw. But that wasn't done in this case.'

'You're talking about Kalista Jordan?'

'Right. Here, the amputation of the arms and legs was done clean, at the joints. Somebody knew right where to go, and they used a sharp instrument to get all the ligaments and tendons.'

'And this clean amputation, at the joints, is what causes you to believe that the killer possibly had medical training?'

'Correct.'

'Therefore, you don't believe these earlier cases are related?' Tannery is driving a wedge, anticipating that we may try to defend using the age-old SODDI, *Some Other Dude Did It*, in this case some crazed serial killer. If we could produce an alibi for

Crone in the earlier cases, this would present complications for the state.

'No. But we think that's why the killer left the head attached. Because it was reported in the press in the earlier two cases. It was also reported that the arms and legs were not attached to the bodies, but there was no report as to how this was done. The killer screwed up,' says de Angelo. 'And it wasn't the only mistake they made.'

'What else?'

'We don't want to get into too many details. The other two murders are still open.'

'Unsolved?'

'That's right.'

'But there are other discrepancies?'

'One in particular,' says de Angelo. 'The use of cable ties around the victim's throat. It was reported in the earlier cases that the victims were strangled with a nylon ligature and that a similar nylon tie was probably used to bind the hands and feet. In those cases, we found a set of arms and hands. They floated up on the beach. These were tied together at the wrist. The item used to tie these was referred to as, and I quote, "a nylon tie," in one of the local papers. Actually it was a piece of nylon rope. The paper was using the word *tie* in the general sense,' he says. 'We didn't correct it because we didn't want to get into the details. We think that whoever killed

Kalista Jordan read that newspaper article and assumed that a nylon cable tie was used.'

'In other words, they tried to copycat and got it wrong?' says Tannery.

'That appears to be the case.'

'Let's talk about the cable tie, the one found around Dr. Jordan's neck. Did you have an opportunity to examine that cable tie?'

'I did.'

'Was it still affixed to the body when you first observed it?'

'It was.'

'Did you remove it?'

'No. The coroner, at the time of the autopsy, removed it.'

'Was there anything unique about this particular cable tie?'

'It was an industrial tie, if that's what you mean. It was heavy-duty. Used for bundling things together. Almost anything,' he says. 'Old newspapers. Stacks of rags. Industry uses them a lot. Electricians would use these particular ones for bundling heavy loads of wire before they run 'em into a chase on large jobs. As I recall, that particular tie had a high tensile strength. Two hundred or two hundred and fifty pounds.'

'I believe Dr. Schwimmer said it was two hundred and fifty pounds.'

'Then that would be right.'

'So this was not something that the average consumer could find in your ordinary hardware store. Is that what you're telling us?'

'That's right. You'd probably have to order it from an industrial supply house.'

'Do you know where this particular cable tie was purchased? The one found around the neck of Kalista Jordan?'

'No.'

'Were there any other similar cable ties found on the victim's body?'

'No.'

'Did you have occasion to find other similar cable ties during the course of your investigation in this case?'

'I did.'

'And where did you find these?'

'I found two other cable ties. The same length, and width. In fact, after examining them we determined that these two ties appeared to be identical in all respects to the cable tie found around the neck of the victim, Kalista Jordan. We found these in the pocket of a sport coat belonging to the defendant, Dr. David Crone.'

There are a few murmurs in the audience, and the judge slaps his gavel.

Tannery treks to the evidence cart and comes

back with two clear plastic bags. He has the witness identify the first one.

'Do you recognize the contents of that bag?'

'I do. It's the cable tie that was removed from around Kalista Jordan's neck during the autopsy, the ligature used to strangle her.'

'Are those your initials on the evidence bag?'

De Angelo takes a closer look. 'They are. And the date that I placed it in the bag and sealed it, at the coroner's office.'

'This second bag, I ask you to look at it. Are those your initials on the bag?'

'They are.'

'And what is in this bag, Lieutenant?'

'The cable ties that we found in the pocket of Dr. Crone's sport coat.'

'And where was that coat when you found these two ties?'

'It was hanging in a closet near the front door, the entrance to the defendant's house.'

De Angelo tells the jury about the search, that they'd turned the house upside down, found the cable ties in the pocket of what they later discovered from co-workers was Crone's favorite coat, a herringbone tweed with large patch pockets, and leather on the elbows. Tannery produces the sport coat from the evidence cart, and the witness identifies it.

'Now when you found this sport coat, which pocket were the cable ties in? You found this yourself, I take it?'

'I did. The nylon ties were in the left side pocket.'

'Did you find anything else in the coat?'

'A set of keys. To the defendant's car.'

'What else?'

'A cash register receipt.'

Tannery takes another trip to the evidence cart, fumbles with a few envelopes until he finds the one he wants, looks inside, then asks the judge if he can approach the witness.

Coats motions him on.

'Lieutenant, I would ask you to look at the receipt in this envelope and tell us whether you recognize it?'

De Angelo takes out a small white slip of paper, looks at it, then nods. 'It's the one I found in the defendant's sport coat pocket.'

'Can you tell the jury what that receipt is for?'

'It's a cash register receipt from the university dining room. U.C.,' he says. 'Dated April third for . . .'

'Stop right there. April third. Isn't that the day before Kalista Jordan disappeared?'

'That evening,' says de Angelo. 'The receipt is time-stamped at seven fifty-six P.M. We checked, and the clock in the cash register is accurate. It is maintained.'

Tannery has closed the loop, made the connection with the earlier testimony of Carol Hodges, who saw Crone arguing with the victim in the faculty dining room the night before she vanished. He has done this in a way that causes maximum damage, with a document that puts Crone there, date and time-stamped, sharing the same garment with the incriminating cable ties.

Several jurors are taking notes. Like a dazing blow to the chin, Tannery has scored points and he knows it. He takes his time, allowing the testimony to settle in for full effect.

'Now when you searched the defendant's house, did you find anything else?'

'We did. We found a tensioning tool.'

Tannery retreats to the evidence cart once more, and when he returns to the witness stand he is holding a metal tool. It looks like a large pistol with a long triggerlike grip in front of the handle. There is an evidence tag wired to it.

'Do you recognize this item, Lieutenant?'

De Angelo takes it, looks at the evidence tag. 'That's the tensioning tool we found in the defendant's garage.'

'Do you know what it's used for?'

'Yes. For tightening cable ties.'

'Like the ones in these evidence bags?'

'That's right.'

'Where exactly did you find this particular tensioning tool?'

'It was underneath a workbench in the garage, covered up with a small piece of carpet.'

'Did you have an opportunity to test this particular tool to determine whether it worked properly?'

'I did.'

'And did it work?'

'It did. We tested it in the crime lab. Using cable ties similar to those in the evidence bag, we determined that it was possible to achieve tension at over two hundred pounds per square inch using the tool.'

Now Tannery has the tool, the cable ties and Crone's sport coat marked for identification and moves that they be admitted into evidence. We don't object.

'How many cases of homicide by strangulation have you investigated in your career?' asks Tannery.

'A good number.'

'More than twenty?'

'Oh yes.'

'More than fifty?'

'Maybe fifty.'

'So you have some experience.'

'Yes.'

'In your professional opinion, would the tension applied by that tool, the tensioning tool in evidence, be sufficient to strangle a person to death?'

'Easily,' says de Angelo.

'Would it be enough to account for a deep ligature furrow of the kind found around the neck of Kalista Jordan?'

'I would say so. Yes.'

Tannery nods to himself as he paces a little, between his counsel table and a rostrum set up in front of the bench where his notes are.

'Your witness,' says Tannery.

Here the game is to whittle away at the edges. I start with de Angelo's credentials as an expert.

'Lieutenant, you say you've investigated perhaps as many as fifty homicide cases involving strangulation. Is that right?'

'Yes.'

'Not all of those were murder, though, were they?'

'What do you mean?'

'I mean a good number of them were suicides?'

'Oh.' He thinks about this for a moment. 'I suppose.'

'Have you ever investigated a case of murder in which the weapon was a nylon cable tie?'

'No. Not to my recollection.'

'So, in fact, this is the first time you've ever seen a case exactly like this?'

'Every case is different,' he says.

'Still, you never investigated a case involving strangulation with a cable tie. Isn't that right?'

'Yeah. Right.'

'Yet you're willing to assume that a tensioning tool was used in this case?'

'Something was used to gain leverage,' says de Angelo. 'The killer didn't tighten that cable tie with his hands alone. Too much tension,' he says.

'Yes, but does that mean he used a tensioning tool?'

'It seems a likely possibility to me,' he says.

'But that's all it is, a possibility.'

He doesn't respond.

'Let me ask you, Lieutenant, do you know for a fact that a tensioning tool was used to tighten the cable tie around the neck of Kalista Jordan?'

'Like I said, it's likely . . .'

'I didn't ask you what was likely. I asked you whether you knew for a fact whether such a tool was used.'

'No.'

'So it is only surmise, an assumption on your part, the part of your investigating team, that such a tool was even used in this case?'

'Something was used to gain leverage. It seems natural that it would have been a tool designed for that purpose.'

'Isn't it possible that the loose end of the cable tie could have been wrapped around a stick, a piece of wood, maybe a short metal rod, and that this could have been used as a handle to gain leverage?'

'It'd be awkward,' says de Angelo.

'Still, it's possible, isn't it?'

'It's possible. Anything's possible.' It is all the concession I need.

'So as you sit here today, you don't know with certainty whether that tool, the one in evidence, or for that matter any tensioning tool was used in this case, do you?'

'There's not much in life that any of us know with absolute certainty,' he says.

'That's not an answer to my question. Do you know with certainty whether that tool or any similar tool was used to kill Kalista Jordan?'

'No.'

Harry and I could have objected to this evidence, the tensioning tool, at the preliminary hearing before the trial, where Crone was bound over. We didn't. It was a tactical decision. Now the state has relied on a piece of evidence that they cannot tie to the crime. Nor can they prove that a similar device was used. Voids like this can be filled later with reasonable doubt during our closing argument.

'You testified earlier that this particular cable tie, the one taken from around the neck of the victim, is unusual, that you wouldn't expect to find it in your local hardware store. Is that right?'

'I think I said it was heavy-duty,' says de Angelo.

'Would you like me to have the record read back?' I ask him.

'I may have said it would be difficult to find.'

'In fact you stated that you couldn't expect to find it in your ordinary hardware store, that you'd probably have to order it from an industrial supply house. Your words.' I'm reading from a legal notepad. 'Isn't that what you said?'

'I think so.'

'Are you telling us that cable ties of the kind used to kill Kalista Jordan are rare?'

'I don't know how you define "rare," ' he says. 'It's not as common as lighter-weight cable ties,' he says.

'Would it surprise you if I told you I managed to purchase two dozen cable ties just like that one' – I point to the murder tie in the bag – 'at five different stores right here in the San Diego area?' As I ask this, I am pointing to a large paper bag that Harry has picked up and placed in the center of our counsel table.

'Objection,' says Tannery. 'Assumes facts not in evidence. Counsel's trying to testify.'

'I only asked him whether he would be surprised.'

'I'll allow the question,' says Coats.

'I don't know.'

'Well, during the course of your investigation didn't you check the local stores to determine whether this type of cable tie was readily available in the area?'

'We looked.'

'How many stores did you check?'

'I can't remember.'

'Isn't it a fact, Lieutenant, that you don't know how many of these cable ties are sold in this area in a given week, or a month, or a year?'

De Angelo doesn't respond.

'Objection. Compound question,' says Tannery. 'Over what time frame?'

'Fine, let's start with a week. Do you know how many cable ties like this are sold in this area in a week?'

'No.'

'Do you want to try monthly?' I ask.

I can tell by the look on his face that he doesn't. So can the jury, several of whom are still looking at the bag on the counsel table.

'Do you know whether you might have a few cable ties like this one in your basement at home, Lieutenant?'

He doesn't answer, but looks at me with a death wish.

'So you can't tell us how rare they are?'

'I never said they were rare. That's your word.'

'Fine.' I leave it alone. The cable ties aren't rare. 'Do you have any idea what these ties are used for? I mean besides strangling people.'

'Industrial uses.'

'For example?'

'Electrical wiring. To bundle up large groups of wires.'

'And?'

'I don't know. Whatever you need 'em for.'

'Do police ever use cable ties like these?'

He makes a face, thinks about it. 'Sure. They might.'

'What for?'

'Crowd control. In lieu of handcuffs. Sometimes it's necessary to use ties like that.'

'The same kind?'

'Probably lighter weight. They wouldn't be that strong.'

'Fine. So there's a lot of reasons people might keep cable ties on hand that have nothing to do with murder?'

'I suppose.'

'And also the tools to tighten them?'

'Yeah.'

'I mean, isn't it possible that a homeowner might keep ties like this, and a tensioning tool like that one in front of you, at home to tie up old newspapers, or bundle up trash, or to gather branches after pruning a tree?'

'I suppose.'

'I mean, are we all to assume that everybody who purchases cable ties intends to use them to strangle somebody?'

There is actually some giggling in the jury box with this question.

De Angelo doesn't respond.

'Maybe we should license them like firearms,' I say.

'Objection.' Tannery's on his feet.

'Sustained. Mr. Madriani.'

'Sorry, Your Honor.

'Then it's entirely possible that Dr. Crone had the tensioning tool in his house and the ties in his pocket for just such a legitimate purpose? To tie up newspapers, or bundle trash?'

'If you say so.'

'I'm asking you.'

'I suppose.'

'That's all.'

'Redirect,' says the judge.

Tannery is on his feet before I can get out of the way. I seem to have provoked some ire. If he has a weakness, it is a fuse that is a little short for the courtroom.

'Lieutenant, can you tell the jury when you found the cable ties in the pocket of the sport coat belonging to the defendant? The precise date?' he says.

'It was April tenth.' This is on the tip of de Angelo's tongue.

'That was two days after the victim's body was found on the beach. Is that correct?'

'That's right.'

'And the tensioning tool that you found in the defendant's garage. Was it in plain view?'

'No.'

'I mean, was it hanging on a hook over the workbench with the other tools?'

'No. It wasn't.'

'Did it appear to you that this tool was being concealed, hidden from view?'

'Objection.'

'Overruled,' says Coats.

'It did. It looked like somebody had pushed the tool to the back of the shelf under the workbench, and placed this piece of carpet over the top of it so you couldn't see it.'

This begs the question why someone who has used a tool and cable ties to commit a cold, calculated murder would keep such evidence in his garage and the pocket of his favorite sport coat in the closet. But these are questions better posed to the jury in our closing than to de Angelo on the stand, who no doubt would lecture me on the stupid things that perpetrators do, even perps who are highly educated.

# CHAPTER SEVEN

William Epperson is the mystery man in our case. Tonight Harry and I are pondering our notes on this particular enigma. Everything we know about the man is spread out on a dimly lit table in the lounge of the Brigantine. This has become our after-hours conference room, a short walk from the office, down the jungle path.

It is after ten, and the dinner crowd has long since departed. Harry is nursing a Scotch and soda. I am doing soda straight up, avoiding a buzz in the morning when I have to be in court. The era of the hard-drinking trial lawyer is in decline. An older generation, with blown kidneys and liver failure, has imparted its message. The final nail was pounded into that particular coffin by the state bar that now appoints guardians to take over the practice of anybody who comes to court glassy-eyed, with an odor of alcohol on his breath. So I walk the straight and narrow for my own sake as well as for

Sarah's. You think about things when you're a single parent.

'So when do you think they'll put him up?' says Harry. He's talking about Epperson on the stand.

'Not yet. It's too early.'

We know almost nothing about him, so we have some ground to make up.

'According to the bits and pieces,' says Harry, 'he's the closest thing Kalista Jordan had to a friend in the lab. Stood by her during her travails with Crone, at least according to the others. And, besides the killer, he was one of the last people to see her alive.'

This gets my attention. I look at him.

'The argument that night in the faculty dining room, Jordan and Crone,' he says.

'Did Epperson weigh in?'

'Not exactly, though according to one version he put himself between the two of them for a moment and tried to get her to leave. One thing's for sure,' says Harry. 'He's the closest thing to a witness as to what was said.'

'And he won't talk to us?'

Harry shakes his head. Usual criminal process does not permit us to depose him, to take a statement under penalty of perjury outside of the courtroom.

'What do we know about him?'

'Not a lot. He doesn't seem to cultivate people at work. Except for Jordan, that is.'

'Was that platonic?' I ask him.

Harry gives me a 'Who knows?' 'They coulda been hitting the sheets. But if so, neither of 'em kissed and talked. I couldn't get any of the other people at the lab to even speculate. When I asked, it was like I was spreading bad rumors.

'Nobody seems to know him that well. An enigma,' says Harry. 'According to the lab techs, he was a big question mark at work. Didn't say much. Kept to himself.' Harry's reading from notes now.

'Did Crone hire him?'

'That's not exactly clear,' says Harry. 'Some in the lab think that it may have been Jordan herself who brought him in.'

What is troubling here is that there are no statements to the cops as to what Epperson may have told them. At least nothing they've disclosed. Which means they debriefed him verbally and kept it to themselves. There is no doubt a reason for this.

Harry has tried twice to talk to Epperson, and twice has gotten the door slammed in his face.

Harry looks through his notes, takes a sip of Scotch. 'Twenty-eight years old. He appears to have yanked real hard on his bootstraps to get out of Detroit. Went to inner-city schools, never got in any trouble. Seems to have been able to jump well,' says Harry.

I look at him, puzzled.

'Full scholarship to Stanford to play basketball,' says Harry. 'According to the press reports, the kid was a high-school prodigy. Lew Alcindor on his way to becoming Kareem Abdul-Jabar.'

'Really?'

'At seven foot six, it's either that or get a job changing bulbs on streetlamps. Unfortunately for him, the basketball thing didn't work out.'

'Why not?'

Harry reading from his notes: 'They call it cardiac arrhythmia. Real common, I guess, in the very tall. According to the stories, they're doing some studies on it, particularly African-Americans over six feet. Enlarged hearts,' he says. 'Epperson has a bum ticker. He couldn't fulfill the terms of the scholarship, so they cut him loose. But that wasn't the end of it. Seems the kid's pretty resilient and very bright. He didn't get the athletic thing, but they ended up awarding him an academic scholarship, and it wasn't for P.E. or communications,' says Harry.

'What?'

'Math and science. Crushes every myth,' says Harry. 'Kid goes to an inner-city school where he's gotta dodge gunfights in the halls and find an outhouse cuz the urinals are all cracked, and he still gets straight As. He does it again at Stanford. Straight As for four years in the engineering department. Graduates near the top of his class, and nearly gets trampled in the recruiting stampede that follows. Every company on the Fortune Five Hundred and a dozen universities all bidding for his services. One thing's real clear.' Harry takes a sip of Scotch. 'The kid's not going back to Detroit.'

He flips a few pages, finds his place. 'After that, Epperson spends a year working for this corporation. Place called . . . Cyber – genom, genam, genomics.' He looks at me.

I shrug.

'According to what I could find out, they're not on the Internet. At least Cybergenomics Incorporated is not. Gotta be some high-tech thing with a name like that. Anyway, a year later Epperson ends up going to work for Crone at the lab. That's it as far as his resume goes.'

'Is there any indication that he might have known Jordan before he went to work there?'

'Get to that in a minute,' says Harry. 'What's interesting is that I asked Crone that very question. He told me he didn't think so. What's more, neither Epperson nor Jordan has a background in medicine, life sciences or genetics, and yet they're working at this genetics lab. She's into this thing called molecular electronics. His specialty is nanorobotics.'

'What's that?'

'Field of engineering,' says Harry. 'Involves small robots. We're talking microscopic here. Riverdancers doing their fling on the head of a pin.'

'What are these robots used for?'

'Got me. I'm told one application could be medicine.'

'Well, there you go. There's the link,' I say.

'Right.'

'And what does Crone say?'

'What he always says. Fell back on the old "*My lips are sealed*" crap. Like the highest calling of the scientist is to keep his mouth shut. They ought to put this asshole in charge of Los Alamos. He gets my vote. With a client like Crone, who needs a prosecutor? He'll screw himself to the wall before he's finished, and us too. He's already doing a good job of it.' Harry on a roll.

'What are the other people at the lab saying?'

'The same sorry mantra. Almost makes you think somebody got to them,' he says.

'Does, doesn't it?'

'The only thing they would say was in reference to some old sci-fi flick, *Fantastic Voyage*. Ever see it?'

I shake my head. 'Must have missed that one.'

'They shoot this miniature submarine up some guy's nose or something. Inject it through a needle. Inside are people all shrunk down,' says Harry.

'I knew I missed it for a reason.'

'Anyway the plotline . . .' Harry ignores me. 'They're going on a voyage through this guy's body to cure some disease or other. If I could remember what he was dying of, I could replace Siskel and Ebert.'

'Siskel's dead,' I tell him.

'Yeah, well, this tiny sub. It seems we're there.'

'What do you mean?'

'I mean this nanorobotics shit.'

'Shrinking people?'

'No. I don't think so. Just the submarine,' says Harry.

'Really?'

'I don't know. Hell. They would talk and look over their shoulders. A couple of the lab techs. Probably laughing their asses off after I left. I had to pick my time carefully, when the guy Tash wasn't around.'

'Were they afraid of him? These lab techs?'

'I don't know if *afraid* is the word. But he has a certain chilling effect on conversation,' says Harry. 'It's like all these people took a vow of silence. And when Tash is around, you can't even get 'em to do sign language.

'People I talked to were lab assistants. I got one of 'em to go on coffee break with me. Guy said he was speaking only in general terms. And if anybody asked, he wasn't speaking at all. All he would say about this nanorobotics was a reference to this movie.'

'Tiny submarines?'

'That's the one. On a crash dive through some sorry guy's bowels. I don't wanna even know where they come out. I'm feeling like I've already been on that trip with Crone. When I pressed each of the lab techs, they all ended up singing the same old chorus. Trade secrets, in four-part harmony,' says Harry.

'Well at least he's telling us something that's true.' I'm talking about Crone.

'Only if you want to take the time to pick through the lies,' says Harry.

'What do you mean?'

'Remember I told you that I asked Crone whether Jordan and Epperson knew each other before Epperson came to the lab? He told me he didn't think so?'

I nod.

'I wouldn't take it to the bank,' says Harry. 'This company, Cybergenomics. The one Epperson worked for before he joined the lab. I come to find out they're one of the companies underwriting Crone's work at the lab.'

'Really?'

'Corporate grant,' says Harry. 'A big one. And there's more. This same company made a job offer to Jordan about a month before she was killed.'

My eyebrows arch.

'Word around the lab was that it was a point of friction between her and Crone. The offer was for big bucks. I don't know the details. We're looking for documents. I've got a subpoena out to the company to get what I can. According to one of the lab techs, Jordan was letting it be known that they'd offered her multiple six figures to jump from the lab and come on board with the company.'

'Maybe they made overtures to Crone as well?'

'That was the problem. They didn't.'

Pieces are starting to snap into place.

'If we know about this, you can be sure Tannery knows as well.'

'You think he's plying this road, job jealousy?' asks Harry.

'You heard what he told us when we visited him at his office. They were checking out some other angle as to motive.'

'You think that's it? The job offer to Jordan?'

'That, and perhaps she was taking some items of value with her.'

'Like what?'

'Like the papers Crone says she stole, and the grant money that Cybergenomics was pouring into Crone's center.'

'Holy shit,' says Harry. 'You think so?'

'Think about it. She takes working papers from

his office. He goes ballistic. She does everything to get him off her back. She doesn't need him anymore. She knows what he knows about the project. If she goes to work for Cybergenomics, why would they pay twice for the same research? His funds are going to dry up overnight.'

'There's a motive for murder,' says Harry.

I nod.

'You think Tannery knows what's in those papers?'

'I know one thing. We don't.'

'Maybe it's just what Crone's been saying all along,' says Harry. 'Maybe they did have professional differences.'

'Where does Epperson fit into all this?'

'I was getting to that,' says Harry. 'It's only surmise, and it only comes from one of the assistants, the guy I talked to over coffee. But according to him, Epperson may have joined Crone's group as part of a package along with the Cybergenomics grant. Nobody seems to know for sure, but he came on board about the same time.'

'A consultant?'

'Not that I can tell. He seems to have been a salaried employee of the university from the time he went to work there. More like a corporate mole, if the guy I talked to is right.'

'Do we know Epperson's salary, at the U?'

Harry looks up from his papers, quickly getting

to the same place I am. 'If he took a big cut in pay to go to the university, you think there might be a reason?'

'Possibly. Maybe stock options. If Crone's team is developing something hot, and this company, Cybergenomics, has a vested interest, they might send Epperson over to mind the store. To make sure that the research takes the right direction.'

'And make sure nobody else horns in,' says Harry.

'If he was their man in Crone's shop, stock options would ease a cut in pay, and ensure his loyalty.'

Harry mulls this over. 'Interesting you should say that.'

'Why?'

'Epperson has this passion. The only thing anybody seems to know about him. He has an addiction.'

'What's that?'

'Stays up nights researching. Comes to work bleary-eyed and takes frequent breaks to get to his laptop. Seems he lives to trade on line.'

Saturday morning and it's bright and sunny. I can think of a thousand places I would rather be. Instead, Harry and I are planted next to a musty set of code books in our library at the office. We are here to meet with Robert Tucci, who has flown in from San Jose up in Silicon Valley for a conference.

For months Tucci has been just a voice on the

phone. Today for the first time, I have the benefit of seeing a face as we speak, judging what kind of a witness he might make if I have to use him at trial.

He is bald. A ragged fringe of black hair droops over his ears. Tucci has the look of some seventeenth-century notable, short and fat with chubby little fingers. There is a shadow of dark beard submerged just beneath the surface of his face that gives it the kind of bluish pallor you would expect to see on some ancient oil portrait hanging in a European gallery. This is appropriate, for some consider Tucci to be the Galileo of modern electronics.

He is seated in a chair across the library table from me with shelves of legal volumes behind him finishing off the backdrop so that I can imagine this painting come to life as he speaks.

I have hired him to lead us through the no-man's-land of science, the maze of molecular electronics, genetics and nanorobotics that Crone and Tash will not discuss.

Harry asks him if he's ever written about the specific fields we are dealing with.

'Not for publication,' says Tucci. 'I've prepared some memoranda for internal use by R. and D. units inside corporations. But that's another matter,' he says.

Tucci is one of the leading lights in the field of

high tech, a writer and theorist who is reputed to have had a major hand in the development of the silicon chip. He's been published in every major professional journal in the country and holds dual doctorates in physics and biology. Best of all, he has written a number of articles in the general press for the unwashed masses in major national magazines and newspapers. He is possessed of that special gift for explaining things scientific to people like Harry and me, who are still grappling with the magic of fire.

'This memorandum you've written, research and development for the corporations,' says Harry, 'would any of it be helpful for our purposes here?'

'It might. But I couldn't give it to you. It's proprietary information.' What he means is another corporate stonewall, trade secrets. This seems to be an article of faith within the field, making me wonder if these guys sleep with computer disks between their knees at night protecting this stuff.

'Been there,' says Harry.

Harry has spent two weeks scoping out the Internet and ravaging university libraries for anything, scholarly articles or news pieces, that might offer a clue as to what Crone and his compatriots are working on. He has found nothing.

Tucci tells us that we're not likely to. 'The science is cutting edge. You won't hear about it in the popular press until there's a major breakthrough. By then, the company that controls the process will be throwing patent parties. They'll have it locked up.'

'What exactly is the process?' I ask.

'A major scientific merger,' he says. 'A kind of synergy.'

'Of what?' says Harry.

'On the scientific level you've got nanotechnology and molecular electronics, with genetics being the software used to program the whole thing.

'At the commercial level you're talking "pick and shovel" companies, the genetic start-ups that sell devices for generating genetic data. Software companies that specialize in peddling vast amounts of data involving genetic information to the drug companies. And finally you have the giant pharmaceutical companies trying to cash in on new modalities of treating diseases. It's what some are calling the genetic gold rush. And there are, conservatively speaking,' says Tucci, 'hundreds of billions of dollars at stake.'

This catches Harry's attention as I can see his eyes light up. He's wondering how he can invest.

'It all started with gene sequencing, mapping the human gene. The genome project?' He looks at us as if perhaps we haven't heard of this.

'They've mapped it. They're working out the fine

wrinkles as we speak. The question now is how to use it. Which genes on which chromosomes cause breast cancer, or lupus.'

'Or Huntington's chorea,' I say.

'Precisely,' says Tucci.

'The theory, and it's more than that now,' says Tucci, 'is that electronics can play a part in this. It has been proved that electronic circuitry can be taken down to the molecular level, submicroscopic electronic circuits that can be introduced into living organisms. A kind of cellular computer chip. It's believed that this is one way to code and carry genetic information.'

'Molecular electronics,' says Harry.

Tucci points at him with a finger as if to say he's got it.

'Nanorobotics is the other leg. Microscopic robots that can be constructed to carry the newly programmed circuitry inside the organism. This would be the delivery system,' says Tucci. 'Instead of injecting a drug and waiting for it to course its way through the bloodstream or to be absorbed into the tissue, you can insert programmed robotics on a microscopic level that will deliver the preprogrammed genetic information to a precise location, perhaps an organ system, or an isolated tumor in the body, and deal with it at a genetic level. You can turn chemical switches on and off, enzymes that will allow the human immune system to combat disease. To treat conditions that today are terminal, and to reverse them.'

'They think that's possible?'

Tucci looks at him, and nods soberly. 'It's only a theory, but the science to accomplish it exists.'

'A magic bullet,' I say.

'Right. It has all kinds of implications,' he says, 'for good and evil. There are the usual ethical concerns that follow all genetic research. You're dealing with the basic building blocks of life. There's the concern that perhaps we're tapping the fountain of youth.'

Harry looks at him quizzically.

'Issues of overpopulation,' says Tucci. 'If in fact we cure major maladies and suddenly life expectancy doubles. What do we do with all the people? How do we feed them? Who gets the new treatments and who doesn't? Who is given the keys to extended life and who dies? Those are major issues.

'But here there's one more element of concern that may outweigh all of these. We are talking about the creation of an engineered life form, an organism unto itself. It could have the ability to propagate, to regenerate itself. A virus, for example, coded in a genetic string and carried by molecular electronics and nanotechnology, could reproduce itself inside the body. In fact that would be part of the design, in order to enhance treatment. But what if its design were to be a weapon instead of a cure. It could be the ultimate doomsday device. Microscopic nanorobotics, engineered to carry a virus capable of replicating billions of times over a short span of time and invading life forms, or stripping the earth of vegetation to produce famine.

'They already have a name for it,' says Tucci. 'The GNR threat: genetics, nanotechnology and robotics. According to theorists, it has the capacity to replace the NBCs of the last century – nuclear, biological and chemical. In its own way the potential is much more insidious.

'There's always a downside,' he says. 'The other side of the coin of progress. Some people don't want to take the chance. You can see why. The question is, How do you stop it? How do you put the genie of knowledge back in the bottle?'

'And you think this is what Crone is working on?' I ask.

'It's a distinct possibility. Conventional wisdom is that we are five or six years away from a breakthrough. But who knows?' Tucci looks at us with wary little eyes like two olives floating on egg whites.

'One thing is certain. Whoever is first is going to make a fortune. The corporation that controls the process is likely to propel its major shareholders to the top of the Forbes list, overnight. They will become the wealthiest people in the world.' He says this with no question or hint of doubt. 'People will be reciting their names, and the world will be wondering where they came from.'

'And the scientist who develops it?' I ask.

'Is a shoo-in for a Nobel prize,' says Tucci. 'He or she will be able to write his or her own ticket. And the breakthrough's likely to come from some shop like Crone's.'

'Why's that?' asks Harry.

'A small operation. Attached to a university for research and support, but sufficiently independent so that no one, except perhaps the director of operations, knows precisely how all the pieces fit. One day there will be a press release, and the floodgates will open – the ones controlling the fountain of youth.'

# CHAPTER EIGHT

Dr. Gabriel Warnake is a private consultant under contract to the county crime lab. He is a hired gun, and works almost exclusively for police agencies around the country. He holds a doctorate in chemistry and can do a wicked reading in spectrographic analysis, using heat to break down molecules in evidence, exploiting them like fingerprints. He has burned his share of defense lawyers in his time. Warnake is also expert in forensic microscopy, the use of a microscope to identify and analyze hair, fiber and other trace evidence. This afternoon Tannery has him on the stand working on the white nylon cable tie used to kill Kalista Jordan.

'Can you tell the jury what this cable tie is made of?' Tannery is holding up the cut tie in its plastic bag, little rust-colored splotches still evident for the jury to see. They will no doubt take this as blood. It is, in fact, an indelible marker placed on the tie for purposes of identification at the crime lab.

'It's a polymer-based resin,' says Warnake. 'In the industry it's known as nylon sixty-six. It's an old compound developed by Du Pont back in the thirties.'

'Is it always white in color?'

'Actually, what you have there is clear, sort of an opaque. But you can put dyes or pigments in it. Basically make it any color you want. Some manufacturers color-code their ties for purposes of identification as to tensile strength, or to identify certain electrical cables that are bundled together for later reference.'

'That's what they're used for mostly? Tying up electrical cables?'

'They're used for a lot of things, but that's a main one. A major market,' says Warnake.

'Can you tell the jury how these cable ties are made?'

'That particular polymer resin is injected into a mold, under heat and high pressure. In that form it will flow, not like water, more like honey, viscous.'

'What kind of heat are we talking about?'

'Nylon sixty-six melts at around four hundred and sixty degrees Fahrenheit. They'll take it up to around five hundred and thirty degrees. That way, they can get it good and hot in order to work it. The mold temperature is usually lower. Once it starts to flow, it's injected very quickly under high pressure. Five hundred, to fifteen hundred pounds per square inch, depending on the mold and the heat applied.'

'Can you tell us about the molds used for forming the ties, what they are like?'

'They're made of steel. Capable of containing high pressure, and polished to a very fine finish on the inside.'

Tannery smiles, finally getting to where he wants to be. Harry and I have speculated on this, the two areas where their witness might go. Warnake has rendered no formal written report, so we are left to guess. We are figuring tool marks, either during manufacture or after. One presents a very real problem; the other may be less problematic, depending on what the good doctor has to say.

'You've actually seen these molds?' asks Tannery. 'Observed them in production?'

'I have.'

'Have you examined the insides of one?'

'A cross section,' says Warnake. 'Yes.'

'And did you bring that cross section with you today?'

Warnake nods and reaches for his briefcase.

'Let the record reflect,' says the judge, 'that the witness is producing an item from his briefcase. Let me see that.'

Warnake hands it up to the judge on the bench, where a few seconds later we are holding an impromptu conference off to the side.

I tell Coats we're seeing this for the first time.

'Why no notice?' asks the judge.

'We're offering it only as a sample, Your Honor. To demonstrate the process,' says Tannery. 'We don't intend to put it into evidence.'

The judge considers this, then looks down at me. 'You have any objection, Mr. Madriani?'

'As long as it's made clear that it's not the mold used to manufacture any of the ties in question. And subject to an opportunity by our own experts to examine it later.'

Tannery nods. 'No problem.'

'You can use it for that limited purpose,' says the judge. 'Subject to later examination.'

Like that, the prosecutor is back to the witness asking him to describe the mold as Warnake holds it up for the jury to see. 'I don't know if you can see it from there, but there's a small cavity, this line right here.' The polished edges, the tiny teeth of the locking gears cut in steel and polished, glitter like facets in a diamond under the overhead canister lights.

'This is a half section of a full mold. Ordinarily there'd be another half and the cavity would be sealed inside a steel block. You can see how the inside of the cavity has been polished.

'The nylon would be injected here into this port, until the entire cavity was filled, under very high pressure. This would happen in a fraction of a second. The speed ensures what they call uniform melt delivery, and avoids what is known as premature freezing. If the nylon were to harden before it had a chance to fully form, you'd get a defective cable tie.

'Once it's cool, they use water for that, the mold is opened and the finished cable tie is ejected. The whole process takes only a few seconds. Then it starts over again.'

'I assume they can make these cable ties in high volume?'

'One press,' says Warnake, 'has as many as twenty or thirty individual molds. They can produce several thousand cable ties in an hour.'

'Is every one of them the same?'

'Only to the naked eye,' says the witness. 'They look the same.'

'But they aren't?'

'Not under a microscope.'

'Perhaps you can explain to the jury?' says Tannery.

'By examining the individual ties under a microscope it's possible to identify what are called tool marks,' says Warnake. 'In the manufacture of anything involving molds, where uniform pressure is applied, and where metal comes into contact with the item being made, the surface of the metal will impart tiny microscopic marks on the surface of the product. No two molds are exactly the same. No matter how highly polished, or how uniformly made, the surface of the metal will impart its own individual surface characteristics on the item in question.'

'Like fingerprints?' asks Tannery.

'That's a good analogy.'

'In this case, on the nylon cable tie?'

'That's correct.'

'Dr. Warnake, did you have occasion to examine the cable tie in this evidence bag, the one used to kill Kalista Jordan?'

'I did.'

'And did you find individual tool marks on the surface of that cable tie?'

'I did.'

'And were you able to locate the mold used to make that cable tie?'

'By process of elimination and some research, I was.'

'Can you tell the jury where that cable tie was made?'

'It was made by a firm in New Jersey called Qualitex Plastics.'

'Do you know when it was made?'

'No. That I cannot tell you.'

'But you're certain it was made by this company, Qualitex.'

'I am. I was able, by examining other cable ties produced by that firm, to identify ties that had the same identical pattern of tool marks as the tie in that evidence bag.'

'And that would indicate that the sample ties you examined were made by the same mold as the cable tie that killed Kalista Jordan?'

'That's correct.'

'And you're certain about this? To the exclusion of all other manufacturing molds that might be used in this process, that this particular mold at Qualitex made the tie used to strangle the victim in this case?'

'I am.'

'Thank you.' Tannery retreats to the evidence cart and fishes through a couple of cardboard boxes until he finds what he's looking for. He asks permission to approach the witness.

'Doctor, I would ask you to examine the cable ties in this bag.'

Warnake takes it and looks at the ties through the plastic bag.

'Do you recognize them?'

'I recognize the tag tied to them.'

'Are those your initials on the tag in question?'

'They are.'

'And did you examine the ties in that bag?'

'I did.'

'Your Honor, for the record, the ties in question

are the cable ties found and previously identified by Lieutenant de Angelo during his search of the defendant's house,' says Tannery. 'They were marked for identification, and the record will reflect that they were discovered in the pocket of Dr. Crone's sport coat hanging in the hall closet.'

Coats doesn't even look up. Instead he nods his assent as he makes a note on the pad in front of him on the bench.

'Dr. Warnake, can you tell the jury what you did to examine the cable ties in this bag, the ones found in the defendant's coat pocket?'

'I examined them separately, placing each of them under a stereo microscope. I looked for tool marks on the surface at specific locations along each of the ties.'

'And what did you discover?'

'I determined that they were made by the same manufacturer as the cable tie used to strangle the victim, Kalista Jordan.'

There are noticeable murmurs in the courtroom. Whispering by people beyond the bar, some press types and the media sensing blood in the water.

'Were they produced by the same mold that produced that cable tie? The one used to kill Kalista Jordan?'

'No. They were made by other molds in the same

production run. Molds in the possession of that same manufacturer.'

'Let me get this straight.' Tannery starts motioning with his hands as if drawing a picture for the jury. 'There's a whole line of these molds at the factory where they're made? Not just one.'

'That's correct.'

'And each one of these molds is giving off different tool marks as they're injected with molten plastic?'

'That's right.'

'And after the ties are injected and cooled, what happens to them?'

'They're packaged and shipped to distribution points around the country, wholesalers in some cases, retailers in others.'

'So if you went to the store and bought one of these packages of cable ties, you'd get ties that could be traced back to a whole line of manufacturing molds, probably in the same plant?'

'Yes. I believe that's true.'

'And that's what you found here?'

'Yes.'

'You were able to trace the production mold that made the tie used to kill Kalista Jordan?'

'Yes.'

'And in that same manufacturing plant you were able to identify molds that produced the two cable ties found in the coat pocket of the defendant' –

Tannery points with an outstretched arm and an accusing finger – 'the coat belonging to Dr. David Crone?'

'That's right.'

Coats is now sitting up straight, looking down at the witness for the first time, his dark robe and gleaming bald head like an inverted judicial exclamation point to this evidence.

'Were you able to conclude from this that the tie used to kill the victim, Kalista Jordan, and the cable ties found in the coat pocket of the defendant had been purchased at the same time, from the same location?'

'Objection.' I'm on my feet. 'Calls for speculation.'

'I'm only asking as to the probability,' says Tannery. 'The witness has surveyed manufacturers and points of sale. He should be allowed to testify on the issue.'

Coats is not sure about this. He wants to talk to us. He calls the lawyers up to the side of the bench.

'Mr. Madriani, it seems as though the witness has already testified to this.'

'Then it's been asked and answered, Your Honor. There should be no need for the question.'

'No, it's not quite the same.' Tannery wades in. 'I asked him about production runs, and shipping practices. I'm only trying to tie it all together,' he says.

'There's no way this witness can know whether the tie used to kill the victim and the ties found in the defendant's pocket were from the same store.' I am red out to the tips of my ears. 'This exceeds any issue of expertise. It raises questions of factual knowledge.'

'It raises issues of probabilities,' says Tannery. 'We know all the ties came from the same factory. They came from the same press run of machines. Is it not probable they were purchased at the same store?'

'That calls for speculation.'

The judge is shaking his head. I can't believe it.

'You'll have your chance to cross-examine him, Mr. Madriani. I'm going to allow it.'

We step back from the bench. Harry's looking at me, like What gives? I simply shake my head. It's how you feel when you've lost a call that you know is wrong.

'Is there not a good probability, Doctor, that the tie used to kill Kalista Jordan and the cable ties found in the coat pocket of the defendant, David Crone, were purchased at the same point of sale?'

'I believe so.' Warnake is actually smiling. He knows there is no way he can prove this. Tannery has pressed it too far. It is just the kind of error that can lead to reversal on appeal.

'Perhaps they were part of the same package?' says Tannery.

'Your Honor, I have to object.'

'Sustained.' I can see it in the judge's face. He has made a mistake, and he knows it.

'Let me ask you this, Doctor Warnake. From what you now know, can you exclude the possibility that all of these cable ties came from the same package in the same store?' says Tannery.

He has turned it around so that there is no basis to object, though I do it anyway.

'I'll allow that,' says Coats.

'No, I cannot exclude that possibility.'

Crone is looking up at me from the counsel table. His hand comes over on my arm as if he is actually consoling me. His expression says he is not surprised, the scientist accepting the conclusions of science. From Harry I get a different look: one that says, *I told you so*.

Within seconds of the judge's gavel coming down, a phalanx of county jail guards moves in to escort Crone back to the holding cell. There he will change from his suit and tie back to jail togs and rubber flip-flops for the shackled walk across the bridge that links the criminal courts building to the jail.

Harry and I collect our papers as the courtroom empties. A few bystanders, court hangers-on, chew on the events of the day. Most of the reporters have headed back to the pressroom where they will file their stories by e-mail, driving one more spike into our client's reputation, and tallying one more brick on the scales for the state.

Tannery's evidence is beginning to come in cleanly, the outline of a case taking shape like a Polaroid print developing in front of our eyes. Lawyers can sense when an opponent hits his stride. It's a feeling that brings on heart-pounding panic, even as you are pulling all the legal levers in court with simulated confidence, and spinning a web of lies to the media outside.

The challenge, as always, is to lie to yourself and to do so convincingly. That is the art of a true believer, who will accept every deceit, even his own, on faith. Neither Harry nor I is of this religion. We are cockeyed pessimists with a cynical twist. I have my own unspoken doubts about the case. I am convinced that at the heart of it lies some corrosive deception, though I still cannot accept that my client killed Kalista Jordan.

It isn't until I turn to stash my copy of West's softcover *Penal Code* in my brief box that I see him, sitting alone, forlorn in the back of the courtroom. Frank Boyd has been watching our case unravel from the shadows of the last row.

He is wearing a pair of white painter's overalls, bits of sawdust on one shoulder that he has missed in brushing off. Some splotches of what look like dried glue on one pant leg.

Frank is a finish carpenter. He is an artist with wood. He has shoulders like a linebacker and forearms like Popeye. The man can move beams the size of tree trunks, notch and carve them into place, single-handedly with nothing but a hand-cranked come-along to hold the weight while he dangles from a ladder: the kind of guy you would want on your side if you had to go to war.

In another life he'd been a teacher until he learned he couldn't stand the confinement of the classroom. Frank took a job as a woodworker's apprentice in a shipyard and over six years he mastered the skills of a shipwright, finishing the interiors of yachts, until the federal luxury tax crushed the industry and threw him out of work. Ever resilient, he started his own business, and for the past fourteen years has worked by hiring himself out to contractors on large homes that require an artist to finish the wood.

It runs in his blood, independence and art. I have seen charcoal and pencil drawings of his children framed in the hallway of their modest home. Doris tells me that these are Frank's work. He had taken anatomy courses to better understand the articulation of the human body, how it moved and functioned. He now produces drawings with such a flourish of confidence one might think they were ripped from the sketch pad of da Vinci. It causes me to wonder what might have been, had he turned to oils or other media. Doubtless he would have been no more affluent. Unfortunately for Frank, he is also hobbled by the mercantile tin ear of the artist. He has no sense of his own worth.

Like a vagabond he now travels in his beat-up Volkswagen pickup, a sixties-vintage van, working on its third engine and for which the only spare parts can be found in wrecking yards. The rear springs sag under the load, tools of his trade assembled and collected over thirty years. Chisels and power saws, miters for angles, and small curved handsaws of Japanese steel mail-ordered from Asia. He uses these for cuts of microscopic precision. I am told that he has assembled whole staircases in homes that might qualify as castles, only to dismantle the entire structure, risers, treads and railings, just to shave a little more wood until the pieces fit like the parts in a puzzle. Frank's signature in wood is perfection.

He is an addict when it comes to his craft. He will drive a thousand miles in the broken-down van with his ladders on top to labor for a month on a log mansion in the wilds of Montana, for some eastern investment broker with the palace appetite of the Medici. For Frank it is the work, not the client, that is critical. It is not difficult for a man like this to find himself laboring at art for which he will not be paid. The fact that contractors will hunt Frank down for these special jobs is a testament to his skill, even if what he receives barely covers his gas. He is today's equivalent of the ancient metal smith hammering gold on a pharaoh's mask. No one will ever know his name, even as they marvel at his craft.

Today the dust on his work clothes reflects the dull pallor of his face, which is lined with deep furrows as if some gnome had pulled a plowshare through the gullies under his eyes. I would bet he hasn't shaved in three days, five-o'clock shadow gone to seed. He has lost forty pounds in the months since our last meeting, so that I have to recalibrate the register of my recognition before I am sure I have the right person.

What passes for a smile these days edges across his face and then is gone just as quickly. He gets out of the chair and moves forward slowly, down the center aisle, then sidles sideways across the front row of chairs on the other side of the bar railing to approach.

'Frank. I haven't seen you in a while.'

He extends a hand and we shake, somewhat shy. His large hand engulfs my own so that I have the feeling that it has been enclosed in a sandpaper glove. The flesh of his hands is tough enough to grind glass.

There has always been some social distance between us; Frank the blue-collar man, Paul the lawyer. He is constrained by self-imposed social divisions of another era. I suspect that doctors would unnerve him, like talking to God. For Frank this would be an added point of stress in dealing with his daughter's illness.

'Been a long time,' he says

'It could have been under better circumstances.' I motion with my head toward the judge's bench and smile.

'Tough day?' he asks.

'They're all tough. You know my partner, Harry Hinds?'

'Don't think we've met,' says Frank.

Harry gives him a mystified look and offers his hand.

'Frank Boyd. Harry Hinds.'

They shake hands, and Harry finally connects the name. 'Oh, you're the little girl's . . .' then catches himself.

'Right. Her father.' There is something about Boyd that brings to mind the actor William Devane. It is in the sad-sack eyes, and the face that seldom changes expression, as if the load of life were simply too oppressive to permit any real relief. It is the look of a man who is not allowed emotionally to come up for air, who is quietly drowning.

'How's Doris?' I ask.

'Oh, good. Good. She's tough.'

And then the inevitable: 'Penny?'

To this he gives me an expression, sort of turns away. 'Not too bad,' he says: the big lie. What he means is for a child who is dying.

'I need to talk to you,' he says. 'If you have a minute.'

'Sure. You want to do it here? I'm finished for the day.'

He looks around a little at the room, daunting formality, walnut railings and fixed theater chairs. 'Maybe we could get a drink,' he says. 'I'll buy.'

Harry offers to clean up, to haul our files back to the office. He has hired some enterprising teenager with a hand truck and a van in the mornings and afternoons to help us with the cardboard transfer boxes filled with documents. These seem to propagate like rodents as the trial goes on.

Harry and I check signals for the morning, then Boyd and I take off. It is clear that Frank is suffering from more nervous agitation than usual this afternoon. When you know someone as long as I've known him, not intimately, but through periods of calm and frenzy, it becomes obvious when there is a favor to ask and the person is uneasy about asking it.

He follows a half step behind me, across State Street, to the Grill at the Wyndham Emerald Plaza.

Frank is uncomfortable here and shows it.

'I'm not dressed for this,' he tells me.

'Don't worry about it.'

I suspect he's wondering whether he has enough in his pocket to spring for the drink he has offered. Though Frank has all the work he can handle, I suspect that he and Doris have never made more than fifty thousand in a single year.

After leaving the personnel firm, Doris held a seasonal part-time job for a while, with a small company, but had to give it up when Penny became too sick for day care.

We shuttle between tables as the after-work crowd starts to settle in for drinks and embellishments on the day's war stories: secretaries on the flirt, young lawyers on the make. The only ones you won't find in here are the bondsmen from bail row a block away. They are too busy making money chasing tomorrow's clients.

We find a table in the back, dim light and wood relief. I order a glass of wine, the house Chablis, and give the waitress my credit card to start a tab. Frank argues with me, but it is halfhearted. He accepts a drink, orders a beer, Bud, and thanks me.

He is a big man, sinewy and strong as a bull. He is a full inch or more taller than I am, even sitting here, hunched over the table.

He looks as if he hasn't had a good meal in two

days. I order up appetizers, chicken wings and some stuffed mushrooms.

Frank kills time with small talk, his latest job, a mansion for some software mogul. He's been hauling one-ton beams into the basement for a mammoth hearth single-handedly. Using leverage, he moves the hundred-year-old timbers that he has salvaged from some closed-down mill in Colorado. Anyone wondering how the pyramids were built might want to discuss the matter with Frank.

I can tell he is waiting for the waitress to come back so that we won't be disturbed. The drinks come first. Five minutes later the food, and Frank doesn't hesitate. He's into the mushrooms and chicken wings. 'These are good,' he says, then notices that I'm not eating. He puts the chicken wing down on the little plate in front of him, self-conscious eyes looking around.

'You gonna have some?' he says.

'Sure.' I pick up a wing to keep him company.

'You're wondering why I need to talk?' he says.

I smile.

'It wasn't to get a meal. Or a free drink.'

'I didn't think it was, Frank. You probably want what we actually owe you for your work in the office,' I tell him. Frank had handcrafted some bookshelves for us into some tight spaces in the office, and charged us five hundred dollars for two thousand dollars' worth of work. When I tried to pay him more he wouldn't take it, saying that what I had done for Penny was more than enough.

'I need a divorce.' He says it just like that. Like 'Pass the salt.'

I don't say anything, but he can read stunned silence when he sees it.

'It's the health insurance,' he says. 'I need a divorce because of the medical-insurance thing. Crazy, isn't it?'

'Why don't you start at the beginning?' I tell him.

'Fine. But I'm not gonna eat unless you do.'

I spear a mushroom with a toothpick, if only to make him feel comfortable.

'It's Penny,' he says. He picks up the chicken wing and starts to nibble on it, but I can tell his heart is not in it. He has lost the yen to eat and drops it back on the plate. Instead he goes to the drink, something to dull the senses. Takes a swig from the bottle, ignoring the glass that the waitress poured and is half full, shrinking by the head.

'Her medical expenses are huge.'

'I can imagine.'

'I don't know that you can. Last month it was twenty-five thousand dollars.'

He's right. I didn't have a clue. He looks at me over the bottle caught by the neck in his large hand.

'You're wondering where would I get that kind of

money? Until last Tuesday, from the insurance company. But that's about to end. A lifetime million-dollar cap,' he says. 'We've bumped up against it with Penny. That's why we need the divorce.' He puts the bottle down on the table and leans forward, a salesman about to make his pitch.

'Doris and I talked about it. She didn't want to do it either, but you see, it's really the only way. We were up 'til three in the morning, talking.'

I can see it in Frank's bloodshot eyes.

'She wants to divorce you?'

'God knows why she didn't do it years ago,' he says. 'I haven't been a great provider. A lot of squandered opportunities. If I'd stayed a school-teacher, at least they'd have health insurance. Doris and the kids. Most of the wood I work on has more brains than I do. I've made a lot of bad decisions.'

I tell him he's being too hard on himself.

At this moment I wish I had a few million in the bank I could loan him. Fact is I'm tapped out, new practice in a new city.

'I've looked for jobs. But who's gonna hire some burned-out termite? Besides, as soon as they find out about Penny they always come up with some reason not to take me on. Suddenly they've filled the position. No longer hiring.'

'You have your own business.'

'Yeah. Right.' He laughs.

'This is the extent of my business.' He holds up his leathered hands. 'My only assets. According to the bank,' he says. 'And I can't sell them or mortgage them, not even for body parts. So where does that leave me? Where does it leave Doris and the kids?' He's looking at me now, leaning across the table, whispering like this is some secret cabal.

'The insurance guy tells us there's nothing he can do. Hell, if I hadn't had the policy for years before Penny came along, they would have canceled us years ago. Fact is, we're uninsurable,' he says. 'That means the house, everything is on the block. They'll take it all, every dime. My kids are gonna end up on the street,' he says. 'I'd be better off dead.'

'Don't say that.'

'It's true,' he says. 'At least they'd have a roof over their heads. I've got a million-dollar life-insurance policy. Paid up.' He tells me his parents had bought this for him years before, in case something happened on one of his jobs.

'Borrow against the cash value,' I tell him.

'There is none. Straight term policy.'

I tell him to relax, to calm down. But my words sound like what they are, the bravado and encouragement of the unaffected.

'Let's think about options,' I tell him.

'What options? There aren't any.' He finishes his

drink, and raises his bottle toward the waitress. 'This one's on me.'

The waitress comes over. I order a beer. Frank needs the gesture, if only to buy some pride back.

'When did you find out about the medical-insurance cap?'

'The million-dollar cap I've known about, but I didn't know we were hitting up against it until last week. I guess I just didn't think. The hospital bills went to the insurance company. We got copies and stuck 'em in a drawer. Went on for what, I don't know. Two years, maybe.'

'Do you have any kind of appeal, to the insurance company?'

'I don't know. You look at it.' He reaches under his coat, to the inside pocket, and hands me an envelope, ripped across the top like somebody opened it in a hurry with a finger.

'It's been burning a hole in my pocket for two days,' he says. 'You keep it. Please.'

I read the letter. It is a notice of cancellation for the reason that the maximum lifetime benefits of the policy are about to be exhausted.

His second bottle comes, and Frank starts on it.

'Do you have a copy of the policy?'

'At home,' he says. 'Someplace.'

'We need to look at it.'

'Why? I suppose I could argue with them over the

numbers. But I don't think I'd win.'

'You think you're into them for that much? A million dollars?' I ask.

He nods. 'Yeah, all the experimental stuff. The treatment at the university. She was hospitalized four times last year with respiratory problems, three times the year before. She can't control the saliva. It goes down her windpipe and gets in her lungs. She gets pneumonia and then she's in there for a month, sometimes six weeks.'

'And a divorce will solve this?'

His eyes light up like those of some grifter with a good idea. He sits up straight in the chair and leans across the table toward me, salesman about to make a close.

'Here's what we figured. The hospital bills are gonna break our back. In two months our savings will be gone. We'll be broke. We have the other children to worry about. I talked to Doris, and she agrees. If we get a divorce, she takes the house, my retirement and custody of the other two kids. I'll agree to it. Division of property. That's what they call it, right?'

'Assuming some judge is willing to accept this,' I say.

'Why wouldn't they? If I agree to it.'

'Judges are funny,' I tell him. 'Especially if they think you're doing this to defeat creditors' claims.'

He ignores me. 'I'll have to pay support from my salary, whatever I take home in pay. They can't touch that. Right?'

I make a face, like maybe. 'Who're "they"?'

'The state,' he says. 'Here's the deal. I take Penny and all the bills. That would qualify her for state aid. I'd be broke.' He smiles at the thought of being destitute and immediately reads the negative response in my eyes.

I start shaking my head.

'There's no other way,' he says.

'Even if you did it, it wouldn't work,' I tell him. 'The state would see through it in a heartbeat. The Medicaid auditors would be all over the two of you before you could cash the first check.'

It is a fact of life that some cagey live-on-the-edge con artist might get away with it, drive a Mercedes and live the high life on somebody else's laundered checks using a different name each day, bouncing from state to state always one hop ahead of investigators. But Frank and Doris Boyd are not cut out for this kind of life. I can see them in jail togs with their kids in tow.

I tell Frank this. From the desperate look in his eyes, I can tell immediately that this was a mistake. He looks at me like the enemy.

'That's okay,' he says. 'If they put us in jail, then the county could take care of Penny and the other kids, while Doris and I do time.' He is serious. It is the kind of mindless escape the middle class, people who have never seen the inside of a jail cell, might come up with when they are desperate. Frank has now sold his wife on this.

I argue with him, but he doesn't want to hear it. Frank feels he's found the only way out of a desperate situation. If I say no, he'll sell his van and his tools to come up with a retainer and find some low-life shyster who will take his money to file for this ill-conceived divorce. If I can keep him under my umbrella, and talk some sense into him and Doris, maybe I can convince them not to do it. Frank is the mover here, the shaker in the family. Doris would follow him to hell if he told her this was the way out. She's too busy trying to raise three kids, keeping one of them alive.

We talk some more. I tell him I would have to think about it, look at the insurance policy first to see if there is any other way.

'Carriers get dicey when you threaten lawsuits, especially for bad faith. There's a chance that you haven't hit the cap yet. They are notorious for inflating costs. It could be you've got some more time.'

His eyes light up with the thought. 'You think so?'

'It's possible. Even if you don't, we may be able to buy you some.'

He reaches across the table, his hand cold and wet from squeezing the bottle of beer, and cups his palm over my forearm. 'You'd do that for us?'

I nod and for the first time, he settles back in his chair and takes a deep breath, a moment of relief, eyes cast up at the ceiling.

# CHAPTER NINE

We are headed north on I-5, Harry at the wheel of his new Camry, the air conditioner humming. My partner is beginning to draw the line at riding in 'Leaping Lena' my ragtop Jeep with its isinglass windows pulled out in good weather.

But the quiet hum of the tires on the road is not enough to dispel the growing sense of dissatisfaction I feel from Harry. Warnake's testimony put a hole in our boat. The only question is whether it's below the waterline.

As we work our way up toward La Jolla and the university, Harry finally breaks the silence.

'You realize we dodged a bullet on the tensioning tool? We owe the gods of evidence on that one.'

According to Harry, if Warnake had been able to link the tool, the one from Crone's garage, to the killer tie around Jordan's neck, Crone might as well start packing for the trip to Folsom.

'It doesn't make any sense,' I say. 'If he did it,

why leave the cable ties in his coat pocket for the cops to find?'

'Maybe he forgot them. People tend to panic,' says Harry. 'Especially if they've been busy cutting off arms and legs. And he is forgetful. Remember, he's the one who couldn't remember arguing with the victim the night she disappeared.' This is still sticking in Harry's craw. 'You can chalk up the cable ties in his pocket with the other things he forgot.'

According to Crone, the cable ties in his coat pocket were probably there from trash night the week before. It was a ritual. He would come home from work, don a pair of work gloves he kept in the garage, gather up the trash from the house and dump it in the can then take the can out to the curb. Newspapers and cardboard he would bundle and tie up with the cables using the tensioning tool he kept under the workbench. According to Crone there was no intention to hide the tool. It must have gotten pushed under an old piece of carpet when he put it away the last time he'd used it. It is a plausible story. Whether the jury will buy it may depend on how many people on the panel put out their own garbage.

'I'll admit it defies common sense,' says Harry. 'But then the man's a little frizzy. University type. You know what I mean. A lot of aptitude and not much judgment.' Harry's looking at me from the driver's seat offering a sideways glance. 'He's stuck with the evidence, and so are we.'

'Still begs the question why the cops didn't find his prints on the ties or the tool,' I say.

Harry has thought about this. 'The ties were too small, too narrow to take an identifiable print,' he says. 'And remember, they did find smudges.'

'And the tool?'

'He wore gloves?'

'Did you ever try to put one of those cable ties together wearing gloves?'

Harry shakes his head.

'I did. It's not easy. If he took his gloves off to work the tie, why did he put them back on just to use the tool to tighten it?'

'He's eccentric? I don't know. It's a hole we're gonna have to plug,' says Harry.

'It's possible he wiped the tool clean after he used it to kill Jordan. But if he did, if he thought about it enough to wipe off prints, why didn't he go the extra step and just get rid of it? Drop it off some dock, or better yet put it in the bag with the body, weigh it down and deep-six the whole bundle?'

'Maybe he didn't have time,' says Harry.

'Maybe he didn't do it,' I say.

He smiles, never one to commit himself.

Before Tannery finished with Warnake on the stand, he had him testify regarding the tensioning tool found in Crone's garage. But his strategy here was not to link Crone to the tool. Instead he wanted to shore up a weakness in his own case. Tannery couldn't link the death tie to the tensioning tool found in the garage based on tool marks. He wanted to tell the jury why.

It seems whoever killed Jordan pulled so hard on the tool that the cable tie got twisted in the process, deforming the edges and stretching the nylon before it was cut. Successive tests performed by Warnake were unable to replicate the precise tool marks left along the edge of the cut tie. Tannery explained this to the jury, distilling this imperfection from his own case before we could exploit it.

He left me only one thing to talk about on cross: the fact that the heavy-duty cable ties used in this case marked them as unique. His survey of manufacturers limited the number of producers of that particular tie to fewer than a half dozen nationwide. Consequently, anyone who purchased these particular kinds of ties would be limited to those same sources.

My point: There was a good chance that anyone purchasing the ties in San Diego would likely obtain them from the same point of manufacture, with the same tool marks as those found in Crone's pocket. After I flogged him with this thought several times on the stand, Warnake finally threw up his hands and gave me the great concession – '*Anything's possible.*' This was as good as it got, and according to Harry it wasn't good enough.

'I was looking at their faces,' he tells me.

'Who?'

'The lawyer's dozen. Who else? Jury in the panel,' he says. 'And they weren't buyin' it. There was only one thing moved 'em,' says Harry. 'Tannery's question about the tie that killed Jordan. His inference that it came from the same package as the ones in Crone's pocket.'

Harry is right. The judge may have kept Warnake from answering it, but the fact that the witness started to, and wanted to, was palpable in the courtroom. The jury could sense it.

'Tannery can take that to the bank,' says Harry.

I have a sinking feeling this morning as we trek to the genetics lab at the university, for a meeting with Aaron Tash. We are being forced to spend valuable time trying to get inside our own case, to discover the facts that our client won't tell us, mostly about relationships; and in particular the one between himself and Kalista Jordan.

University medical facilities abound in this county. There are two hospitals, both teaching institutions, and a list of research and graduate programs that would be the envy of any city in the country. But unlike the Salk Institute and Scripps, the University Genetics Center, known to all who frequent it merely as the center, is not funded by any perpetual endowment or foundation. In fact, it exists in rented quarters, a four-story office complex just off campus, a measure of its precarious existence that is reviewed every year.

It is left to its own devices when it comes to funding. We are told that Crone has had run-ins with university administrators, and a few regents who have tried to monitor his largely private fund-raising efforts. The fear is that because of the center's ties, the university could get a public black eye if Crone were to take funds from the wrong people, entities that might be political lepers. Crone took offense at this questioning of his judgment. According to observers, Crone is jealous of his independence, the freedom to pursue research and its funding as he sees fit. This has been a continuing source of friction between Crone and the university. This may answer the question why it was that Kalista Jordan received offers of employment with lavish salary increases from other universities while David Crone was passed over. He has a reputation as being difficult to deal with. There is even a rumor that some in the university hierarchy were eyeing her as a possible replacement to head up the center. We have done everything possible to hunt this story down and drive a stake through its heart. If true, it could supply a damaging motive for murder.

Harry parks on the street, at one of the two-hour meters. Whatever the reticent Dr. Tash has to tell us, it can no doubt be covered in that time.

Tash has been excluded from the courtroom since he appears on our witness list, and though we have interviewed him twice, Harry and I both sense that he is holding back. Getting information from Tash is like distilling water from an iceberg in a blizzard. He is cagey. Get your tongue too close and it may stick like a kid licking a water fountain in winter. If I were preparing him for a deposition, I would tell him only one thing: Act normal. As Crone's number two, he is keeper of the office flame, the man to whom all secrets are most probably known.

We take the elevator to the fourth floor. When the doors open we are standing in a small reception area, nothing fancy, antiseptic white walls and an industrial carpet to absorb the sound of heels that would otherwise be clicking on concrete. There are six chairs, black plastic institutional seats with chrome arms and legs. These grace the otherwise-bare walls, three on each side of the room. A stack of old magazines, what look like science journals, is spread on a low table next to one of the empty chairs. Straight ahead is a desk, a clean surface with nothing behind it except an open door, hallway to the inner sanctum. There is no receptionist, simply the barricade offered by the desk. Harry's first instinct is to go around it, just walk right in.

'You did make an appointment?' he says.

'On my calendar for ten o'clock.'

Harry glances at his watch. 'On the dot.' He waltzes up to the desk. 'Hello. Anybody home?' Harry knocks on the Formica surface.

Like a tomb, all I can hear is Harry's echo. We wait a couple of seconds, and Harry does it again. Nothing.

'What say we go in?' he says.

Then, before we can move, there's a slow shadow in the hall, followed an instant later by a tall, lean figure. Tash appears in the open doorway behind the desk. Slender and bald, he gives us an expressionless look from over the top of a file he is holding. I can't tell whether he is expecting us, or has forgotten about the meeting. With Tash you can never tell much, a stone face, expressions that never seem to change. You are left to wonder if it is academic reserve, or arrogance, or whether Harry is right and the two are the same.

Tash is wearing a black cotton turtleneck under a dark herringbone sport coat and dark slacks, so that he looks like a character from a sci-fi flick with undersized production values. *Thin* is not the word. The turtleneck hangs on him with wrinkles like ribs on a skeleton.

He looks at his watch. 'You're on time.'

'Guess that's why we're lawyers and not professors,' says Harry.

Tash gives him a look, sly, off centered, everything dead from the eyes to the mouth, John Malkovich.

'Come in,' he says. No greeting or handshake. He is not a social animal. Tash would not think to offer coffee, or small talk. He lacks the social grace of his boss. There is not the slightest hint of warmth from the man. From our few meetings his most admirable quality appears to be loyalty. He reports dutifully to Crone at least once a week. This to a man who is under indictment for murder, and who has been suspended without pay by the university. If Tash feels threatened by fidelity to his mentor, he shows no sign of it.

He's had easy access to Crone at the jail since our earlier meeting, traveling there twice, once with Harry and the second time with me. On both occasions Tash was silent to a fault, all the way up in the elevator and into the small cubicle with its inch-thick acrylic partition they use for attorney-client consultation in the slammer. I had to assure Tash that it was safe to talk on the receiver hanging from the wall, that no one would monitor this during meetings with counsel.

On each trip Tash treated Harry and me as if we

were furniture. Even with his antennae up, Harry was unable to pick up anything. He told me that Crone and Tash perused more numbers, scientific mumbo jumbo, according to Harry. Tash pressed a single sheet of paper up against the acrylic so that Crone could read it. Then Crone wrote a few formulas on a sheet of paper on the other side and held it up while Tash made notes. It was a repeat of the session I'd had a week earlier with the two of them. Tash would then leave, as silent as a six-foot mouse, while Harry or I spoke to our client.

We follow Tash down the long, narrow hallway, past a door with a small plate-glass window in it. Inside I can see stainless-steel tables, glass beakers and electronic equipment. This, I assume, is one of the laboratories.

'We'll use Dr. Crone's office,' he tells us.

The university has not yet tried to replace Crone. Caught in a pickle, wondering which way to run, university administrators take a wait-and-see attitude. The official word is 'no comment while the case is in the courts,' though they have engaged in some fast footwork over Jordan's sexual harassment claim. 'Maybe we should have looked into it sooner.' This was one of the comments reported in the press from an unnamed source close to the administration. Defending Crone has definite downsides. Abandoning him publicly might push the case toward a conviction, leaving the university facing wrongful-death, or some other civil crisis. Love him or leave him, they are caught in the middle.

Tash unlocks the office door with a key from his pocket, and flips on the lights. Inside, Crone's office has the look of a museum. There is dust on the desk thick enough to plant potatoes, along with a few scraps of paper that haven't been moved since the day the cops searched the place. They would have swept everything into plastic garbage bags and rolled all the filing cabinets into a waiting van, except for the fact that I and two lawyers from the university rode herd, forcing them to adhere to the particulars of their warrant. The search took four hours and was not pleasant. Several torrid arguments erupted along the way. I recognize the notes on a yellow tablet in the center of the desk, the same pad that was there that afternoon. Now it has dust around it to mark its footprint on the wooden surface.

Tash looks at me staring at the pad on the desk and reads my mind. 'We have orders from the chancellor's office not to touch anything. Just in case the police want to come back and look again. The university seems to be treating this place like the scene of the crime. You would think they would have more confidence in their own people.'

'You would, wouldn't you?' says Harry. 'Just the

same, maybe we shouldn't be in here.' As he says the words, Harry starts picking through some books left on a stand on the other side of the room.

'I figure to hell with the cops,' says Tash. 'If they can't do a good search the first time, they shouldn't be in the business.'

As soon as the words clear Tash's lips, I notice Harry smiling. A university man he can finally agree with.

'The chancellor's lawyers can talk to the D.A. if they like. None of my concern,' says Tash. 'Besides, my office is far too cramped for meetings like this.'

He takes out a handkerchief and wipes the dust from the executive swivel-back chair behind the desk, then takes a seat and leans back. The high top with its black leather makes a stark contrast to the white baldness of Tash's head, like an inverted exclamation point.

Harry takes one of the chairs across from him and I slide into the other.

'So what is it you want to know?' asks Tash. 'You do understand that if it has to do with our work here, I can tell you nothing.'

'What is it with you guys?' asks Harry. 'Sooner or later you're gonna be called to testify. If not by us, by Evan Tannery. What are you going to tell him when he asks you what you do here all day long?'

'We do genetics research,' says Tash.

'And what if he wants particulars?'

'Then he will be dealing with an army of university lawyers. I would imagine in conference in the judge's chambers. That is what they call it? Chambers?' Tash looks at me.

I nod.

'They're prepared to obtain court orders, from other judges, to protect the substance of our work if that becomes necessary. I believe that Mr. Tannery will ultimately be persuaded that the specific nature of our work is irrelevant to anything in this trial. If he persists, all that will happen is that he will delay a verdict.'

'The way you say that, it sounds like you don't believe Dr. Crone is going to be acquitted,' I tell him.

'On the contrary. I don't think they have a thing on him.'

'You haven't been in court,' says Harry.

'You don't sound terribly confident yourself,' says Tash.

'My confidence level when it comes to clients,' says Harry, 'is in direct relation to the truths they tell us.'

'And you think Dr. Crone is lying to you?'

Harry doesn't answer, except with his expression that says it all.

'Why don't you start by telling us about Kalista Jordan and your boss? What kind of working relationship did they have?' I ask.

'Is that what you came here for?' says Tash. 'You could have saved yourself the trip. I would have told you that over the phone. What do you think went on?'

'Why don't you tell us?' I say.

'Actually it's a very dull story. It was the typical problems you have in any organization. David Crone is brilliant. Kalista was ambitious.' He reaches into his coat pocket and pulls out an apple, shines it on the sleeve of his coat, and from the pocket on the other side takes a small Swiss Army penknife.

'What about the complaint?' I ask.

'You mean the sexual harassment thing?'

I nod.

'I saw it. Reads like a fairy tale. The woman would have said anything to get ahead. She was claiming a hostile work environment. If there was any hostility in the office, she brought it with her when she came. Unless, of course, you think they were having an affair.' He looks up at me and smiles at the very thought. 'Trust me, the only part of her David ever saw that was naked was her ambition, and he only saw that when it was too late.'

Methodically he opens the razor-sharp blade on the knife and just as quickly cuts the apple in half, then quarters it deftly with all the pieces in one hand.

'Was she after his job?' I ask.

'That and other things.'

'Other things?'

'The product of his work. The fruits of his labor.' He slices the skin off the apple with thin precision so that you can see the reflection of light through it as it lands on the desktop in front of him in curling sinews.

'The papers she took from his office?' I ask.

'That was part of it. And don't ask me what they were, because I won't tell you.' He hasn't been looking at us for over a minute, concentrating on the apple.

'Of course not. We wouldn't think of it,' says Harry.

'It's not that she was above using sex to get ahead,' says Tash. 'It's just that she was an icicle. If she touched you, you'd get frostbite.' Listening to Tash describe her is like hearing an iceberg describing a cube. 'And she knew how to manipulate the system.'

'What system is that?' asks Harry.

'The thought-control process that now passes for liberalism in higher education. And I'm not talking open-mindedness,' says Tash. 'In the sciences you live in a political bunker. You constantly measure your words for fear that you might utter some political blasphemy that can end your career. Undergraduate courses are the worst. Fortunately for us, we don't do any of that. Some of the students are like the Red Guard: ready to report you to the administration at the first sign that you're not sufficiently inclined toward proper dogma. You can find yourself enrolled in a mandatory course of thought correction just to keep your job. Of course they call it "sexual harassment guidance" or "minority sensitivity training." And they can never get too much women's studies,' he says. 'Today if you want to take a survey course in biology, you're required to take Women's Political Thought and Marxist Ideology as prerequisites. Jordan was into all that crap. She used it whenever it suited her needs. When David gave her a subpar evaluation after her first six months at the center, she had the regular roster of feminists calling the chancellor's office to complain. She played the gender thing like a harp, and when the tune went sour she tried sexual harassment. You want my guess, she was working her way up the chain toward race discrimination when somebody did us all a favor.'

'Sounds like you didn't like her,' says Harry.

'I didn't. I told the police that when they asked me.'

Harry and I have seen this in the police reports, Tash's statement the day after they arrested Crone.

'In some ways she was like many young women today. Focused on what she wanted.'

'Sounds like a lot of the men I know,' I tell him.

'Hardly,' says Tash. 'The young men we see, even the best ones, are constantly distracted by the pursuit of sex. No, no. Most women of Ms. Jordan's generation view that as simply one more gift, like brains, or grades or a good degree from a name university, just another arrow in their quiver. And they know how to use it.'

'Are you saying Jordan was loose around the office?' says Harry.

'I'm saying she was ambitious, to a fault.'

'Did she ever try to come on to you?'

Tash gives Harry a look as if this doesn't merit an answer. 'No. She was self-absorbed, arrogant and dishonest, and absolutely shameless in the pursuit of publicity. The university would hype her to the alumni in their publications. Dr. Crone was never mentioned, nor was anyone else at the center. You would think she worked here alone. I remember the blazing headline, DR. KALISTA JORDAN ON THE CUTTING EDGE OF THE HUMAN CELL. Her picture on the cover. She was not the slightest bit embarrassed or apologetic. As far as she was concerned, it was her due. She got the cover photo framed and hung it in her office. You would have thought it was the cover of *Time*.'

'We want you to be candid,' says Harry. 'We wouldn't want you to sugarcoat it.'

Tash grimaces at him. 'You wanted to know what I thought, so I'm telling you. The fact is I told David, Dr. Crone, not to hire her. He wouldn't listen to me.'

'Why not?'

'I don't know. You'd have to ask him.'

'No, I mean why did you tell him not to hire her?'

'Call it instinct. I sat in on the interview. There was just something that wasn't right about her. Besides, I felt we could have had someone more qualified.'

'In her field?'

'That's right.'

'And what was her field?' I ask.

'You know very well.' Tash looks at me directly for the first time. 'Molecular electronics.'

'Which is?' says Harry.

'If I'm going to do all your homework, I'm going to want a consulting fee,' says Tash.

'How about we just put you on the stand as a percipient witness and ask you?' says Harry.

Tash gives him a look, nothing you could call friendly. 'It's a new field. Basically, it involves the use of atoms and molecules to replace more conventional transistors in electronics.'

'And how does that fit into genetics?'

'It holds promise for medical science,' says Tash. 'And that's all I'm going to say on the subject.'

'Fine. Tell us about Jordan and Dr. Crone?' I ask.

'What do you want to know?'

'What was she like when she first came to work here?'

'She was personable. She seemed eager to get along. Worked long hours. She was often here when I closed up.'

'By herself?'

'Sometimes.'

'How well do you know David Crone?' says Harry.

'As well as anyone here at the center. We've worked together, let's see' – he looks up at the ceiling tiles – 'I guess it's going on fifteen years now.'

'Did he and Dr. Jordan socialize at all, outside the office?'

'No.'

'You seem pretty sure,' says Harry.

'I am. Outside of work they had nothing in common. Different types completely.'

'In what way?' I ask.

'She was a social climber, into cultivating friends who could do her some good, move her career forward. David hated that crap. You couldn't get him to attend a chancellor's function, a dinner or cocktail party if his life depended on it.'

'Maybe he had a secret side? A life you didn't know about?'

'If he did, it didn't involve Kalista Jordan. As far as I know, all their contacts were here at the center.

I don't think either of them even knew where the other lived.'

'Still, there must have been some social interaction between the people who worked here,' says Harry. 'I mean, a drink after work? Christmas parties? Beer and pizza? Something to celebrate, a birthday party, new breakthrough in whatever it is you do here?'

'Oh, sure.'

'But you never saw Dr. Jordan or Dr. Crone socializing?' I ask.

'Not in the way you mean,' says Tash. 'They were sociable, at least in the beginning. What you would expect of professional people. They would talk, chat.'

'About what?'

'Who knows what people talk about? Hobbies. Work.'

'What kind of hobbies?'

'I don't know. I didn't pay that much attention. David plays tennis. I don't think she did.'

'But at some point the relationship deteriorated?' I say.

'Yes.'

'And when was that?'

Tash thinks for a moment, scans the ceiling with his eyes as if the answer is printed there. 'I think it was about last January.' He is now nibbling at the edges of the quartered and peeled apple. 'David told me that he'd had a problem with Kali. He called her Kali.'

'Was that usual? Did he call other people by their first names or use nicknames?'

'Sometimes.'

'Who?' says Harry.

Tash thinks for a moment. He can't come up with anyone else off the top of his head. It's an issue to stay away from if we can when he's on the stand.

'And the problem?' says Harry.

'She had taken some papers from David's office, without his knowledge. He knew she had taken them because someone saw her do it.'

'Who?'

'I don't remember, but it wasn't important, because Jordan admitted it. She told David that she needed the papers to complete some of her work. He was furious. He told her that if she wanted something from his office, she should have asked him for it. They had an argument, here in his office.'

'Were you present?' says Harry.

'No.'

'Did anybody else see or hear this argument?'

'See it, no. Hearing is another matter,' says Tash.

I look at him from the corner of one eye.

'Voices travel,' he says. 'Walls are thin.'

'And what did you hear?'

'Bits and pieces,' he says. 'Snarling and snapping.

Mostly from Kalista. Dr. Jordan. We all knew there had been a problem between them, but I didn't know the precise nature until Dr. Crone told me.'

'And what did he tell you?' I ask.

'That she'd taken papers from his office.' We are now back to where he started. Tash has a satisfied look, as if pleased by the fact that he's given nothing we didn't already know.

'Did he threaten her?' says Harry.

'Excuse me?'

'During this argument, did Dr. Crone threaten Dr. Jordan?'

'Did somebody tell you that?'

'Just answer the question,' says Harry.

'You mean threaten with violence?'

Harry nods.

Tash finds the question humorous. 'Oh, I'm sure she often felt threatened, but it wasn't by violence.'

'What's that supposed to mean?'

'Let's put it this way. If there were two people at any meeting and Kalista was one of them, she usually wasn't the most competent person in the room. Her problems with Dr. Crone came down to insecurity.'

'How so?'

'David wanted to get rid of her. Dismiss her. It took him about a month to realize she was in over her head. She knew it. That's what the sexual harassment thing was all about. She figured if she filed the complaint, it would be more difficult to fire her. But the fact is, she couldn't do the job. Her work had been substandard almost from the day she joined us. Gradually she began to come to work late and go home early. Wouldn't show up for meetings. There's no doubt in my mind she felt threatened by the people around her. Their quickness and superior intelligence. She simply didn't fit in.'

'Well, one thing's for sure,' I tell him.

'What's that?' says Tash.

'Kalista Jordan's arms and legs weren't severed by a sharp wit or piercing intellect.'

This only draws a stone-cold look.

'He would never have threatened her. David doesn't operate that way. He is very controlled. Everyone will tell you this. The fact is, I've never seen him lose his temper. He may have been upset. But even when he's upset, David tends to be understated.'

'And you heard all this understatement,' says Harry, 'from behind a closed door?'

'Mostly her voice,' says Tash. 'Some people have that irritating nasal thing. You know what I mean? She had a voice that tended to carry.'

'So you only heard one side of the argument?' says Harry.

Tash concedes the point.

'Without divulging the contents or precise nature of these papers, how important were they?' I ask.

Tash thinks about this for a moment, and measures his answer. 'What I can tell you is that our work here is quite compartmentalized. Different members of the staff work on different aspects of any project. It is designed so that their knowledge and responsibility are limited. Only the project director would be in a position to know how all the elements fit together.'

'And that would be Dr. Crone?'

'Correct.'

'So what you're telling us is that these papers taken from Dr. Crone's office allowed Dr. Jordan to know more about how all the pieces of the project fit together than she was authorized to know?'

Tash snaps his fingers, still moist with apple juice. 'You got it.'

'And this created a big problem?' I ask.

'In a word, yes. How big it was I will leave for others to determine. You have to understand that confidentiality in our work is paramount. There's a great deal of competition, patent rights and sizeable sums of money at stake. It's the reason for all the security.'

'Yeah, we noticed it at the door,' says Harry.

'First impressions can be deceiving,' says Tash.

'If you tried to get into any of our computers, you would find it more difficult than invading the Pentagon. There are multiple passwords for every level of access, and a firewall guarding the entire system from the outside.'

'And yet Kalista Jordan was able to walk out of Dr. Crone's office with sensitive materials.'

'He didn't think she would steal things.'

'Do you know whether Dr. Jordan passed these papers or the information on them to anyone else?'

'How would I know? She could have sold the information to a competing lab for all I know.'

'Do you have reason to believe that's what happened?'

'As I said, I don't know. And I really shouldn't be discussing this stuff with you.' He's talking about the center's work product.

'One last question,' I say. 'If Dr. Crone was the genetics expert and Dr. Jordan was in charge of molecular electronics, who was in charge of the other aspects of the project?'

He considers for a moment, weighs whether he will answer a question that can easily be sorted out by reference to an organizational chart. Tash knows this and so he answers: 'That would be Bill Epperson.'

'Nanorobotics, right?'

Tash doesn't say a word.

## *CHAPTER*

# *TEN*

Harry and I are alone, mired in our differing assessments of Tash and his story of the moment as the elevator doors slide closed behind us.

It is difficult to get a clear picture of Kalista Jordan. Everyone seems to have a different take, perceptions being what they are. According to Tash, she was a self-serving viper lying in wait.

Harry's view is that Tash might be useful. 'It may be our best defense. Putting the woman herself on trial.' Harry is talking about Kalista Jordan.

This is not a novel approach in criminal cases where defamation of the dead seems to thrive. Raise enough eyebrows in the jury box, and murder can become a victimless crime.

'The question is whether Tash's take on her is accurate. An African-American woman and a high achiever, someone with the title of doctor in front of her name. There's certainly nothing in her background that looks bad on paper,' I remind him.

'You're thinking there was some jealousy on Tash's part?'

'There is that possibility. She may have been ambitious, but that's not a crime. We take off after her, and we're going to alienate every woman on the jury. That's just for starters. We haven't even begun to consider the issue of race.'

'You think our friend Tash was troubled by the color of the woman's skin?'

'I don't know. But the way he talked, I think Tannery could make it sound that way. According to Tash, Jordan was predatory, but she's the one who ended up dead. He tells us she was incompetent, but doesn't give us any specifics. If we put him on the stand, Tannery is going to make it look as if Tash felt threatened, jealous of her position and access to Crone.'

'Maybe that's not so bad,' says Harry.

I look at him, a question mark.

'We could put Tash on the stand and let him twist. The other man,' says Harry.

'You think Tash had something going with her?'

'Doesn't matter what I think,' says Harry. 'Question is whether we can sell it to the jury.'

'The man has the metabolism of a reptile,' I tell him.

'Maybe they got it on.'

'What? And Crone got between them? Tash got jealous?'

'Maybe,' says Harry. 'Stuck his fangs in her. It's better than what we have right now. Listen. Tash is an angry man. Angry with the system. Angry with Kalista Jordan. That anger is rooted in something besides mere loyalty to his boss.'

'And your point is?'

'Maybe he's the proverbial angry white male. Maybe he can't deal with a woman. Particularly a black woman. He sees her undercutting him with Crone.'

'So he kills her.'

'Stranger things have happened,' says Harry. 'And who would have better access to Crone's garage for the tensioning tool, or to his coat pocket for the cable ties?'

'It's all good except for one thing: Tash has an ironclad alibi for the night Jordan disappeared.' According to police reports, Tash was at a meeting, a homeowners' association gathering, until close to midnight. After that, he went to a local coffee shop with two neighbors where they talked until nearly one in the morning.

'That's just it,' says Harry. 'We don't know exactly when she was killed. We only know when she was seen last.'

'Without something more, it would be a tough sell to a jury.'

From Harry's look, he is chewing on this in silence as the elevator slows to a stop. He takes a step toward the door before I can grab his arm. The light overhead has stopped at two.

The doors slide apart, and Harry's way is blocked by a soaring figure standing in the hall waiting to enter.

Harry looks up at the man with an expression one might use to estimate the altitude of a mountain, smiles and steps back out of the guy's way. The man has to actually cant his head, just a little, off to one side in order to clear the header over the door.

When he looks up he is again smiling under the canister lights of the elevator car. Silent, he looks both of us in the eye, first Harry and then me. His expression is pleasant, passing the time. If I had to guess, I would say that William Epperson doesn't place us.

We have been chasing him for more than six weeks, Harry specifically, trying to get a statement from him, some clue as to what he will say if he is put on the stand. Now fate has placed him in the elevator with us, and I can read it in Harry's eyes, the look of opportunity.

Epperson is barred from the courtroom as a prospective witness, since his name appears on the prosecution's list. In the weeks before trial Harry made several attempts to talk to the man, once at his apartment, and two more times outside the D.A.'s office, all to no avail. Epperson had been shielded by investigators from the D.A.'s staff, and while they couldn't order him not to talk to us, they made it clear that he was under no compulsion to do so.

Under these circumstances, most witnesses decide that the prudent course is silence. And so it is with Epperson. Several months have now passed. If he remembers us, he shows no sign of it.

Once inside the elevator, Epperson works his way to the left side of the car and leans against the wall, his head nearly touching the ceiling. I can see his reflection dancing in the gleaming brass plate that covers the inside of the elevator doors as they close. Harry and I stand there in silence, elevator etiquette, pretending to ignore the giant standing next to us.

Under the canister lights I finally look over and up, studying him, as he looks at me in the reflective doors. We descend.

Epperson is not what you would envision from the hurly-burly of basketball. He is big, a sinuous athletic build, his hair closely cropped. There most of the similarities of size end. He wears his clothes, shirt, tie and neatly pressed suit, with a quiet dignity. You would have a difficult time seeing him in the key, jostling with the bad boys of the NBA.

The fine and delicate lines of his face, high cheekbones, look as if they were carved using a sculptor's knife in earth-toned clay. He has a prominent chin that finds its strength below generous, sharply defined lips. These are closed in silence, causing you to guess at the tones that might issue from the voice that lies within. It is the kind of face that would prompt you to listen, the features of some ancient bronze mask. It would not be a reach to imagine that the blood of nobility runs through William Epperson's veins, royalty of some timeless African tribe. He has the bearing and stature of a Tutsi warrior; perhaps the narrowing genetics of aristocracy that resulted in his stature, and left him with an inherited cardiac condition.

'Nice weather, huh?' Harry can't restrain himself. He breaks the silence, confident that Epperson hasn't made us.

The tall man looks down at him. There is nothing imperious or arrogant, only gentle eyes and a kind of confidence that comes with knowing you are probably the tallest man in this part of the state.

'It has been pretty nice, hasn't it?' His voice fits the image, a deep resonance with no wasted effort.

More silence, and Harry has to work at it. 'A regular Indian summer,' he says.

'I suppose.' Epperson is smiling. Tight-lipped, he looks at Harry.

I'm getting worried that my partner might pull the red button, jerk us to an emergency stop so he can give Epperson the third degree on the spot. Bad heart condition and all, the man could pound both of us through the floor like bent nails.

Harry now looks at him, and engages the bigger man's eyes directly. 'Have we met?'

Epperson studies Harry for a brief second. 'I don't think so.'

'You're Bill Epperson, aren't you?'

He doesn't answer him, but instead looks at Harry with an expression that says, *Who wants to know?*

'I saw you play a few years ago. High-school game back in Detroit. You scored forty points if I remember.'

'Thirty-four,' says Epperson.

Leave it to Harry. Master of the file trivia. He has combed all the documents, including the press clippings that earned Epperson his scholarship to Stanford. He gets the figures wrong just enough to make it believable.

'You were there?' Epperson leans away from the wall. You can read the gleam in his eye. His feet may be on the floor, but his mind is somewhere in that ethereal moment of fame and lost glory.

'Never forget it,' says Harry.

'You don't look like you'd be from Motown.'

'Just visiting,' says Harry. 'I have a sister back

there. Lives in Ann Arbor.' Harry making it up as he goes. Now he has Epperson talking about the old days, his Detroit roots. 'We ended up at the game. Lucky for us,' says Harry.

'Really?'

The elevator slows to a stop, and the doors begin to open.

Epperson is still smiling. He takes a step toward the opening. 'Well, it was good meeting you.' Epperson heads out the elevator door.

'You know, my son would kill for an autograph.' Harry's not going to let the conversation die that easily.

Before Epperson can turn around, Harry is on his tail, pen in hand.

'Would you mind?'

They step outside the elevator into the building's lobby. Epperson is embarrassed. The first graceless moment I have seen. He's not sure whether to take the pen, what to do. He holds his hands out, palms open as if warding off somebody wielding a knife, shaking his head, out of his depth.

'No. No. I really don't do that.'

'Why not? You don't have to charge me for it,' says Harry.

They both laugh.

'It's just, I'm never asked.'

'Well, you are now.'

Not knowing what else to do, and not wanting to appear rude, Epperson looks at me, then takes Harry's big Mont Blanc.

Suddenly he's all thumbs. Can't get the cap off. Harry explains that it is a fountain pen, and shows him how to unscrew it. They're at a loss for something to sign. Finally Harry hands him one of the case files, a legal-sized manila folder. Fortunately he has the presence of mind to turn it over, so that the tab with the label is facing the other way, the one that reads PEOPLE V. DAVID CRONE.

'What's your boy's name?' Epperson is finally regaining some composure. He's willing to personalize it.

This catches Harry flat-footed.

'What would you like me to say?'

'Just a signature would be great.' Let Harry think about it for a minute, and he'll drag Epperson to a stationery store for a clean sheet of paper and have him put his John Hancock on it so that we can type an alibi for Crone above it.

'My boy won't believe that I actually met you,' says Harry.

'How old is he?'

'Twenty-six,' says Harry.

With this, Epperson actually rocks on his heels. He lifts his gaze in mid-signature to check Harry out, to make sure all the gum balls are still in the machine. Epperson may be flattered, but his ego doesn't match his stature. What in the hell does a twenty-six-year-old man want with an autograph from a has-been high-school star, even if he does hold a state record?

'High-school heroes were his big thing. He's got a collection of autographs.' I'm waiting for Harry to say, *People who never made it big – a truly rare collection*, but he bites his lip.

'He never forgot that game.' Harry tries to patch it up. 'He's even told his boy about it.'

'Kids of his own. Really?'

'Oh, yeah. It's funny how some things just make an impression. Sports moments,' says Harry. 'You always remember them. Like the catch made by Clark in the end zone. The Forty Niner playoff game they beat Dallas. The one that sent 'em to their first Super Bowl. You always remember it, don't you?'

Epperson makes a face. Nods. He remembers.

'Well, that game where you scored forty points' – Harry's back to inflating the numbers – 'that's the same kinda thing.'

Epperson hands Harry the signed folder and his pen. 'Good meeting you,' he says. He shakes Harry's hand and heads for the door.

'You know, I wonder, cuz he's sure to ask me . . .'

'Hmm?' Epperson stops again and turns.

'Why didn't you play in college?' Anything to keep him talking.

'Injuries,' says Epperson.

Suddenly Harry turns toward me. 'I told you it had to be something like that.'

Epperson's looking at me now, wondering who the hell I am.

'We had a bet. I told him that you'd have been in the NBA unless you got hurt. He wouldn't believe me. Oh, excuse me. You guys haven't met.'

The fact that Harry hasn't introduced himself doesn't seem to bother him.

'Paul Madriani. Bill Epperson.'

Oh, shit. I do the best I can to smile.

Epperson looks at me, thinking about the name, taking time for it to register. Then it does. He's not sure whether to hold out his hand.

'You're the . . .'

'The lawyer,' I say.

'Yeah. Listen, I gotta run. I'm late. Really.'

'I told Paul you'd have been a major star,' says Harry. 'That you must have gotten injured somewhere along the way. What was it, knees?'

'Heart,' says Epperson. He's still looking at me.

'You know, it's a good thing we ran into you. We'd been meaning to call you anyway. The trial,' says Harry. 'You don't mind if we talk to you, do you? I mean, in fairness.'

The vacant look on his face makes it clear he doesn't know what to say.

Harry doesn't even slow down to take a breath. 'The D.A.'s people didn't tell you that you couldn't talk to us, did they? Cuz if they did, they're gonna be in big trouble with the judge,' says Harry.

'No. No. Nothing like that,' says Epperson. 'They just said I didn't have to talk to you.'

'Well, then, in the interests of fairness . . .' Harry gives him one of his better looks, arched eyebrows over the top of his half-lens cheaters, with just enough of a pause. 'You do want to be fair?'

'Oh. Oh, sure.'

'Great. Then why don't we go get a cup of coffee?'

'I can't right now. I've got a meeting.'

Harry and I are thinking the same thing – *Yeah, with a telephone booth or his cell phone. Hotline to the D.A.'s office.*

'Well, we can talk for a couple of minutes right here,' says Harry. He's not about to let Epperson out of his clutches.

Harry looks at the signature on the manila folder one more time. 'You know, my boy really is going to be happy.'

Epperson gives him a sick smile, wishing I'm sure that he'd taken the stairs.

Harry flips the folder open, finds a legal pad and has the cap off the pen again.

'You were a friend of Kalista Jordan's?'

Epperson looks at us shifty-eyed, not sure if he should answer, then says: 'Yeah, sure.'

'How long did you know her?'

Epperson thinks for a moment. 'I don't know.'

'You don't know how long you knew her?'

'Five years. Maybe six. We met in college.'

'Good,' says Harry. A little encouragement. 'Did you meet socially, or were you in the same classes?'

'It was social.'

'Did you date?'

'I don't know if I'd call it that. We went out a few times.'

Harry with the pen in the file. 'Dated,' he says.

'I didn't say that. We had some mutual friends. We always went out with friends. I was a couple of years behind her.'

'Yeah, I always liked the older women, too,' says Harry. 'Must be that maternal touch.'

If a black man can suffer from rosacea, I would say Epperson has it now.

Harry is scratching out notes on the yellow legal pad. 'Why don't we move over here?' He finds a ledge of polished granite that lines the wall of the foyer like a stone wainscot and lays the notepad on it for a harder surface.

'I really have to go,' says Epperson. 'I'll give you my card. You can call me at the office.'

Harry gives me a look like *sure*, and ignores him. Epperson doesn't want to be rude. It is the only thing keeping him from walking on us.

'The night Kalista Jordan disappeared.' I cut to the chase. 'You do remember that night?'

'Hard to forget,' he says. Epperson now looks down at me.

'You had dinner with her in the faculty dining room on the campus?'

'That's right.'

'Did you overhear the conversation between Ms. Jordan and Dr. Crone that night?'

Epperson is now not sure if he should answer. 'Listen, I don't think we should be talking about this.'

'Why not?' asks Harry. 'You don't want to be unfair to the defendant, do you?'

'No, but I don't want to get in any trouble either.'

'How are you gonna get in trouble?' asks Harry. 'Certainly not by telling us the truth.'

'Okay, sure,' he says. 'They had a conversation.'

'Did you hear any of it?'

He shakes his head.

'Is that a no?' I ask.

'Crone took her by the arm. Moved her away from the table. I couldn't hear any of it.'

'But you could see it?'

He nods.

'Was it a friendly conversation?'

'Depends on what you mean by "friendly." He didn't hit her, if that's what you mean. They had some words.'

'An argument?'

'Probably. As I said, I couldn't hear. They kept their voices down. At least Crone did.'

'So he didn't shout at her?'

'Not that I heard.'

'But Kalista, what did she do? Did she raise her voice?'

'Might have,' he says. 'I can't remember.'

Harry can't believe our good luck.

'Besides taking her arm to move her away for privacy, did Dr. Crone ever touch Kalista Jordan that evening? Did he put his hands on her?' I ask.

This is how I would couch the question in the courtroom, preface it with a little softening context.

'No. Not that I remember.'

I look to Harry to make sure he's gotten every word, my question verbatim, and Epperson's response. Harry would be the witness if Epperson says anything different on the stand, merely to verify the accuracy of his notes.

'Would you be willing to give us a signed statement to that effect?' Harry pounces on it.

'I don't know if I could do that,' he says.

'Why not? We'd make it very brief. Just the

questions we've asked you here. We could call to clarify over the phone if we have anything more.'

'Yeah. Right. You call me,' he says. 'Right now, I have to go.'

'There is one more thing?' I say.

'What's that?'

'Those papers. The ones Kali . . .' I'm talking and suddenly I notice that he's no longer looking at me. Instead his gaze is fixed on something in the distance, over my shoulder.

I turn, and see the elevator doors are open. Standing in front of them is Aaron Tash. He is taking a particular interest in the three of us on the other side of the foyer, though he doesn't make a move to join us.

'Listen, I'm late for my meeting. Gotta go,' says Epperson.

'You will give us a signed statement? Under oath?' asks Harry.

Epperson is already halfway to the door. 'Call me,' he says. With that he is gone, out the door, disappearing onto the sidewalk and around the corner in strides that Harry and I couldn't match if we ran.

'You'd think we'd come down with a sudden case of the plague,' says Harry.

'Yeah.' I'm looking at Tash. 'I wouldn't be offering any odds that we'll catch him at the office.'

# CHAPTER ELEVEN

A good trial lawyer is a magician, one who excels at the art of misdirection. Tannery is good at this. He has kept us focused on William Epperson in order to distract us. This morning, in the judge's chambers, he plucks a surprise from his other sleeve.

It is Tannery's mystery witness, Tanya Jordan, Kalista's mother. She has been on the prosecution's witness list for months, we had assumed for other purposes.

Harry makes the pitch that while the witness may have been disclosed, her testimony, which is now highly prejudicial, was not. 'The state is obligated to disclose,' he tells the judge.

'I know the law, Mr. Hinds.' Coats is not impressed.

We are asking him to exclude the testimony, and from the look on the judge's face this may be an uphill battle.

'She was on our witness list,' says Tannery. 'The defense had every opportunity to approach her to obtain a statement. If they failed . . .'

'How could we obtain a statement? According to your own proffer, she lied to your investigators at least three times before she finally came up with this story.'

'That's a good point,' says Coats.

Harry finally scores one.

'We kept after her, and she finally told us the truth,' says Tannery.

'Right. You browbeat her until she made up a lie you could live with.' Harry turns back to the judge. 'Besides, we tried talking with several of their other witnesses and got stonewalled.'

'Are you saying that we instructed them not to make disclosures?'

Harry looks at Tannery for a brief instant, frustration etched in the lines on his face. 'Yes.'

'Do you have evidence?' asks Coats.

'No.'

Tannery is smiling.

'That brings us back to the conflicting stories,' says the judge. 'What about that?'

'It goes to credibility,' says Tannery. 'They are free to raise it before the jury. Ask the witness why she changed her story.'

'What have you told her to say?' says Harry.

'I resent that.'

'Gentlemen, please.' Coats is getting irritated.

'Mr. Madriani, we haven't heard from you.'

I am shaking my head. 'What can I say? This is the ultimate eleventh-hour surprise. A bombshell,' I tell him.

'Do you have any suggestions?'

'Exclude it.'

'Sure,' says Tannery. 'What do you expect him to say?'

Harry and I had passed on Tanya Jordan for a simple reason. We assumed she was on the state's list as a setup, probably a victim-impact witness, somebody they could use if Crone was convicted to solidify their case in the penalty phase.

According to police reports, except for two brief telephone conversations, she had no contact with her daughter during the month before the killing. I have seen her only once, outside the courtroom. An attractive woman in her late forties. The family resemblance was striking. It was not difficult to imagine this statuesque woman as related to the victim. A neck like a swan, high cheekbones, even in middle age she possessed all the qualities magazine editors might covet in a cover model. And like her daughter, she had opted for other things. She is a teacher at a Michigan high school, a single woman who put her only child through college and grad school, and is now left with nothing but memories. Why she is doing this we can only guess, but bitterness is high on our list of conjecture.

'We were right all along,' says Tannery. 'It was a crime of passion. Admittedly it wasn't romantic, but passion nonetheless.'

'What are you saying?' asks Harry.

'Merely that the murder of Kalista Jordan was motivated by emotion, call it rage if you like. In this case, it was racial.'

'Now we have a hate crime.' Harry is beside himself. 'Your Honor, you can't permit them to do this.'

'I admit it should have been charged earlier. We would have asked for a capital sentence, death qualified the jury, but we didn't know all the facts,' says Tannery. 'The state is prepared to live with the consequences.' This is the bone he is trying to throw Coats to get the evidence in.

Harry points out that it is an empty bag. 'You're not charging it as a hate crime because you can't. The law is clear on that point. Unless you want to dismiss and start over. And if you dismiss, we'll argue jeopardy has attached.'

'As I said, we're not interested in recharging. But we want the evidence in.' Tannery ignores Harry and makes his argument to the court.

'What evidence? The ranting of a distraught

mother who will say anything to convict the man the state says killed her daughter?'

'Again, you can argue that to the jury,' says Tannery.

'Mr. Madriani.' The judge tries to move around them. 'Have you looked at the state's offer of proof?'

'I've scanned it. It was delivered to us only this morning.'

'Understood. That isn't much time. And the court is sensitive to the defense's need to prepare.' This is not a good sign. Coats is trying to fix the problem, patch it up and sail on.

'We only confirmed the information ourselves late last evening,' says Tannery.

The judge puts up a hand. He doesn't want to hear anything more from the state. The judge's problem is fundamental fairness. Can the defendant, in light of the new evidence, get a fair trial? If not, he has two choices: exclude the evidence or declare a mistrial.

'How much damage does it do to your case?'

I'm not going to discuss theories of defense in front of the prosecutor. Coats knows this. He is merely inquiring as to a general assessment of damage.

'Try a torpedo below the waterline,' says Harry.

'Do you agree?' Coats looks at me.

'It's a serious matter. I would consider it highly prejudicial.'

Coats turns his attention back to Tannery. He walks a fine line. A court on appeal has twenty-twenty hindsight.

'How long have you known about this?'

'As I said, we confirmed it only late last night.'

'That's not what I asked. How long have you had reason to know there was additional incriminating evidence?'

'The witness lied to us. It's all right there,' says Tannery. 'We exercised due diligence, but you can't discover what is being affirmatively withheld by a witness.'

Tannery has provided a witness statement, a transcript, a copy to the court and separate copies to Harry and me. We scan these as Tannery pitches the judge.

'The first time we talked to her, she knew nothing. We interviewed her three times, and each time she told us the same thing. It wasn't until we got an inside tip,' says Tannery, 'another woman who'd known her back in college, that we got the information. That was two days ago.'

'You told us a week ago,' says Harry.

'We told you we had a lead, nothing definite,' says Tannery.

'What was the lead?' asks Coats.

'There was a history with Mrs. Jordan, the victim's mother. It seems she attended college in

Michigan, the university. This was at the same time that the defendant was a member of faculty.'

'And you discovered that when?'

'About ten days ago. It took us a day to schedule a meeting with the defense.'

'So when did you get some notice?' Coats turns this on Harry.

'I doubt that a court on appeal would call it that.'

The judge takes the question under advisement, and turns back to Tannery for more.

'At the time, back in the seventies, Dr. Crone had drawn considerable controversy. He issued some papers, research documents that resulted in a great deal of disruption on the campus. Student demonstrations,' says Tannery.

'Surely this is not news,' says Coats. He is looking at me now. 'This information was in the file. I believe I saw newspaper articles from the period. Why didn't you check it out?'

'We knew about Dr. Crone's background,' I tell him. 'We didn't know about the victim's mother attending the same school.'

'Go on.' Coats to Tannery.

'Anyway, our source . . .'

'Who was?' The judge wants all the details.

'Her name is in our brief. Jeanette Cummings. She was a student with Mrs. Jordan at Michigan back at that time. They were both active in civil rights. They participated in student demonstrations against Dr. Crone's research. And the research is the key,' says Tannery. 'A kind of genetic racial profiling. Dr. Crone was in the vanguard of some studies . . .'

'Which he has since disavowed in writing,' I remind the court.

Coats cuts me off with a raised hand.

'Whether he's disavowed them or not, it goes to the issue of motive,' says Tannery. 'Motive as to why Kalista Jordan went to work for Dr. Crone, and why she was murdered.'

This catches the judge's attention. He wants to know more about the studies.

'Your Honor, if I might.' I break in rather than have Tannery fill in the blanks. 'The data was skewed. The people collecting it, mostly undergraduates and some hired help, violated protocols. The result was that my client, Dr. Crone, based his findings on faulty data. He has acknowledged this.'

'Which begs the question of why he was studying the stuff to begin with. But we won't get into that.' Tannery smiles at me.

This is exactly what the prosecution wants to get into, something to poison the jury.

'The defendant's studies dealt with so-called cognitive abilities of different racial groups,' says

Tannery. 'It was dynamite then and now.'

'That was over a quarter of a century ago,' I argue. 'He hasn't done anything in that area since.'

'How do you know?' asks Tannery. 'A lot of people thought there were serious ethical issues raised.'

'My client is a scientist. He goes where the science takes him.'

'Are you saying he is involved in this research?' Coats is now inquiring.

'No, I'm not saying that.' I don't want to tell him the truth, that I don't have a clue as to what Crone is involved in.

'He published two articles in a very embarrassing study and took a lot of heat. It nearly ended his career. He has acknowledged his error in this regard. He has done so repeatedly over the years. And now to use this against him over twenty years later in order to inject race into this trial would be a gross miscarriage.'

'I understand your position,' says Coats. 'Still, I have to look at what is before me.' He motions Tannery to continue.

'We don't contend that Dr. Crone is a racist.'

'No, you only imply it,' says Harry.

'The evidence goes to the issue of motive. According to our information, Kalista Jordan went to work for Dr. Crone principally at the behest of her mother. There is independent evidence to support this.

We know, for example, that the victim received a number of higher-paying offers for employment. But she went to work for the Genetics Center. She turned them all down in order to take the job for less money. Some would argue less of a future. Why?

'We know why. Mrs. Jordan will testify that she had conversations with her daughter at the time. She will testify that Kalista Jordan was socially motivated. Like her mother before her, she was interested in civil rights. Both mother and daughter were convinced that David Crone was again working on theories of genetic racial profiling.'

Harry looks at me. I can tell what he is thinking. The reason why Crone and Tash have refused to tell us anything about their work.

'The reason Kalista Jordan went to work for Dr. Crone was to uncover these facts and to expose them,' says Tannery. 'This is the reason she was killed. To keep her quiet.'

'Why? It doesn't make any sense,' says Harry. 'If he was doing research, clearly he intended to publish the results.'

'There might not be any results if his funding was cut off,' says Tannery. 'He knew this was dynamite. He knew the university would want no part of it.'

'A lot of conjecture,' says Harry. 'A grieving mother will tell you a lot of things.'

'It's a point,' I tell the judge. 'Where's the evidence?'

'Where are the documents the victim took from Dr. Crone's office?' Tannery turns it around. 'The papers are missing. Why was the defendant so intent on getting them back? Why was he so angry with Kalista Jordan for taking them? We contend that the killer has these papers, and that these documents will bear out our theory, that David Crone was hard at work on theories of racial intelligence.'

'You have the documents?' Harry's into him.

Tannery hesitates for just an instant. '*Mmm*. No.' The way he says it makes me wonder.

'But I don't believe we need the documents in question. We have witnesses,' he says.

'Who?'

'Tanya Jordan.'

'Not if the court doesn't allow her to testify. They're trying to bootstrap themselves,' says Harry.

'There is also Aaron Tash.'

Now Harry's head whips to take in Tannery. Suddenly Harry is quiet.

'Dr. Tash has been with the defendant a long time. They have known each other from the days of those earlier studies. They have been colleagues.' Tannery says *colleagues* as if it is a dirty word. 'We propose to put him on the stand and find out what they were working on. After all, there is no privilege here.'

'We're informed that there are serious trade secrets involved,' says Harry.

'We're prepared to deal with that,' says Tannery. 'The needs of justice take precedence over mere commercial interests. The court can evaluate it and decide whether the witness must answer.'

Tannery already knows the result, a criminal courts judge faced with questions involving a potential life sentence. It is not a close call. He will order Tash to answer the question.

It's a neat strategy, knowing as Tannery does that the papers taken by Kalista Jordan from Crone's office are likely never to be found. He also knows that Tash has made a point about the nature of his work, that it is off-limits, that he would rather go to jail for contempt than answer questions about the center's research. If the state puts Tash in front of the jury, he will no doubt refuse to answer questions regarding his work, thereby raising questions about what he has to hide. No matter what he says, questions of racism are likely to overwhelm any other evidence. Even a bald denial of racially related research, without some indication of what they were working on, is not going to satisfy the jury. And the specter of Tash, Crone's number two, being hauled off in chains to serve time for contempt does not augur well for our case. We are about to be called on the very issue Crone has studiously avoided from the beginning, the nature of his work with Kalista Jordan.

'It's time to cough it up,' says Harry.

We have wasted no time. It is early afternoon, and we have Crone in the little cell off the courtroom. Coats is looking for a way out. He has deferred a decision on whether Tanya Jordan can testify until tomorrow when he will allow us to voir dire her outside the presence of the jury, put her on the stand under oath and see what she will say. Harry and I are now like blind men wandering through a minefield.

Tannery's position is that it doesn't matter whether racially charged research was involved or not. The mere fact that Kalista Jordan believed Crone was back delving into this field was sufficient to motivate her to take the job. Where the prosecution may fall short is on the second issue. Was it the motive for murder? Without some showing that our client was actually involved in what might be construed as politically volatile research, why would Crone kill her? On this issue Tannery may have to make some showing, link his suspicions with at least some hard evidence.

It is now imperative that Crone tells us what he

was working on so that we can sweep the racial issue off the table.

'I can't do that. I've told you repeatedly . . .'

'Why? Are you telling us that you were working on this?' Harry is in his face.

'No. I'm telling you that my work is not a subject for public disclosure.'

'Trade secrets?' asks Harry.

'If you like.'

'I don't like.'

I tell Crone that the rules have changed. There's a new wrinkle.

'Not as far as I'm concerned.'

He can hide behind the Fifth Amendment, refuse to take the stand. Tash does not have that luxury. 'If he refuses to testify, he's gonna end up in the bucket,' says Harry. 'And his refusal would work against you. The jury would draw conclusions you don't want them to draw. Believe me.'

This slows him down. Crone thinks for a moment. Looks at Harry. 'It had nothing to do with race,' he says. 'Not in a direct fashion. Not in the way that you think.'

'What does that mean?'

'I can't say anything more. You'll just have to trust me,' says Crone.

Harry is now beside himself. 'Not likely.' He's pacing the little room. 'It's been a surprise a minute and you expect us to trust you? I'm telling you, we should have withdrawn.' Harry puts this to me. 'The first time he lied to us.'

'I never lied to you.'

'The argument with Kalista the night before she disappeared?'

'That was an oversight. I forgot. I told you. And besides, the police are making more out of it than it was.'

'Great,' says Harry. 'Fine. We'll tell the jury that. What do you know about Tanya Jordan?' He changes gears.

Suddenly shifty eyes from Crone. Who says you can't read demeanor?

'Nothing.'

'She certainly knows about you,' says Harry. 'According to Tannery, she toted the tar and feathers when they rode you out of Michigan on a rail.'

'Nobody rode me out of anywhere. I received a better offer out here. More freedom to do my work, so I came. That's the truth.'

'There were a lot of students,' says Harry. 'They had to use tear gas to keep them from storming the walls of your classroom building. They didn't like what you were doing.'

'They didn't understand. They didn't have the first clue about academic freedom, the need for free and independent research. A scientist goes where the science takes him.'

'You tell 'em that on the stand,' says Harry, 'and they're gonna hang a great big sign around your neck that says RACIST.'

'I'll have to live with it,' says Crone.

'Perhaps in an eight-by-ten-foot cell for the rest of your life.' I finally come into the conversation, and Crone looks at me.

'You think so?'

I give him an expression that it's anybody's guess. That I would not be surprised.

'Five hundred years ago that same kind of mentality, those same people, put Galileo in front of the Inquisition,' says Crone.

'You're no Galileo,' says Harry.

'Like it or not, it's a political world,' I tell him. 'Offend people at a cocktail party, and they'll give you a dirty look and walk away. Offend people on a jury, and they may lock you away for the rest of your life, or worse.'

Crone thinks about this for a moment. Silence, then he offers a distant look, somewhere halfway between here and hell. 'That's the price we pay for truth,' he says.

Outside the courthouse, I have a sinking feeling in the pit of my stomach, wondering who I represent:

the Dr. Jekyll who laid himself on the blocks to help Penny Boyd, or the Mr. Hyde who dabbled in racially charged research.

Crone has been tethered to a line of other jail inmates for the walk back to the county lockup. Whatever it is he isn't telling us may come rolling out of the witness box like a bomb. In criminal law, your biggest enemy too often is your own client, based on the lies they tell or the truths they withhold.

It is verging on darkness, the shortening days of early winter, as Harry and I assess where we go from here. We have few alternatives. Tomorrow we face Tannery's offer of proof with Tanya Jordan. Unable to really prepare for her testimony, we will scramble to take notes and follow up with questions.

Harry is tired, depressed. It has been a while since he's had a client as unyielding as David Crone. Criminal defendants usually see the light, even the most hardened liars. At some point they are forced to deal with the reality of facing stiff time, and the fact that no lawyer can help them unless they come clean. Usually they crack like a clay piñata. But not Crone. He may take whatever secret he possesses with him to the joint.

Harry doesn't like it. He thinks we're being used. 'There're a lot of ways to lose a case,' he tells me. 'Our name is out there. New boys on the block in a new city, with our reputation riding. There's a lot of publicity. And don't think I'm not worried about the client. But he's making his own bed.'

Harry getting wound up, moving toward his usual rendition of 'Maybe we withdraw.'

'You know we could tell Coats he won't cooperate with counsel.' I listen under the yellow light haze from the streetlamps overhead. At the curb, a block away, a lone blue van is parked across from the steel-gated garage of the county jail waiting to disgorge its passengers chained inside.

The conversation with Harry finally starts to run down. Harry has vented his spleen. No resolution, but he feels better. He says good night and heads for his car. I am parked in the other direction. Five minutes later behind the wheel of Leaping Lena I am lost in the streaming sea of headlights caught in the rush on I-5, inching my way toward the arching Coronado Bridge and home.

Like half of the world, twice each day I am left alone on a crowded freeway with my private thoughts, modern man's equivalent of the religious experience of solitude, eyes straining into the rearview mirror at the headlights blinding me from behind.

On mental autopilot, I grapple for some reason why Crone will not level with us. I have long since dismissed the excuse of commercial secrets. No sane person is willing to go to prison for life to protect such interests. David Crone may be accused of a lot of things, but being mentally unbalanced is not one of them. He is hiding something and has a good reason. I can only hope that it is not a glaring motive for murder.

The lights in the mirror are giving me a headache. The vehicle behind me has its high beams on, like flares exploding behind my eyes. I flip to the night mirror to cut the glare. In the summer it is the setting western sun that blinds you. In fall and winter it is headlights, approaching and behind. Now all that is left in the mirror from behind are little yellow parking lights, the one on the left burned out. And so it goes, the nightly evacuation of the city.

Sarah will be waiting for me at home. We touch base daily in the afternoon by phone. Quite the little lady, she now fixes dinner. I have learned that my daughter loves to cook. My chore is the dishes, the nightly domestic task that I actually enjoy. Unlike my job, interminable delays and unfinished projects, it is a task I can complete in minutes and view with satisfaction, mundane as it sounds.

I take the off-ramp to the bridge. Over the span it is stop-and-go, vehicles backed up for the tollgates on the other side. This takes twenty minutes. Stalled lights behind me as far as I can see. I look at myself in the mirror. The stress of a trial takes its toll. There are times in the morning when, just out of bed, I do not recognize the face looking back from the mirrored door of the medicine cabinet.

Sitting here stalled in traffic, I keep turning over in my mind all the pieces, like a puzzle, looking for the ones that fit. Tash and Crone, Kalista Jordan and William Epperson. And Jordan's mother, popping out of the weeds as she has. I haven't seen her much around the courthouse, now I know why. Tannery has been keeping her under wraps.

I make my way to the tollbooth and through, then head for the last stretch, the few blocks home. Within minutes I am in the driveway. It is now totally dark. I step down out of Lena and reach for my briefcase on the passenger seat. As I do, I notice a vehicle pulling up a few houses down on the other side of the street. It is a dark van; its headlights out, parking lights on, except for the left one that seems not to be working. It is the absence of lights as it slides to a slow stop at the curb that draws my attention. In that brief and absent observation, it registers. It is the same van that was parked across from the jail where I left Harry.

# CHAPTER TWELVE

This morning I am sleep deprived, the result of a recurring nightmare, three nights running. It always starts the same way. I am in the courtroom, but instead of wearing my coat and tie I am dressed in a baseball uniform. I can feel the bat in my hand, preparing for the pitch. Bases loaded. A jury of scowling and angry umpires is in the box. Each night I draw closer to a verdict, but never quite get there, hanging on the edge just as I wake. So vivid is this dream that I have no difficulty remembering the details even as Harry and I make our way to the courthouse down the side street from the parking lot this morning.

We edge toward the front steps of the courthouse as we see the trucks with their video satellite dishes parked just around the corner. Another day, another dollar, we run the gauntlet.

By the time we reach the steps they've engulfed us, soundmen with their boom mikes jousting while the cameramen wield their lenses like bazookas. It is the latest rage in entertainment, anything salacious from the courthouse. Crone's trial is now hot news. In this case, there is the added undercurrent of race; unstated in the press or on the tube, it is conveyed by constant photographs of Crone and the victim, profile shots facing off on the same page. Two of the local network affiliates have crafted these into their nightly logo for the so-called 'Jigsaw Jane murder case of Dr. David Crone.' Harry is thinking of having these printed on his business cards.

The cry for racial justice, while not heard in the courtroom, is openly discussed on the talk shows at night and in sidebars in the newspapers. Assurances from Judge Coats to the contrary, Harry and I can only wonder whether the jury is properly insulated from this. We could demand that they be sequestered, locked away in some hotel under lock and key with bailiffs to watch over them for the duration. This inevitably would cut against us. It is a fact that jurors incarcerated for trial will invariably hold it against the defendant.

Harry and I fight our way up the steps past the cameras, push and shove.

'Who's today's witness?' One of them sticks a boom mike in my face. I shove it aside with a shoulder and walk by.

'Why is the session closed to the press?'

'You'd have to talk to the judge,' says Harry.

'Is it true that there's a witness to the murder?'

This last stops Harry in his tracks.

'That's news to me,' he tells them.

'Then it's not true? Are you telling us it's not true?'

'I'm not telling you anything.' Under a gag order, Harry has said all he can. The rumor has been floating for days.

'Then you're not denying it?'

I say nothing. Harry is mum, responding only with looks to kill.

There are a thousand ways your client can be tried in the press. One of the least enviable is to be gagged by the court as false stories begin to spread on the airwaves. We can't be certain that jurors won't hear these and begin to engage in their own speculation.

We push our way through the throng. As in medieval combat, two of the soundmen employ their boom mikes like pikes, dangling them in our faces as we surge forward up the steps. Harry uses his briefcase like a shield to ward them off.

'Can you tell us who the witness is?'

'Can't tell you anything,' says Harry. 'And if you don't get that damn thing outta my face, you're gonna be wearing it where the sun don't shine.'

Tonight's sound bite if they don't find anything more interesting.

'Would we be wrong to report that there is a witness to the killing?'

'Has being wrong ever bothered you before?' Harry is starting to get hot.

'Are you saying we'd be wrong?'

One of the bailiffs just inside the courthouse lobby sees our plight. A burly guy, he opens the door and uses an arm, cutting a swath through the working press like Moses parting the Red Sea. Inside is the metal detector, a line with guards checking brief-cases, sanctuary and some sanity.

I am fighting off a headache, and the day hasn't started. I was up most of the night prepping for the unknown, periodically watching the dark van parked across the street from the house. It left a little after three, pulling away from the curb and rolling almost to the end of the block with its lights out, then rounded the corner and disappeared.

It was too dark to see any occupants inside. Maybe I'm getting paranoid. It was probably somebody visiting in the neighborhood. This morning I say nothing to Harry about it.

We make it through the line, and take the elevator. By the time we reach the courtroom we are down to the usual suspects, lawyers with their clients engaged in last-minute deals out in the hall, forlorn witnesses and family members lost in the sea of department numbers. There are two local reporters outside Department 22, newspaper regulars with space in the pressroom. Here the action is less frenzied. There is no need for frenetic film at five.

They pose the expected questions: 'What's going on?' 'Can you tell us who the surprise witness is?'

One of them, Max Sheen, has worked here for two decades. He has carved out a beat so that he knows every lawyer in town. He's on a first-name basis with every judge, at least those who want to get reelected. It is rumored that Sheen has his own key to the courthouse, with access to the clerks' filing room downstairs.

I tell them no comment, that we're under a gag order, and Sheen takes his appeal to Harry. 'Can you at least tell me how long she's likely to be on the stand? Something for the one-o'clock deadline,' he says.

Sheen may already know more than we do about today's activities.

Harry knows him, the kind of person my partner would cultivate if he wanted to drop his own news bomb in the middle of a trial and not have his fingerprints all over it. They step to one side, Harry and the two reporters, a conversation out of earshot.

Harry has always entertained such types, with

private phone numbers in his Rolodex in Capital City. He has been busy making new friends here. It's all very cordial in the corner between them, intent looks and a lot of scribbling off by one of the benches. I don't want to hear what Harry may be telling them. Ignorance is bliss. When they're finished, Sheen flips his notepad closed and casts an eye at the courtroom door. It is locked, with heavy brown paper taped over the long slit windows from the inside. We have to knock to be admitted.

'I hope you didn't step in it,' I tell Harry.

'What? With Mr. Sheen? Never! At least not so's Coats could track my shoe size.'

This is not much comfort. If Harry gets caught violating the gag order, it is not likely that the judge will make fine distinctions between Harry and me when he starts handing out fines or jail time.

Finally the lock turns on the other side of the door, and we are admitted to the courtroom by the bailiff inside.

Evan Tannery is already at his counsel table, seated next to one of the investigating detectives. I have seen this cop scurrying with notes into the courtroom, whispering with Tannery during breaks. If he is here today, as a representative of the people, my guess is that he is the one who finally nailed down Tanya Jordan's testimony. Tannery would want him front and center so that she is less likely to recant and change any of the details of her story.

'Counsel, you have a second?' Tannery wants to huddle.

'Sure.'

He comes over to our counsel table as we unload our briefcases and Harry starts to pore through one of the boxes delivered earlier by his delivery boy.

'Our witness is a little traumatized,' he tells us. 'You can understand. She's lost her daughter.'

'I understand perfectly.' He wants a stipulation. I can smell it. Some area of inquiry he wants to put off-limits on cross.

'We should go easy on her.'

'We have no interest in beating her up,' I tell him.

'I didn't think you would. Would you be willing to shorten her testimony a little?'

'In what way?'

'Accept declarations in lieu of certain portions of her testimony?'

Harry wants to know how we can stipulate to anything until we know what she is going to say.

Tannery insists these are not contentious areas, but merely intended to reduce the stress on the witness.

'Certainly you'd be willing to accept that she is the mother of the victim, that they had a close familial relationship? These are painful areas. No need to drag the witness through the details.'

'If she testifies at trial, are you willing to forgo testimony in this area?' I ask.

Tannery has to huddle with his friend the cop. They debate the issue. I can tell the detective isn't happy. Finally Tannery turns back to us.

'Agreed.'

I look at Harry. He shrugs his shoulders. This sounds good. The details of a close family relationship would highlight emotional issues that could inflame the jury. If we can temper them with a stipulation, so much the better.

'And one more,' says Tannery. 'It would be pointless to drag the poor woman through her personal background. Her political affiliations, social acquaintances – ancient history,' he says.

'What are we talking about?' asks Harry. 'How ancient?'

'We're talking about the period of time when she was a student in Michigan. We'll stipulate that she was involved in demonstrations, what some might have called, at least at that time, a radical movement.'

Harry looks at him askance. 'Are we talking a conviction here?'

'No felonies,' says Tannery.

'But she was arrested?'

'Minor disturbance,' says the prosecutor. 'A

refusal to disperse. She was arrested with a number of other people. She did no time.'

'Was she a minor at the time?'

Tannery shakes his head. This means that the conviction is not sealed. He would have to disclose it even though we could not impeach her testimony on this basis alone.

'And where did this violation take place?' I ask.

'On the university campus,' says Tannery.

My eyebrows rise a little. 'Exactly where on the campus?'

'Near the defendant's faculty office.'

'She was picketing him?' asks Harry.

'With a number of other people,' he says.

'So she has a prior history with the defendant?'

'No history,' says Tannery. 'She didn't like what he was working on. She made her feelings known just like a lot of other students at the time.'

He has a prepared stipulation, one page. He hands it to me and I read, but before I finish the bailiff is on his feet.

'Please rise. Superior Court in and for the County of San Diego is now in session. Honorable Harvey Coats presiding.'

Coats comes down the corridor leading from chambers in a swirl of black and ascends the bench. He takes his seat, a tufted high-back executive chair. 'Be seated.' We all sit down. I am still reading

Tannery's stipulation, with half an eye up on the bench.

Coats shuffles through a thin sheaf of papers he has carried with him, looking for his starting place.

'The record will reflect that the jury has been excused, that the press and public have been excluded from these proceedings. Mr. Tannery, are you prepared to make an offer of proof?'

'I am, Your Honor. If we could have a moment. Mr. Madriani is reviewing a document. It may save the court some time.'

Tannery is getting his ducks lined up, his own yellow legal lined notes in order, waiting for me to finish reading.

'Mr. Madriani, am I to understand that your client has opted not to be present today?'

'That's correct, Your Honor.'

Coats makes a note. Because today's proceedings are in the nature of a motion to admit evidence, Crone is not required to be present. He will have an opportunity to hear what Tanya Jordan says if she is allowed to testify in front of the jury. For a man who has kept a virtual diary of the trial up to this point, he has a curious reluctance to confront the victim's mother. Harry thinks it is the doctor's guilty conscience, though he says he is not certain Crone possesses one, guilty or otherwise.

'The people call Tanya Jordan,' says Tannery.

The bailiff does not call her name but instead heads toward a side door, the one that leads to the holding cell. They have brought Tanya Jordan in this way so that she wouldn't have to run the gauntlet of the press out in the hall. A few seconds later, she enters the courtroom.

Tanya Jordan is tall, stately. She wears a gray business suit, skirt and jacket, and a blouse with a plain white collar. Despite Tannery's depiction of the distraught mother, there is no air of trepidation on her part. If she is intimidated by the formal surroundings of the courtroom or the specter of cross-examination, she doesn't show it.

Nearly six feet tall, she is slender and carries herself with a grace and assurance that is likely to impress a jury. Her eyes are straight ahead, fixed on the judge up on the bench as she walks toward the counsel tables and the clerk. She raises her right hand and takes the oath, swearing to tell the truth, the whole truth and nothing but, then climbs the two short steps into the witness box and takes her seat.

Tannery moves to the lectern that is positioned between the counsel tables.

'Your Honor, if I may. We have a stipulation outstanding.' He turns toward me for an answer.

'Do I have a copy?' says the judge.

Tannery has forgotten to give him one. The

detective forages at the counsel table, and finally gives up his own copy so that the bailiff can hand it up to the judge.

'What is this?' Coats looks at it as he asks the question.

'It deals with the witness's background, Your Honor. I think we can shorten her testimony if we agree to certain facts.'

'Your Honor, given the limited information we have concerning this witness, I don't think we can accept this portion of the stipulation.' Harry and I are conferring at the table as I address the issue.

'I don't see why not, Your Honor. The information is probably irrelevant,' says Tannery. 'These activities involving the witness took place over two decades ago.'

'If the defense isn't comfortable with the stipulation, you know the drill, Mr. Tannery. You can object, and we'll deal with it then.'

'Your Honor, this was part of a package. Two stipulations.' Tannery isn't happy. 'If we're not going to agree as to the one, then the previous stipulation offered by the people must be withdrawn.'

Tannery looks over at me, dangling this. He knows that the family history, the relationship between mother and daughter, is a measure of damages he can draw out in front of the jury for emotional impact. That he is willing to offer this up makes me wonder why he is so anxious to avoid the witness's history as an undergraduate at Michigan. Harry has the same thought. He is making a note to himself on a legal pad.

'We're willing to accept the one,' I tell the court.

'We're not,' says Tannery.

'Very well,' says the judge. 'There are no stipulations. Proceed.'

'Would you state your name for the record?' Tannery finally turns to the witness.

'Tanya Elizabeth Jordan.' She spells her first and last names for the court reporter. There is no nervous hesitation. She is cool – almost businesslike.

'I know this is difficult for you,' says Tannery. Though you wouldn't know it from her demeanor.

'We will take it slow. If you need time to collect your thoughts, just tell us. You are the mother of the victim in this case, Kalista Jordan?'

She nods. 'I am.'

'When was the last time you spoke with your daughter?'

She doesn't have to think long. 'It was spring, this year.'

'Can you tell the court, did you have a close relationship with your daughter?'

'Very close. I was a single parent. Kalista and I were the only family either of us had. She was my only child.'

'Is her father alive?'

'No. He died when she was an infant. Kalista never knew her father.'

'So you raised her alone?'

'Pretty much. My mother was with us for a time, when I was in college. She would watch my daughter when I attended classes, or had to go to work.'

'But you would characterize your relationship with your daughter as close?'

'Very.'

'And it remained close even as she became an adult? Your daughter, I mean.'

'Yes.'

'How often did you see her?'

'Objection, lack of specificity as to time.'

Tannery looks over at me, and before the judge can rule he reframes the question.

'Within the last year before her death, how often on average would you see your daughter?'

'At least four times a year, perhaps five. We would spend vacation time together, Christmas and Thanksgiving. Given the distance sometimes I would travel out, sometimes she would come home.'

'And on the phone, how often would you talk? During this same time frame?'

'At least twice a week. Sometimes more.'

'Did she confide in you?'

'We didn't have any secrets, if that's what you mean.'

'Did she come to you for advice?'

'Usually. Children don't always ask, but Kalista is . . .' For the first time Tanya Jordan breaks her concentration, looks up at the ceiling and amends her answer. 'She was a good child.' Her voice catches a little as she places her daughter in the past tense.

'Yes.' Tannery glances over at Harry and me as if to say there will be much more of this if we don't take the stipulation.

'When she was young I take it she would talk with you about boys, her friends, what she was doing at school?'

'Oh, yes. We discussed almost everything. She never kept any secrets from me.'

'And I assume you shared things with her?'

'I did.'

Tannery shuffles a page to the top of the stack from the papers in front of him on the lectern.

'Did you ever discuss with her your experiences in college, at the University of Michigan?'

'I did. We talked about the fact that I'd done some things, made some mistakes, but that she was not one of them.'

'What do you mean she was not one of them?'

'I mean having my daughter was not something I

had planned. But I would never have changed it for the world.'

'You weren't married to Kalista's father?'

'No.'

'Was she troubled by this?'

'I don't think so. I mean, I'm sure there were times in her life when growing up without a father was difficult. But she didn't dwell on it. And, as I said, he died long ago.'

'So she would have been without a father whether you had been married to him or not?'

'Objection.'

'Yes.'

'Sustained. You're not supposed to answer the question if there's an objection,' says the judge.

'Sorry.' She looks up at him, only a few inches shorter than Coats even though he's on the bench.

'Let's concentrate on your days at Michigan.' Tannery now starts to lead her into ancient history. Harry and I are looking at each other wondering why, unless Tannery is just trying to take the sting out of an old arrest, something we are not likely to raise in any event.

'Did you talk to your daughter much about your undergraduate days?'

'We talked about it. She was interested in the period. Student activism. I think it held a certain nostalgia for her. Kids today have it much easier, but they think they missed a lot, in the sixties and seventies.'

'Civil rights?' says Tannery.

'That was a big part of it. Yes.'

'And you were involved back then when you were in college.'

'I was.'

'You were active in civil rights activities?'

'Yes.'

'You engaged in demonstrations? So-called sit-ins?'

'I did.'

'And Kalista was interested in this?'

'Yes. She always wanted to know what it was like. I think to her it was' – she thinks for a second – 'like history. Curiosity driven by nostalgia. Kalista was born when I was in college, but she was only an infant when I graduated. She had no recollection of that time. It was very difficult. The only reason I was able to attend the university was that I had a scholarship, and my mother provided child care so I could attend classes. We lived in a small apartment off campus. Kalista wanted to know about it. She was very curious.'

'And you would talk about this with her?'

'We would discuss it.'

'Your mother, is she alive?'

'She died four years ago.'

'I'm sorry.' Tannery is laying it all out, life leveraged from the bootstraps. He takes her through her studies in college, her jobs on the side to support the family while she went to school, a time punctuated with bouts of social activism. What Tanya Jordan calls her 'period of commitment.' She says it with a somewhat cynical grin as if she has grown up since then and come to realize there is no such thing as justice.

'And you say you participated in demonstrations when you were at the university?'

'I did.'

'Did you consider yourself highly active in this way?'

She thinks for a moment. 'I considered myself committed.'

'To social justice. Civil rights?'

'Right.'

'Do you believe you are still committed in this way? To these goals?'

'Yes.' She says it, but the conviction is gone from her voice. What kind of social justice can exist in a world in which her child has been savagely murdered and dismembered?

'And can you tell the court, did your daughter share this same interest? This commitment?'

'Yes, she did.'

Tannery pauses, looks through his sheaf of

papers, finds the one he is looking for and studies it for a moment. 'I'm going to hand you a document. Your Honor, may I approach the witness?'

The judge motions him on.

'I want you to look at this document and tell the court what it is.' Tannery hands her what looks like three stapled pages. The witness looks at it briefly, then looks up.

'It's a police report. A record of my arrest on May second, nineteen seventy-four.'

'And what were you arrested for?'

'I'm not sure what the exact charge was. Disturbing the peace, or unlawful assembly.'

'What were you doing when you were arrested?'

'We were picketing. It was a sit-in at the university. In the faculty offices.'

'Why were you picketing?'

'Because of research being done at the university.'

'What kind of research?'

'It was a kind of racial profiling. Intelligence quotients, based on so-called genetic research.'

Tannery, who is still at the witness box, now turns to look at Harry and me.

'And who was performing this research? The head of the project at that time?'

'Doctor David Crone.'

'The defendant in this trial?'

'Yes. That's correct.'

'Had you ever met the defendant at that time?'

'Yes.'

'And when was that?'

'I took a class from him.'

'He was a faculty member and you were one of his undergraduate students?'

'That's correct.'

'This was a science class in genetics?'

'Right.'

'And why did you take this class? I mean, I assume it wasn't a required course?'

'I took it to get information.'

'What kind of information?'

'At that time it was suspected that he . . .'

'Doctor Crone?'

'Yes. It was believed that he was gathering information to show that blacks, African-Americans, lacked certain cognitive abilities based on their genetic makeup.'

'The ability to reason, to form judgments.' Tannery is leading her shamelessly, but Harry and I don't object. We want to see what the witness has to say. It will be another thing if she gets in front of the jury.

'That's correct.'

'And I take it this was controversial?'

'Dynamite,' says the witness. 'It was not something they wanted out in the public, at least not until they were finished, until he had his studies done. Then it would take time to refute the findings. While that was being done, Dr. Crone would have been all over the airwaves promoting his study, giving it wide publicity.'

'Which takes us back to the question of why you took the course from the defendant in the first place.'

'Because I was asked to.'

'By whom?'

She takes a deep breath. 'We were activists. We called ourselves Students for Racial Justice. Some were grad students. Others undergraduates.'

'And you were a member of this group?'

'I was.'

'Why did they pick you? I mean, why not some graduate student who was doing research with Dr. Crone?'

'There weren't any minority graduate students involved in his project. He wouldn't have them. At least that was the rumor.'

'Objection. Move to strike.'

'Sustained.'

'Were there any black graduate students working on Dr. Crone's project?'

'No.'

'Were there any minorities of any color?'

'He had one Asian graduate student, and the rest were all white.'

'So the only opportunity to get close to the project was as an undergraduate?'

'That's correct.'

'Now, with reference to the undergraduate class that you took from Dr. Crone, were there any other African-American students in that class, besides yourself?'

'No.'

'Why not?'

'The word was out on campus that this was not a class that African-Americans would want to take.'

'Why was that?'

'It was believed that Dr. Crone had a racial bias.'

'Objection. No foundation. Speculation on the part of the witness.'

'Let me rephrase the question,' says Tannery. 'Did you have occasion to talk to other black and minority students at the time about this class?'

'I did.'

'And based on those conversations, did you form any conclusions as to why minority students might not want to take this class being taught by Dr. Crone?'

'Yes. I concluded that there was a general feeling that Dr. Crone was racially biased.'

'And what was this based upon?'

'Stories regarding his work.'

What the witness means is rumors, since none of

the students were close enough to know the nature of his work.

'How many students were there in the class?'

'Roughly a hundred, maybe a hundred and twenty.'

'And you were the only African-American?'

'That's right.'

'Now you say you were selected by this group. This Students for Racial Justice. Why were you selected to do this?'

'I majored in education, minored in science. I had good grades. Also I worked at the university part-time, which gave me access to certain information, and to some offices.'

Harry looks at me as if the shoe has just dropped.

'This access, did it involve faculty offices?'

'It did.'

'Including the office of Dr. Crone, the defendant?'

'Yes.' She looks at me and smiles as she says it.

'Except for your daughter, have you ever told anyone else about this?'

'Only the people involved in our group.'

'You're talking about this organization you belonged to, Students for Racial Justice?'

'That's right.'

'And during this period, did you actually enter Dr. Crone's office?'

'I did.'

'When?'

'I can't remember the exact date, but it was in the spring, near the end of the academic term.'

'And did you take anything from that office?'

She looks directly at me, Crone's alter ego, before she answers. 'I did.' She says it with purpose, as if this was the culmination of some mission.

'And what was it that you took?'

'I copied some research papers. Handwritten notes in a binder. There were also printed forms with raw data and some conclusions written by him in his own hand, based on that data. I copied all of it.'

'By "him," I assume you mean the defendant, David Crone.'

She nods.

'For the record,' says Tannery.

'That's correct.'

'Why did you copy these papers?'

She hesitates an instant before responding. 'They were evidence.'

'Evidence of what?'

'Of what he was working on.'

'And what was that?'

'Racist studies,' she says.

'Objection.' I'm on my feet. 'Your Honor, this is irrelevant, prejudicial. It is hearsay. It's beyond the scope of any evidence before this court. The worst kind of speculation by this witness.'

'We're not offering it to prove the truth of the matter,' says Tannery. 'That these documents or that Dr. Crone's work was racist, but only to show the state of mind of this witness. As a motivating factor.'

'Motivation for what?' I ask.

'We're getting to that,' says Tannery.

'I assume there is some relevance?' says the judge.

'Absolutely,' says Tannery. 'If you'll just allow me a few more questions . . .'

With the jury out of the box, on an offer of proof, there is little harm to be done, so Coats permits Tannery to go on an evidential safari. It is little wonder the prosecution gave up so easily on the theory of a love tryst. Intimation of racial bias would be far more damaging. From a tactical point, it is also better because it doesn't sully the reputation of the victim.

'These documents, these copies, what did you do with them?'

'I turned them over to some people.'

'The people from your organization?'

She nods, then remembers about the court reporter and gives an audible 'Yes.'

'And what did they do with them?'

'They turned them over to the newspapers. The campus newspaper was the first, but then there were demonstrations, and the major press got involved. I believe the *Trib* picked it up, and then it went national. The wires got the story. The Associated Press.' She says this with a smile.

'And what happened?'

'There was a mighty furor,' she says. Her voice rises an octave in indignation. 'All hell came down. On the university. On Crone. He was called in by the administration. There were meetings of the academic senate. There was an investigation, a lot of questions. In the end the research stopped.'

Harry looks at me, trepidation in his eyes, an expression of *I told you so* from the lips up. Harry is thinking what I am: mother and daughter, history repeating itself, only Mom had the good grace and foresight to copy the papers from Crone's office, instead of taking them.

'Did Dr. Crone ever find out that you were responsible for obtaining these documents and releasing them to the press?'

'Not that I know of. I don't think he did.'

'So it was never made public? At least not until today?'

'That's right.'

'And you were never arrested?'

'How do you mean?'

'For taking Dr. Crone's papers?'

'Oh. No.'

Tannery shifts gears, shuffles papers at the podium. 'Now, can you tell the court, did you subsequently, years later, have occasion to tell your daughter about this episode in your life, the fact that you had taken documents from one of your professors while in college?'

'I did.'

'And when did that conversation take place?'

'About two years ago.' There is a certain intent look in her eyes now as she stares at me from the stand. Message to Crone.

'And how did this conversation come about?'

'Kalista had just completed her doctoral thesis. She was looking forward to employment opportunities, some field of research. That's where her strength lay. She had an excellent academic record. There were a number of offers, and one in particular that caught my eye. It was from the Genetics Center.'

'That's the research institute directed by the defendant, David Crone?'

'That's correct.'

'And how did you come to realize that the center had made an offer of employment to your daughter?'

'She showed me the letter. His name was very prominent on the letterhead. He had signed the letter soliciting Kali to apply. She told me that she'd actually met him at the university, when he was recruiting. I thought it couldn't possibly be the same man. But his curriculum vitae was included in the literature that came to the house. It mentioned his time on the faculty at Michigan. It was him. I couldn't believe it. Of course it didn't say anything about his earlier research into racial genetics. He needed money, and he wasn't going to get it . . .'

'Objection.'

'Sustained. Just answer the question,' says Coats.

'But you told your daughter about the defendant's history in this area? The fact that he'd been involved in controversial research regarding racial genetics in the past?'

'I did.'

'When you talk about controversy,' says Tannery, 'let's get into some of the specifics. What exactly was Dr. Crone working on back then?'

'Objection, Your Honor. This is irrelevant.'

'Overruled. You can answer the question.'

'He was working on *racial graying*.'

'And what is that?'

'He was researching racial markers, enzymes that distinguish one racial group from another, with the goal of finding ways to neutralize them, to blur them. He wanted to create a kind of genetic melting pot in which there would ultimately be no racial distinctions, no unique characteristics of race.'

'And you considered this to be unethical?'

'Absolutely. He was playing God, or getting ready to. It was clear that he was leaning toward the elimination of minority characteristics.'

'And you stopped him?'

'Yes, I did. Fortunately for us,' she says, 'the science of genetics was not as advanced back then. We were able to find out what he was working on and expose it.'

'And you told this to your daughter?'

'I did.'

'What else did you tell her?'

'I told her about the demonstrations back in the seventies. About Crone's published studies, and how they were discredited.'

'Did you tell her that you were in large part responsible for uncovering the information that led to this?'

'I did.'

'And what was her reaction?'

'Objection.'

The witness sits upright in the chair and looks at me. There is a long sigh, as if she didn't hear the objection.

'She was proud of me. She said I did the right thing.'

'Objection. Move to strike.'

'Sustained.' The judge admonishes her that she is

not to answer the question when there is an objection.

The witness looks at him but doesn't indicate one way or the other whether or not she accepts his instruction. Coats presses the issue, and finally Tanya Jordan acknowledges that she understands.

Hearsay is the law's final insult in a murder trial. The victim's voice is silenced forever. Now the rules of evidence, with narrow exception, erase every comment she made before death. This is sufficiently broad as to include Kalista Jordan's feelings regarding the incidents related to her by her mother.

Tannery asks the judge for a moment. He confers with the cop back at the counsel table. The problem here is that they have run into a wall. The witness cannot relate to the jury things told to her by her now-dead daughter. Tanya Jordan can only testify as to her part of any conversation, and the jury, without more, cannot fill in the gaps with guesses. If it comes down to that, it is likely that the judge will not allow her to testify at all.

The prosecutor comes back to the podium. 'Let me ask you, did you discuss with your daughter this employment opportunity? The job with the Genetics Center?'

'I did.'

'And can you tell the court what you told your daughter in this regard?'

'I told her I didn't think it was a good idea for her to take the job.'

'And why not?'

'Because of Dr. Crone's history.'

'You mean his perceived racial attitudes?'

'Objection. There has been no testimony as to his attitudes, only his work.'

'Sustained. Rephrase the question.'

'Is it fair to say that you didn't want your daughter to take the job with Dr. Crone because of your knowledge regarding the history of his work in racial genetics?'

'Yes.'

Tannery smiles at my having made the point, one that he is likely to expand upon for the jury.

'But she took the job anyway?' he asks.

'Yes.'

Why? The unasked question lingers in the air like the acrid smell of smoke from a spent fire. Tannery can't pose it because it would call for hearsay, but the jury will no doubt conjure it in their silent thoughts.

'But so that we're clear, you didn't want her to take this job?'

'No.'

'And the reason?'

'Dr. Crone's history. What I considered, my view, my opinion that he had been involved in what I considered racist genetic studies.'

The witness is a quick study. I object, but this time the judge overrules me.

I can object to a statement of fact, but not to her considered opinions, especially when they relate to the witness's motives.

'I didn't think Kalista should get involved with someone who had that kind of a history.' The witness drives the point home.

There are a dozen avenues of attack on cross: What makes Tanya Jordan an expert on racial genetics? How can she be so sure Crone's research wasn't legitimate? How is it possible to pursue science if certain topics are taboo? All these are poison. Tannery would watch with glee as I got tangled in each of them. The witness has already characterized Crone's earlier work as 'racist.' There was enough of a sting to these charges at the time to draw controversy, to bring an abrupt end to his research back then. To parse words with the dead victim's mother now, an African-American, over what constitutes racism is not a dispute I am likely to win. One thing is sure: If the issue becomes racism, the verdict will no longer be in doubt.

Tannery moves closer to the question.

'Did you have reason to believe that Dr. Crone

was involved in racially related research at the time he was recruiting your daughter?'

'I didn't know.'

'Is it fair to say that you were concerned about this?'

'I was concerned. Yes.'

'And did you come to learn later that this was in fact the case?'

'I did. I received a message from Kalista that she wanted to turn over documents that she had taken to her people.'

'Objection, Your Honor. Hearsay.'

' "Her people." Those are the words she used?' says Tannery.

'Sustained,' says Coats.

'She used those words? She wanted to turn these documents over to her people?'

'That's exactly what she told me.'

The judge is now pounding his gavel. 'The question and the answer will be stricken. The witness is instructed not to answer a question when there is an objection pending. Do you understand.' Coats points his gavel at her like a gun, then aims it at Tannery.

'And you, sir. You know better than that. The only reason I am not imposing sanctions is that the jury's not in the box. Try that when they are, and you'd better bring your toothbrush. You're gonna be spending the night in the bucket.'

'Sorry, Your Honor. I got carried away.'

'Yes. You're going to be carried away by my bailiff, you keep that up.'

Tannery feigns a little mock humility. Eyes downcast, feet shuffling, body English substituting for an apology. He shuffles through a few papers, then picks up without missing a beat.

'Let me ask you,' he says. 'This information concerning the nature of Dr. Crone's current research, were you able to obtain information regarding this matter from another source? A source other than your daughter?'

Coats is looking at him over the top of his glasses, ready to swat him with his wooden hammer.

'Yes.'

'And what was that source?'

'Another employee at the center.'

Tannery turns to look at me as he poses the final question. The hair on the back of my neck stands up. I can feel it coming; lawyer's coup de grâce.

'And can you tell the court the name of that employee?'

'His name is William Epperson.'

# CHAPTER THIRTEEN

Crone is waiting for us at the jail. Harry called ahead to make sure the guards would deliver him to one of the attorney-client consulting cubicles over the dayroom where the 'professor' has been pumping iron and putting miles on the treadmill while we were in court.

The news that Epperson served as a source of information for Kalista's mother hit us out of the blue. Harry has tried and gotten nowhere with Epperson. Now we are faced with the prospect of hostile testimony, what we have feared from the former basketball star from the inception.

'What did Crone say when you gave him the news?'

'If he was surprised, he didn't voice it,' says Harry.

'You think he knew?'

'If he didn't, he's the coolest character since James Dean. Didn't seem to faze him in the least. Said he had absolute confidence in us.' Harry looks at me with a crooked grin.

'Maybe he didn't know what else to say.'

'He could have shown a little fear,' says Harry. 'That would be a nice change.'

'So the man's got ice in his veins.'

'He's a fucking snow-cone. Which leaves us right where we started. Kalista Jordan being dead, anything she told her mother we can keep out. That's hearsay,' says Harry. 'But Epperson's another matter. He's alive and available. If Tannery puts him up on the stand and Epperson testifies that Crone was mixing some genetic stew with the entrails of wombats to come up with a new formula for African IQ, our closing argument is gonna resonate like the Nazi national anthem. It wouldn't be a long leap for the jury to conclude that Kalista was killed because Crone found out she was about to go public on some hair-raising racial experiments. You're going to find yourself defending the angel of death,' he tells me.

'That doesn't make sense,' I say. 'Why would he hire her in the first place if he was working on something that was racially charged? Why take the chance?'

'Who's he going to hire?' says Harry. 'There's not a lot of skinheads running around with Ph.D.s in whatever it was.'

'Molecular electronics,' I tell him.

'Whatever. Crone needed qualified researchers to

get funding. And the presence of a minority or two didn't hurt. He knew how to play the game. Maybe he didn't have a choice. You have to remember Crone had to get the funding, the corporate grant from that company.'

'Cybergenomics.'

'That's the one. If he had to take Epperson to obtain a research grant, it could be he was induced to hire Kalista Jordan for the same reason. They knew each other before they went to work there. Epperson was still with the company when Kalista was hired. He didn't come on board at the center until after,' says Harry. 'What if they were working together to get information on Crone? If Kalista's mother is telling the truth, and she fired up her daughter with tales of activism from the days of yore, the daughter could have gone to Epperson, enlisted his help.'

'And you think they were out to set him up?'

'If the mother is to be believed. And if Epperson comes through for him on the stand, Tannery's got a good chance of selling it to the jury.'

I think about this for a moment. 'There's something wrong, which doesn't fit.'

'What is it?' says Harry.

'Why would a corporation like Cybergenomics touch anything like that? I mean if Crone was engaged in research with a social and political downside why would they get involved, sully their corporate image? I can't imagine there would be that much money involved in it.'

Harry mulls this over for a moment, deep in thought as we walk through the courthouse lobby. 'What if . . .' He's thinking out loud. 'What if their funding was for something else? What if Crone was working on the racial stuff on the side? Something the company didn't know about? If news of it got out, think what would happen to his funding.'

'Dry up overnight,' I say.

'It could be worse than that,' says Harry. 'If Crone was diverting funds for something else, playing hide-and-seek with grant money, you're talking some nasty criminal shit. Now there's something to kill for.'

Harry and I suffer the same thought instantly. We utter the words in unison: 'A financial audit.'

We turn to look at each other, stopped dead in our tracks. Anybody watching us from the top of the escalator, looking down, might half expect by body language alone to see some luminescent green light flicker on behind our eyes.

'Was there one?' I ask.

'I don't know.'

Then I remember I had some of the documents, working papers on the early grant request for the Huntington's study on the children.

That would give us something to start with. The project number and the name they used for the principal research. It was on the grant request.

'What do we know about the funding?' I ask Harry.

'Squat,' he says. Suddenly the sickening thought: We've been looking in all the wrong places.

I think maybe I might have filed them in one of the cabinets back in the office, but then I realize where I left them. They were copies only, and when we finished with them I left them with Doris Boyd.

I tell Harry I'll call her in the morning. He can stop by and pick them up. 'That'll give you a start, anyway. Tell you where to begin looking.'

'If that's it,' says Harry, 'Crone would be under a legal hammer.'

'Like a moth under a mallet.'

'He could have been personally liable for the funds,' says Harry.

'That's if they were feeling charitable. Didn't nail him criminally for diversion, embezzlement,' I say.

'That wouldn't look too good on his resume next time he goes out fund hunting. And it's tough to get a grant when you're in the joint,' says Harry. Though I suspect Harry has known a few clients who have done it.

'You think this is what Jordan and Epperson were doing, chasing the money trail?'

'I don't know.' Harry doesn't want to think about it. 'Maybe we're just worried about nothing,' he says. 'I mean, we can't connect all the dots.'

'Let's just hope Tannery can't. I don't need any more surprises. Find out everything you can about any audits. Track the trail of the grant money, especially anything coming in from Cybergenomics.'

Harry makes notes as we walk, then clicks the top of his pen and sticks it back in his vest pocket. 'If there's anything there, I hope you have an answer for them.'

'Me?' I look at him as we stride across the lobby. I'm half a step behind.

'You're the one Crone has all this confidence in,' he says.

'What about you? You're the one who's dreaming up all this shit to worry about.'

'That's probably why he doesn't have any confidence in me.' Harry smiles.

Walking fast, we're at a near jog, down the front steps of the courthouse and around the corner toward the jail. Harry is out front, the two of us angling toward the curb. It's like one of those surreal dreams. I'm listening to Harry talk, but my brain isn't in it, as the tumblers of recognition turn, clicking into place.

It is almost by us before I realize. The driver could have turned around in the middle of the block, pulled a U-y, but he was already committed; it would have been too obvious. The best he can do is lift an elbow to shade his face as he glides past, headed for the larger herd of vehicles on Broadway. The elbow up was a good effort, except that I have seen the move too many times on the basketball court, and it's hard to be inconspicuous when you're seven foot six.

'You see that?' I say.

'What?' Harry looks up, at me, then at the sky – it's a bird . . . it's a plane.

'The car,' I tell him. 'That van.'

By the time he turns, the vehicle is at the corner sixty yards away.

'I didn't see it.'

'Epperson was behind the wheel.'

Harry gives me a dull look, then finally stops to turn and get a fix. 'What do you think he's doing down here? A long way from work. And he's excluded from the courtroom.'

'Yeah. I know.' But what is most troubling to me is the vehicle itself, the dark blue van with a sizeable dent in the left front fender, its parking light smashed on that side: the same van that was parked in front of my house last night.

By the time we get to the jail Crone is waiting, and Harry and I are in no mood for games. We are positioned on the other side of the thick acrylic that separates us from the jail holding area. Though we can hear every word and see each gesture, we can't touch Crone, and Harry at this moment is ready to. There are no smiles from either side of the screen.

Crone is the picture of concern, as anxious as I have seen him from the start of the trial, though this isn't saying much. What we are getting is mostly denials.

'I don't know what she's talking about. I had a lot of students over the years. I can't remember them all.'

'She remembers you,' says Harry.

'I probably gave her a bad grade.'

Harry and I have decided not to mention Cybergenomics or questions regarding the grant until we know more. We confine ourselves to Epperson and Tanya Jordan's testimony.

'The fact is Bill and I had a good working relationship,' says Crone. 'We got on well. I have nothing but wonderful things to say about him.'

'Let's hope the feeling is mutual,' I say, 'when they put him on the stand.'

'From what we're hearing, I doubt it,' says Harry.

'There's nothing that I know of. Believe me.'

'Where have we heard that before?' Harry is starting to get short with Crone. 'We're not interested in stories about collegial working relationships or academic mutual respect. What we want to know is whether you were working on anything with a racial edge.'

Crone looks at him over the top of his glasses. 'We're back to that.'

'We've never left that,' says Harry. 'Apparently this good working relationship you had with Dr. Epperson included his disclosure of information to Kalista Jordan's mother that involved some – how do I say it? – "socially divisive issues." '

Crone looks at him from beyond the screen.

'Racial genetics,' says Harry. 'And we're not talking a cure for sickle-cell anemia. Tell us about this racial graying.'

Crone shakes his head. 'There was a misunderstanding back then.'

'Back when?' says Harry.

'When I was at Michigan.'

'We're not talking about Michigan. We're talking about now.'

Crone actually looks mystified, as if he doesn't understand. 'What is she saying, that I'm doing it now?'

'That seems to be what she's saying, and according to her, Epperson is prepared to substantiate it on the stand.'

'No,' says Crone. His eyes suddenly flash toward me. 'Paul, you have to believe me. I don't know what the woman is talking about.' He has both palms laid flat on the countertop in front of him, leaning toward the acrylic partition, staring intently into my eyes as if to emphasize the truth he is telling.

'Tell us about racial graying,' says Harry. He's not about to be put off.

Crone is a bundle of frustration. Eyes darting, looking at everything but us. 'Where do I start?'

'Try the beginning,' says Harry.

'Fine. Let's go back to the beginning, back to the Middle Ages when there were dynastic wars, when armies fought under the banner of Christendom to blot religious differences from the map. They butchered in the name of God: a higher calling than what we are about to engage in if we continue heading in the direction we're drifting.'

Suddenly his eyes are on us, cutting through me like twin lasers. 'Do you have any idea how many people over the ages have lost their lives as a result of religious strife?'

No answer.

'You're wondering what this has to do with genetics?'

'It crossed my mind,' says Harry.

'The sectarian wars of religion were merciful compared with the racial and ethnic conflicts that will engulf man if we don't deal with them now. People could convert to new religions if presented with the sharp blade of a sword or the heat of the flames as an alternative. But how do you change the pigmentation of your skin, the shape of your nose, the texture of your hair?

'We are already engaged in the new Inquisition; if you don't believe me, just look at the racial composition of our prisons. We are headed for the new Crusades and if you don't buy that, witness what is happening in the Balkans.

'You know,' he says, 'the great thinkers, the masters of intellect from the earliest writings, lectured on the equality of the species since long before Christ and yet we have lived through eons of slavery.

'Here in the Land of the Free it took seventy-five years, a Civil War and six hundred thousand dead before the preamble of Jefferson's declaration became fact, that all men are created equal. And still there are those who don't accept it.

'Yes, that's what I was working on. Back in Michigan. I admit it.' He looks at Harry. 'You don't get it?'

There is only the sound of silence from our side of the screen. Harry and I are now confronted with the thought, *How do we put Crone on the stand to talk about this?*

'No matter how well intentioned, no matter how much we crave social justice,' he says, 'we are never going to be color-blind. Face the fact. We are always going to be cognizant of those differences that mark us physically. And it's not just racial,' says Crone. 'In an age of scientific enlightenment and technological miracles, we judge our leaders on their physical stature and television presence and we select fools and the false priests of corruption to govern us. We embrace diversity but engage in white flight. We want to smile, hug minorities because it makes us feel good. We want to revel in those differences, and yet the very act, the recognition of difference, separates us. Yes, I was working toward erasing those differences. I don't know that I am proud of that. The very endeavor is a damning admission that our species has failed in the one single act that should have come naturally, the act of accepting one another on faith. The knowledge that we all put our pants on the same way each morning, one leg at a time.

'It's a subtle thing,' he says. 'The recognition of difference. How do we tell the brain not to form a system of classification that is impressed on us daily by economics, by the neighborhoods in which we live, by the media in which we are immersed and that we seem to absorb almost by osmosis?'

He looks at me. 'Tell me you have no twinge of anxiety when five or six young black men, or a group of macho Mexican teens, walk toward you on the sidewalk. Would you have the same fears if those kids were white?

'Would they feel compelled to engage in the secret rites of gang graffiti, or don gang garb, clothing that sets them apart? These are tribal instincts as old as man. Archeologists will tell you there is evidence of this on the steppes of Africa dating back nine millennia. But that's where we're headed,' says Crone, 'back to the tribes, back to the darkness. What I hoped for was a way out.'

He looks at us, stone-cold from the other side of the screen. 'I admit it was controversial. There is no so-called race gene,' he says. 'We know that. It is much more subtle. There's more genetic difference within racial groups than between them. We're dealing with a hundred, maybe a thousand, genetic differences. Melanin for skin color, but even that is no indicator of race. Some might call it unethical to even be looking at this. But you tell me a better way to deal with the problem, and I'll change my views.'

'How about leaving the decision to nature?' says Harry.

'That's not going to cut it,' says Crone. 'I'm afraid we don't have a million years to allow evolution to take its course, to blur the distinctions and make us one family. We are very likely to destroy one another in that time. Racial strife is going to devour us.'

'I like the way I look,' says Harry. 'I wouldn't want you screwing with it.'

'Future generations,' says Crone. 'If it worked, it would only work on them.'

'Maybe they'd like to be the product of nature, too,' I say.

'Nice thought,' he says, 'but it doesn't address the problem. As a matter of science, as a genetic factor, race doesn't exist; it is purely a social concept. Wouldn't it be nice if society caught up with science? Maybe the race could survive. I'm talking about the human race,' he says. 'Instead of filling census forms with meaningless data regarding race and ethnic origins, we should be moving away from that. All we are doing is further ingraining racial stereotypes.'

He considers for a moment, looks at me, pondering how to get through.

'Let me give you an example. You're a pilot in a small plane. You take off and within minutes you find yourself engulfed in clouds. You look out through the windows and all you see is white. You trust your eyes to tell you which way is up. You rely on your inner ear. Two minutes later you fly the plane into the ground. Why? Because your eyes and your inner ear deceived you. That's how it is with race. We're trusting our perceptions and ignoring the science. Look at the instruments of science and they will tell you there is no genetic difference, no such thing as racial markers. But people believe what they see. So how do you deal with that?'

I have no answer for him.

'People are so stupid,' he says. 'It's like when you ask someone what it takes to be great, the first and most fundamental element of making a mark on human history, they always think about it, though they never think long enough, and then they start rattling off the characteristics of the great, whittling down the list, looking for that one essential common ingredient. They talk about persistence, and brilliance, education and eloquence, natural talent and acquired skills; some of them even come close and mention luck. But they never get it right. They always miss the most essential and obvious element of them all. And it's so simple.

'In order to be great, in fact in order to achieve anything in this life, first rule – you have to survive.' He smiles. 'Bet you didn't get it.'

He knows by my look I didn't.

'And yet we all take it for granted. Do any of us know? Do we have any idea how many Einsteins or Picassos there might have been but for the fact that they didn't survive to realize the promise of their greatness? How many Churchills or Roosevelts died in their infancy because of disease, war or famine? We'll never know. The world will never know who they were. They never made it into the history books because of the simple fact that they failed the first test of greatness. They didn't survive long enough. And that's where we're headed as a species,' he says. 'In the race for greatness in the cosmos. Other beings on other planets will never know we existed, because unless we solve the problems here, we'll never survive long enough.

'Do you know that in the last five months, since I've been in here, I've been recruited, at least two dozen times, by Nordic Pride, the Caucasian gang that provides protection?'

What he is telling me I have already heard from jailers whom I know. Places of incarceration are the modern equivalent of the state of nature. You band together or you die.

'It's a caste system constructed on color: brown, black and white. So far, I've refrained,' he says. 'How much longer I can afford this luxury I'm not sure. If I'm convicted and end up at San Quentin or Folsom, I'm going to have to stop thinking about it and act. My time for commitment will have arrived,' he says. 'I will have to join the tribe, or die. You can take it on faith,' he says, 'that I am a survivor.'

These are no longer academic questions for Crone. I can tell that he has considered them at night in the dark on his bunk.

For a moment there is just silence. Then he looks at us. 'Funny, isn't it?'

'What?' asks Harry.

'That the petri dish growing the culture for modern American society is not the schools, or the corporations or even the family. It's the prisons.' He laughs a little at the thought.

'Make no mistake,' he says, 'the tribes that are growing there aren't going to stay there. We can't lock them up fast enough or hold them long enough to isolate the problems and to fix them. We'd better do something, and do it quickly.'

'And that's what you were doing,' says Harry. 'Dealing with the problem.'

'Trying to. At least coming up with an option,' says Crone. 'In Michigan.'

'We're back to that,' says Harry.

'Because it's the truth. My views have not changed,' says Crone. 'But I was not engaged in racial genetic research at the center. That is a fact. If you don't believe me, bring Bill Epperson into the courtroom. I'm sure he'll tell you that I wasn't working on anything of the kind.'

'We won't have to bring him in,' says Harry. 'The prosecution is taking care of that.'

'Then talk to Bill if you don't believe me.'

'We've tried,' I tell him. 'He doesn't want to talk to us.' Harry had followed up on a meeting with

Epperson after our encounter in the elevator. As soon as Epperson found out that we represented Crone, he got cold feet. He asked Harry to leave.

'I don't understand.'

'That makes three of us,' says Harry.

'Why wouldn't he talk to you? I know Kalista's death hit him hard. They were close. But I don't think Bill believes I had anything to do with it. In fact, I know he doesn't. He told me so.'

'When was that?'

Crone thinks for a moment. 'A week or so before they arrested me. We were talking in my office. Everybody at the center knew the police were nosing around, that I was a suspect. They let the word out, tried to destroy my reputation. I think they wanted to see if I would run.'

'And what did you say to Epperson?'

'I told him I didn't know why the police kept questioning me.'

'And what did he say?'

'He couldn't figure it out either. He said he couldn't think why anyone would want to hurt Kalista. He said he knew that we'd had some disagreements, but that he was certain I had nothing to do with her death. He didn't hold me responsible. I know he didn't. And believe me, if he had any suspicions he would never have talked to me.'

'Why not?'

Crone suddenly looks away as if maybe he's crossed the line, said something he shouldn't have.

'Listen,' I tell him. 'If you're holding something back, now's not the time. We can't represent a client who is holding out.'

'It's not something that's important,' says Crone.

'Let me decide that,' I tell him.

He thinks about how he's going to say it, tries to measure his words, then just blurts it out: 'Epperson was in love.'

I don't say anything, but he knows the question.

'With Kalista,' he says.

'Next you're going to tell me the feelings weren't mutual?'

He seesaws his head back and forth on his shoulders as if he'd rather not say, then does. 'She liked him. They were friends.'

'But nothing more.'

Crone shakes his head.

'And Epperson was looking for more?'

'He wanted to marry her.'

'Did he ever ask her?' says Harry. Something we might confront Epperson with on the stand.

Crone now gets out of the chair on the other side of the screen. He is in a small, enclosed cubicle, the guard on the other side of a closed door. I can see the uniform through the acrylic partition that separates us and the glass in the door over Crone's shoulder.

'Don't talk with your back to us,' says Harry. 'They can read lips.'

Crone turns around. 'He'd tried to give her an engagement ring.'

'Epperson?' I say.

He nods.

'She turned him down.'

'When?' asks Harry.

'About three weeks before she disappeared.'

'Why the hell didn't you tell us?' I say.

'Because it had nothing to do with her murder.'

'How do you know that?' asks Harry. 'It seems to me only two people could be as certain about that as you seem to be: Epperson if he didn't kill her, and if he didn't whoever did.'

Crone ignores him. 'Kalista took her troubles to a friend, an older woman at the center; the friend came to me. She told me Kalista didn't want to ruin a good friendship with Epperson.'

'When?' I ask.

'A few days after he tried to give her the ring.'

'Who was the intermediary?' asks Harry. 'The older woman?'

'Carol Hodges.'

Hodges has already taken the stand in the state's case. She was one of the witnesses to the argument between Crone and Jordan in the faculty dining room the night Jordan disappeared.

'She was close to Kalista. She thought maybe I could help.'

'How could you have helped?' I ask. 'You and Jordan were at war. She'd taken the working papers from your office. She'd filed a sexual harassment complaint against you?'

'At the time, Hodges didn't know that. Hodges thought I could talk to Bill, try to make him understand that she simply didn't love him, but that she wanted him as a friend. I did what I could.'

'You talked to Epperson?' I ask.

He nods.

'Where did he buy the ring?' asks Harry.

'What?'

'The engagement ring.' Harry has a notepad open on the counter in front of him, pen at the ready.

'I don't know. Why is it important?'

'Did he show it to you?'

'No.'

Nothing we can check out. No evidence with which to confront Epperson on the stand. With Kalista Jordan dead, anything Hodges has to say on this point is hear-say.

'Did Epperson ever talk to anybody else at the center, maybe somebody he might have confided in?'

'Some of the younger staff,' says Crone, 'a few of the younger guys ran together, partied.'

'Why the hell didn't you tell us sooner?' I ask.

'Because I was sure he didn't kill her. He was in love with her.'

'Yes, and she'd rejected him,' says Harry.

'He didn't do it.'

'How do you know?'

All we get is a shrug and a stare from the other side of the acrylic.

Harry wants to talk outside, where Crone can't hear. He tugs me by one arm. I tell Crone to sit tight. Harry and I step outside and close the door on our side of the cubicle, and stand there to make sure that the guard doesn't take Crone away.

'Question is,' says Harry, 'do we talk to Epperson now or hit him on the stand?'

'We have nothing to hit him with. You think you can run down the ring?' I ask.

'If it exists.'

'You don't believe him.'

'I don't know what I believe anymore. Gotta admit it's pretty far-fetched this woman coming to him to do his impression of Cyrano. How many jewelers do you think there are in San Diego?' he asks.

'I'd start in La Jolla, out near the center, work my way this way. Try the places around where Epperson lives.'

Harry nods, a sour look on his face. This is a thankless task. He now has a full plate, following the audit trail for Crone's research and delving into Epperson's love life.

'We have an approximate date for the purchase of the ring. Besides, maybe there were other people at the center who saw it. He may have shown it around. Young man in love,' I tell him.

'Yeah. Just my line of work.' I can tell what Harry is thinking: Crone is sending him out chasing geese.

We step back inside. Crone has calmed down enough to sit, waiting for us at the acrylic partition.

'If we wanted to talk to Epperson,' I say, 'how would we go about it?'

Crone thinks about this for a moment. 'Aaron, I suppose. I could have Dr. Tash call him.'

'It would have to be voluntary. Epperson's conversation with us. No inducements,' I tell him. 'If he doesn't want to talk, he has to be told that he is free to decline.'

'Understood.'

There is no doubt that if we talk to Epperson, Tannery will find out, and will explore the conversation with Epperson on the stand. Anything that looks like duress would cut against us.

'Do you want me to call him? Aaron, I mean.'

I nod.

Crone picks up the jailhouse phone and waits for the operator to answer. 'Bill's the only one who can set this straight. I don't understand why he won't talk to you.'

'He's been told by prosecutors to stay clear,' says Harry.

'Can they do that?'

'They can tell him he doesn't have to talk to us if he doesn't want to. If they wink and nod in all the right places, most witnesses get the message. Don't complicate your life if you don't have to. The rest is up to him,' says Harry.

'Then maybe he just doesn't want to get involved.'

'He is now,' I tell him.

'Well, absolutely. And he's going to have to tell the truth.'

'Yeah, that's what we need. Some truth telling,' says Harry.

Crone takes this as the shot it is intended to be, but doesn't respond.

'I need to have a call placed.' The operator is on the line. 'No, it's a local area code. Yes, it's at the request of my lawyer. He's here. You want to talk to him?'

The jail operator must have said no because Crone doesn't ask me to pick up the receiver on my side.

At this moment he is all energy and enthusiasm, finally something he can do in his own defense. He gives the operator the telephone number from memory, Tash's office number at the center.

'Don't say anything else, just tell him to contact Epperson and have Epperson call my office,' I tell him.

Crone nods, winks from beyond the screen, circled finger and thumb like he understands.

We can hear half of the conversation, Crone breathing into the phone from the mike set in the thick acrylic that separates us.

'Aaron, David here. We have a problem.' Just like that. Crone says it as if he's never left the office, like it's something they can handle in a midmorning staff meeting. 'Can you get ahold of Bill Epperson for me, and have him call somebody.

'No. No. It's nothing having to do with the project. It's the case. There's some mix-up,' he says. 'Nothing serious.'

I'm beginning to grimace on the other side of the screen.

'Seems a witness is saying some things . . .'

I tap on the partition with my pen, shaking my head as Crone looks at me. He nods like he understands, then looks away.

'Some garbage about our work,' he says.

Now I'm tapping with my knuckles, waving him off with my hand. Finger slicing across my throat like a knife as if to cut him off. He turns sideways in the chair so that I can no longer make eye contact.

'Nothing to worry about,' he says. 'Bill can straighten it all out.'

I'm hitting the acrylic hard enough to break a regular window.

Crone gives me another bull's-eye, this time blind, not looking at me, with finger and thumb.

'It's that same old crap,' he says, 'from back in the seventies. Yeah.'

Tash is commiserating on the other end of the line.

'Yes. The whole thing raising its head again. You get tired of people misconstruing your work,' he says. 'Especially now. They're saying I'm doing things when I'm not.

'What's that?

'Yeah, it has to do with the same charges.'

I can only imagine what Tash is saying on the other end, hoping and praying that the operator is not recording it on Tannery's orders.

'Let me check.' Crone cups his hand over the mouthpiece, and turns to look at me. He can see the fire in my eyes, but he ignores this.

'Aaron would like to know if he can come by.'

'What? Now?'

'Tomorrow morning. He's got some numbers he wants me to look at. Maybe about nine one of you could be here?'

Harry and I look at him dazed, being from another planet.

'He *is* helping us get to Bill,' he says.

Harry sits in stunned silence, neither of us able to come up with the words before Crone is turned sideways again, and back to Tash on the phone.

'Good. Yeah, that's fine. Nine o'clock,' he says. 'No, it's not something I can get into, at least not on the phone.' Like he's going to discuss what happened in court behind closed doors with Tash. I decide I'd better be here.

Crone turns to wink at me, a look from furrowed eyebrows, a sly smile as if to say he understands the delicate situation here, the risks of tampering with a witness.

'Tell him it's purely voluntary, but that I'd appreciate it if he'd contact my lawyers, in the interest of fairness.' He gives Tash my phone number to pass along. Then he hangs up.

He turns. Big smile. 'You guys don't mind, do you?'

# CHAPTER FOURTEEN

'You get the feeling we're being used?' asks Harry.

Several months behind bars and on matters of common sense David Crone still lives in a criminally artless other world. It causes me to wonder what confidences he may be sharing with his cellmate at night. The gangs may have his attention, but nothing else seems to make a dent.

By nine the next morning I was back at the jail, this time to watch Crone and Tash flash pages with numbers back and forth. The only reason I did this was to ensure that they didn't discuss matters relating to Kalista Jordan or Tanya's testimony, for which Tash has no privilege. This mime act of number crunching took almost forty minutes. Tash would hold up a work sheet against the partition while Crone jotted numbers on a piece of paper with a dull pencil on the other side. Crone would then hold up his penciled sheet while Tash made adjustments on the original. It was Greek to me, though the guard behind Crone outside the door seemed to take particular interest in the doings. At one point he called in a supervisor who observed the antics for a moment through the window. Seeing that legal counsel was present, the supervisor, a sergeant, chose not to interfere. But I can imagine Tash on the stand being pressed by Tannery to explain what was happening. I raised the question myself, posed it to Tash as we left the jail.

All he would say was 'Genetics. The project.'

'That's crap,' says Harry. 'I don't know about you, but I'm getting tired of this hiding behind the high-tech veil. It's like the holy of holies. Only the lawyers can't go inside. How do we know what they're doing?' he asks. 'It's a convenient cover, if you ask me. They don't want to talk about their work, and yet everything always seems to come back to that. Now we have the victim's mother telling the court they're involved in collecting data with a racial tinge. And still Crone won't tell us what's going on. We need to draw a line in the sand. They don't tell us, we withdraw.'

'It's a nice thought, but Coats isn't likely to let us out at this late date,' I tell him.

We are camped in the office, another late-nighter. Epperson is up tomorrow, Tannery's offer of proof and still I have nothing to talk to him about. If our message to Epperson from Tash got through, it has borne no fruit. I have called the answering service to make sure they put any calls through, and will have them forwarded to the house when we leave here.

'I told you he wasn't gonna call,' says Harry. 'What did Tash say?'

'Says he talked to him. That Epperson told him he would make an effort to call us.'

'What does that mean? Makes it sound like it's a marathon to push the buttons on the phone,' says Harry. 'I'm telling you he's not gonna call.'

I look at my watch. It's almost eleven P.M. Harry is probably right.

'So much for Crone's high regard and good working relations,' he tells me.

Harry spent the morning and afternoon chasing geese, trying to get a lead on the engagement ring Epperson supposedly bought for Kalista Jordan, and running down audit trails at the university on Crone's research.

'Let's start with the ring,' he says, 'since that's gonna be a short discussion. Came up with nothing.'

This is a long shot. With no drawing, no picture and no description, we might as well be looking for the Holy Grail.

'If I have to deal with one more jeweler trying to peddle me a watch . . . They all wanna know the same thing: why some old fart is asking questions about an engagement ring.'

'I understand,' I tell him. 'It's not like old farts never get married. Right?'

He looks at me sideways. 'Right. It's just you get tired, everybody putting you in pigeonholes all the time.' Harry hates to be old, white and male. For Harry it was hard enough being young. But then I have a feeling Harry was old even when he was young.

'The world is always making assumptions,' he says. 'Don't you get tired of it?' Harry doesn't wait for me to answer.

'Pisses me off,' he says. He's had a bad day. A lot of shoe leather left on the street, so that his shoes are now sitting in the middle of my desk on top of a stack of papers, as he lets off steam rubbing one foot crossed over his knee.

'So what are you telling them, these shop owners?' I ask.

'That we're trying to verify an insurance claim. I describe Epperson. That seems to do it.'

'And how are you describing him? Tall? Dark?'

'Yeah,' says Harry. 'A detailed description is always best.'

'And of course you're telling them this is a man with a Ph.D.?'

'I think I may have left that part out,' he says.

I raise an eyebrow.

'You let their imaginations fill in the blanks.'

'With assumptions,' I say.

'Yeah. Well.'

I can imagine that the vision these shop owners have of Epperson after Harry's visit is something from a mug shot. God help the man if he tries to buy more jewelry in any of these places. They'll be calling out the SWAT team.

'Spent a lot of time, came up with nothing,' says Harry. 'Squat. *Nada*. Of course, I only covered half of La Jolla. You have any idea how many jewelry stores there are in that town? And that's just the ones selling new stuff. I haven't even started with the antique spots, the fucking boutiques and galleries for the artsy set. I have a call in to get some help from one of the P.I. firms downtown. They'll have a couple of investigators for us by tomorrow.'

'Good. How about the audit? You picked up the file, the papers from Doris Boyd?'

'Yeah. I went by. She couldn't find them, but she turned the place upside down. She finally located them.'

'Where were they?'

'Seems her husband had looked at 'em last. He put the file in a drawer in a cabinet in the dining room. Good place to keep papers, huh? It got sorta touchy,' says Harry. 'Doris wanted to know if maybe the grant application for the daughter was up and running again. I had to burst her bubble, tell her no; that we needed the documents in Crone's case. Nothing like opening old wounds,' says Harry.

'Still, with their file I was able to track the stuff at the university. Only problem, there was nothing there but another dry hole,' he says. 'If there was an audit, I couldn't find it. They do a financial analysis every year for the budget, but that's it. No certification by an accounting firm, and no audit trail of where last year's money went. Everything I was able to get is there in front of you.' He gestures toward the pile of papers he has planted on my desk, under his shoes.

'If there's no audit trail, it's not going to tell us much.'

'There's some stuff from Cybergenomics in there. I saw the letterhead as I was copying. Didn't have time to read it all, but glanced at it. It looks like normal covering correspondence to me. No mention of Epperson, or Jordan. The letters were addressed to the financial affairs office at the university with copies to Crone.'

I pick up Harry's shoes. Hand them to him to get them off the desk, and start pawing through the papers, a stack about five inches thick. I go through fifteen, maybe twenty, pages quickly seeing if anything jumps out. It doesn't.

'They bind all the working papers together each year. Put 'em between covers in those plastic spiral things and stack 'em on a shelf. I get the sense nobody really looks at them. Makes it a bitch to copy, though,' he says.

'*Hmm?*'

'The spiral binding. Gotta turn each page. End up losing the margins in the copier.' Harry sounds as if he's become an expert on this.

'Some of it's gonna be hard to read. The action seems to be in the budget augmentations,' says Harry, 'and new applications for grants.'

'Did you see any references to *genetic graying*?' I ask.

Harry shakes his head. 'Like I say, I didn't read every page. But then I wouldn't expect to find anything in there on that. If Crone was siphoning money from the grant to put ethnic evolution into overdrive, he wouldn't have been likely to document it in a grant application. You think?'

Harry is right.

'What's the process for the money?' I ask. Age-old adage – follow the money.

'From what I'm told, everything from the state goes into the university's general fund. Gets disbursed from there. Grant money is sequestered in separate accounts and doled out by the university in accordance with the written conditions for each grant. The vice chancellor for fiscal affairs has the final word if there's any dispute. Unless it gets into court.'

'How often does that happen?'

'Never,' says Harry. 'Though according to the woman I talked to in the financial affairs office, disagreements happen more often than you might think. From what I'm told flaps over grant money are usually handled at the administrative level. The courts are a little too public for comfort.'

'Sounds like you got a lot of information from this lady.'

'I took her to lunch,' says Harry.

I give him an arched eyebrow.

'Nothing fancy, just the student union,' he says. 'Between soup and salad she tells me there's a lot of stuff goes on people don't know about in higher education. A lot of it comes under the heading of entertainment. Deans and chancellors, it seems, have to entertain. They buy a lot of shit, pianos, and furniture, university logos painted on the bottoms of their swimming pools. This seemed to be a real problem with her, so I listened,' says Harry. 'Give somebody a shoulder to cry on, sometimes you hear something. According to her, some of this stuff may not be entirely necessary.'

'I'm shocked,' I tell him.

'And sometimes it disappears. The university set gets real sensitive about scandal. Seems the chancellor at one of the other campuses took a dive on insurance fraud a few years back. It's one thing to fudge on the state budget, another to screw over an insurance company. Seems this chancellor spent a bundle of state money buying silverware to entertain,' says Harry. 'Somehow they misplaced it between trips to Europe. So they file an insurance claim on behalf of the university. Problem was, when they found the mahogany case with the silverware a month later, they forgot to tell the insurance company. Cashed the check.'

'Oops.'

'To make a long story short, this lady thinks there ought to be more insurance companies involved in education audits. That or the mob,' says Harry. 'Either way.'

'Sounds like she loves the people she works for.'

'According to her the university is anxious to keep a low profile, especially when it comes to gifts, donations and the like. They don't like judges looking over their shoulder, asking accountants to get out their calculators. This makes the givers nervous,' says Harry. 'So disputes are almost always handled in-house. You get two professors pissing on each other over who gets what for research, the chancellor's office steps in like the Pope, resolves it and everybody kisses the ring and moves on. You screw with the chancellor, you find yourself in academic hell.'

'That means finding records of anything rising to the level of an argument is not likely,' I say.

Harry points a finger at me like a pistol and drops the thumb like a hammer. 'Bingo.

'According to the woman in the financial office, you have a director. In this case, Crone. Then you have associates, other people involved in aspects of the same project getting funding.'

'Jordan and Epperson,' I say.

He nods. 'If the money is apportioned and funding gets shifted around like a shell game, somebody finds out theirs was spent on some other part of the study. Well. You see what can happen,' says Harry. 'In that case, whoever got screwed might complain to higher-ups.'

'Do we know whether that happened here? With Jordan and Crone?'

'Exactly what I was thinking,' says Harry. 'I asked the lady in the office. She didn't know. She says it would be in the documentation, but we might have to read between the lines to find it. And that's not all.'

'What?'

'There's no form,' says Harry. 'You'd think these people would come up with some kind of a form you could look for if there was a dispute. But they don't seem to want to do that,' he says.

'For obvious reasons,' I say.

'Right. So what do they do? They just send a letter to the vice chancellor. That's if we're lucky.'

'What do you mean?'

'Sometimes it's just an e-mail message asking for a review of the grant and a ruling on an item.'

'Let me guess. There are no copies of the e-mail messages in your pile of papers?'

Harry nods. 'Academic confidentiality,' says Harry. 'You can't look at anybody's e-mail without a specific subpoena.'

Before I can say a word, he goes on: 'I've already prepared one for Jordan, Crone and Epperson. Problem is, Jordan's computer was reprogrammed after she was killed. The cops got into it, took what they wanted, all under the careful eyes of university lawyers. Then they turned it back in to the university. God knows where it is now. I looked at their evidence sheet. There was nothing in the e-mails that came remotely close to a complaint on funding.

'Crone's machine is still collecting dust in his office,' says Harry. 'But it's not likely he would have complained about anything. And Epperson. I assume he has his. So we'll take a look.'

'There must be a server somewhere.'

'Paul, listen. I'm tired. Worn out.'

'It is the university's e-mail system, right?'

Harry nods.

'There ought to be something in a server somewhere if Jordan complained about funding. See if we can subpoena the server?'

'Fine,' says Harry. A long sigh. He makes a note. I can always tell when Harry's hit the wall. I'm treading on thin ice.

'Too bad there was no federal money involved,' he says. 'In the grant.'

'Why's that?'

Before he can answer, the phone rings. I look at it. It's the back line. This number is not listed. Both of us thinking the same thing – Epperson calling.

I pick it up. 'Hello. Law office.'

'Is Harry Hinds there?'

I don't recognize the voice on the other end, but it's not Epperson.

'Who's calling?'

'Max Sheen.'

'Just a second.' I start to hand the phone to Harry.

'What did you mean "too bad there was no federal money"?'

'Who is it?' he says.

I hold the phone back.

'If there were federal funds, it's more likely there would have been an audit at some point.'

'Ah.'

'Who is it?' he asks.

'The press calling. Your friend Sheen.' I hand him the phone.

Harry takes it. 'Hello.'

I continue looking through the stack of papers on my desk, part of the original grant proposal. There are entire lines of typed print blocked out by black marker. Classified material. No doubt information subject to protection as trade secrets. Arriving at conclusions is going to be like putting a jigsaw puzzle together without all the pieces.

'Why? What's happening?' asks Harry. There's a tone of urgency to his voice that causes me to look up.

'What is it?' I ask.

He shakes his head at me. Doesn't answer.

'When?'

'Are you sure?'

'What's happening?' I ask.

Harry cups his hand over the mouthpiece to the receiver.

'Epperson is dead.'

IN THIS ANCIENT INDIAN VILLAGE OF COSOY
DISCOVERED AND NAMED SAN MIGUEL BY
CABRILLO IN 1542

VISITED AND CHRISTENED SAN DIEGO DE ALCALA
BY VIZCAINO IN 1602
HERE THE FIRST CITIZEN
FRAY JUNIPERO SERRA
PLANTED CIVILIZATION IN CALIFORNIA
HERE HE FIRST RAISED THE CROSS –
HERE BEGAN THE FIRST MISSION
HERE FOUNDED THE FIRST TOWN, SAN DIEGO,
JULY 16, 1769

The original native inhabitants of the place might quibble over how well those seeds of civilization took, especially if they could see the macabre scene here tonight.

William Epperson's body twists in the dark, damp air of early morning, suspended from a rope around his neck that is looped over the horizontal beam of the massive brick cross that forms the monument.

The bronze plaque with its words to the friar rests embedded in the white plaster covering the base beneath the giant cross that stands thirty feet high, faced with red brick.

By the time Harry and I arrive, the medical examiner's office is setting up a ladder, an extension affair lent to them by the fire department that is on the scene with two of its trucks and several big portable lights.

Even from a distance, I can see Epperson's body. Harry and I park at the top of the hill on the street near the colonnade. We slipped in this way to avoid the emergency lights all along the road down below. We drove up past Old Town and came in through the park at the top of the hill. It takes us five minutes to hike down, avoiding the roots of eucalyptus trees and the depressions in the ground obscured by the angle of the bright lights aimed up from the cross and shining in our eyes from below.

Both Harry and I come out of the woods with one arm up to shade our eyes from the light.

As we get closer I can see the rope and crude noose, rough hemp, and hear it strain under the weight and over the hush of voices, as Epperson twists slowly in the still, damp air and the evidence techs work beneath him around the base.

He is clothed in a white dress shirt and suit pants, one shoe on, the other lying on the ground, as if shot by gravity from his foot when the body stopped at the end of the rope. The line suspending him is tied off around the bottom of the brick cross, just above the rectangular base with its plaque.

A painter's ladder, which looks to be ten or twelve feet in length, is tipped over, lying on its side near the path that fronts the monument.

It is a picture worth a thousand words, all of them screaming one thing – suicide, all of it bathed in bright flood-lights with the SID, the Scientific Investigation Division, crime-scene folks, working it and looking for a different message.

One of them is examining the soil near the foot of the base, casting light at different angles over the ground, looking for impressions, footprints, though I doubt they will find much. The compacted river-bottom sand is as hard as concrete.

Several cops are working farther up the hill. They have laid out police lines of yellow tape from tree to tree. One of the uniforms stops us as we approach the tape.

It takes a couple of minutes to explain why we are here, the dead man being a witness in a case we are trying. He takes my business card. This seems to work its way from hand to hand up the hierarchy, until it gets to somebody in a suit farther down the hill. If the man is impressed, he doesn't show it. Gives us a look, then back to the card. Words exchanged with one of the uniformed officers that I cannot hear.

We cool our heels.

Harry nudges me in the ribs with an elbow. When I look over he nods, off in the direction of the parking lot down below toward the museum that sits on the opposite hill.

The lot is crowded with police cruisers, emergency vehicles with strobes flashing, blue, red and amber, enough color to spike blood pressure even if it isn't in a rearview mirror.

Getting out of one of the cars is Evan Tannery. He stops to talk to the brass clustered in the parking lot, spending most of his time and attention on an older guy, gray hair in a uniform. He seems to be in charge. Tannery is pumping him for information. They huddle for several seconds, the cop motioning with his arm up toward the hill behind us.

Until that moment I hadn't seen it. Parked in the shadows under a eucalyptus on a narrow service road leading up the hill toward the cross is the dark blue van I'd seen Epperson driving the previous day. The cops have staked it off with yellow tape and one of the fingerprint guys is giving it a going-over with dust on the driver's-side door handle and window, spreading the graphite liberally with a brush and blowing every few seconds searching for latents.

They've got a problem, and somebody knows it. A key witness in a felony murder is dead, and the cops are telling themselves this is no suicide.

'You Madriani?'

I am interrupted by the detective holding my business card. He has come up the hill behind us and is now looking at Harry and me like something the cat dragged in, interlopers.

'I'm Madriani. This is my partner, Harry Hinds.'

'I understand you knew this man?' He squares off in front of me, legs spread, and gestures toward the dangling body with his head. The coroner's guys have finally got their ladder up, and two of the firemen are giving them a hand, lifting the load so that they can sever the rope near the base and lower the body. They will cut like this to avoid screwing with the knot, hoping that the fashion in which it is tied will tell them something about whoever tied it.

'We weren't well acquainted,' I tell him. 'I talked to him once, about a week ago. I was scheduled to cross-examine him in court.'

'Looks like that show's off,' he says. 'How did you get here so quickly?'

'We were alerted by a phone call,' says Harry. 'He's right over there. You want to talk to him?' Harry has spotted Max Sheen in the distance, reporters in a flock, Sheen trying to work his way toward us around the police tape. The last thing the cops want, a conversation with counsel close to microphones on camera or anywhere near the pad-and-pencil crowd.

'Why don't you come this way,' he says. Open sesame. We are through the police line.

# CHAPTER FIFTEEN

It's Saturday morning, and we are all in the dark regarding Epperson. Coats's courtroom went dark on Thursday. With Epperson dead, Tannery had no one to talk to. The offer of proof is now in suspense while he scrambles trying to figure what to do next.

With no witness to confirm Tanya Jordan's testimony, unless he can come up with another witness, her words are now hearsay. In an early-morning appearance in chambers Tannery asked Judge Coats for time to consider his moves. He had no difficulty getting it. Harry and I didn't even oppose the motion. The judge is as mystified as the rest of us concerning Epperson's death, telling the D.A. he wants details as soon as they are available.

In the middle of a murder trial there is not much that can get your mind off events in the courtroom. But this morning is an exception. Still unhinged by Epperson and events of the last twenty-four hours,

I am also confronted by the fact that the driving force that caused me to take this case is suddenly gone. Penny Boyd has died.

It happened right after Harry's visit on Wednesday. Doris called to give me the news and for the first time since hearing it, I now have a moment to dwell on the passing of a child. It brings back memories of the first death I can remember as a kid. I was seven. A little girl crippled from birth and confined to a wheelchair had passed away. She lived up the block. I saw her often out on the sidewalk, wheeling along trying to keep up with the other kids. A perpetual smile on her face, she would call me by my first name. With her angelic blond hair and sunny disposition, she seemed not to comprehend the injustice dealt to her in life, legs that were dead and lungs that each year filled with pneumonia. I didn't learn until many years later, after talking to my mother, that it was a bout with pneumonia that finally took her. After all these years, I can still picture her face and remember her name, an indelible impression. I remember the day my mother told me she'd died. I said nothing, went to my room and sat there in shock. In my sheltered world of middle-class America, children didn't die.

It seems I have not grown a lot over the years. I was caught completely off guard when Doris called. I would have expected such a message from someone else, a friend or family member. But Doris was amazingly composed, though her voice was strained, a little raw. The news hit me like a bullet in the brow. Penny had died in her sleep.

This morning I sit behind the wheel with Sarah in the passenger seat, headlights on as we motorcade from the church.

We are five cars behind the hearse when we finally park on a gentle curve in the cemetery. I had debated in my mind whether to bring Sarah. The last time she had been to a funeral was her mother's.

Nikki has been dead nearly four years and I feared that cemeteries and caskets would dredge up all forms of memories, most of them painful. But my daughter has come of age. Attending Penny's funeral was not something for me to decide. When I suggested that she might stay home, that the family would understand, Sarah would have none of it.

This morning she wears an ankle-length black dress, gathered in high under her shaping bosom, and black leather pumps with heels. She is changing from a child into a young woman before my very eyes, a transition occurring with the speed of time-lapse photography.

Sarah has thick brown hair, generous and abundant, and has Nikki's long legs, like a gazelle's. Her thick ponytail now bobs above her shoulders as we walk toward the assembling crowd at the grave site.

If it must be, at least Penny goes to God on a bucolic morning, one of those blue Pacific days with transparent wisps of white high in the jet stream. There is only a hint of dew on the grass, and the soulful tune of birds, none of them visible, their songs erupting from the massive oaks and sycamores that shade the graves.

There are more people here than I would have expected for a child who has been largely homebound for two years. There are children here Penny's age – wide-eyed kids, I suspect, from her grade school – and cousins, all confronted, most of them for the first time, with the stark reality of death. Someone they knew, a child, one of their own, is gone.

Folding chairs are set up in two rows under the canopy that covers the casket. Up front in the center is Doris, seated in one of the chairs. Relatives, another woman on one side and her two surviving children on the other, all within touching distance of the coffin, flank her. Frank, it seems, cannot sit. He stands behind her, his large hands on the back of her chair, his head downcast, a giant in pain.

Penny's two surviving siblings. Donald, her little brother who is seven, seems in shock, eyes of wonder. Jennifer, his older sister, Sarah's friend and classmate, is more controlled.

She looks to see Sarah and, actually, smiles. She

has inherited the social grace of her mother. Even under the circumstances irrepressible. The last place she wants to be. She loved her sister. Still, this cloud has darkened much of her life; it is probably difficult for her to contemplate life without this load.

Frank's gaze is fixed on the coffin, his face puffy, signs of grief. He wears a dark suit that doesn't fit him terribly well, something no doubt purchased off a rack at the last minute. The spread of his shoulders would make anything not tailored a tough fit. It is hard to say who is consoling whom here. Doris seems, at least at first blush, to be more in control, though she holds a white handkerchief in one hand and is wearing oversized dark glasses.

For Frank, there is no hiding it. I can see by the way he looks that he is devastated. He had always placed more hope in the magic of medicine, though he never understood it well. For him Penny's placement in any study was seen as a guarantee, a reprieve. I tried to warn him, but he would have none of it. Hope sprang eternal.

If there is a silver lining to any of this, it is that his thoughts of divorce to save the family from financial ruin are at an end.

The priest has traveled with us from the funeral mass at the old mission a few miles in from the coast. I am told he is a longtime family friend. He opens his prayer book and begins the intonation from the head of the casket, sprinkling it with holy water from a gold canister held by an altar boy who has accompanied him for this task.

> Deliver her, O Lord, from death eternal
> in that awful day, when the heavens
> and the earth shall be moved:
> when thou shalt come to judge
> the world . . .

All heads are downcast, except for some of the children, who seem to look on wide-eyed.

> Eternal rest grant unto her, O Lord, and let
> perpetual light shine upon her.
> Deliver us . . .
> Lord, have mercy.
> Christ, have mercy.
> Lord, have mercy.
> Our Father, who art in heaven . . .

As the priest recites the Lord's Prayer he circles the bier with its undersized coffin one last time, sprinkling it with holy water. The collective voices rise in volume and confidence, until in unison they become a single *Amen*.

The gathering begins to break up, mourners

dispersing, many of them making their way toward Doris to offer their final condolences.

At that moment, I notice that Frank is no longer standing behind her. I look for a moment. He has disappeared. Then I see him. He has made his way around the row of chairs, his lumbering body moving as if in pain like a wounded bear. He moves to the head of the casket, leans over and reaches out with his left hand. I think for a moment that he merely touched it, a final farewell.

The priest consoles him, a few words. He takes Frank's large hand in both of his. From the look on his face, it is not clear whether Frank has even heard him. He seems in a daze. It isn't until the priest steps aside that I notice that Frank has placed something on his daughter's coffin. There on top is a single long-stemmed pink rose.

The cops are still trying to put the pieces together. The media is calling Epperson's death suspicious, an 'apparent' suicide.

They have somehow sniffed out that Epperson was scheduled to appear in court behind closed doors. They are now fueling suspicion that Epperson was about to identify the killer when he himself was killed. Speculation is running high that the dead man knew more than the authorities are willing to say about Kalista Jordan's murder.

Harry and I, Tannery and the investigating detectives huddle this morning in Judge Coats's chambers to gather the facts. Tannery's face reveals that from the state's perspective it is not good.

He has already delivered something to the judge in a sealed manila envelope. Printed on the front in large red block letters the words:

SDPD
Police Evidence

Coats opens the envelope in front of us, removing the contents, what appears to be two printed pages, eight and a half by eleven. Coats holds them at an angle, reading.

The judge finishes one page, reads the other, only a few lines at the top, then places them facedown on the desk.

'Where did you find these?'

'They were in the victim's printer, at his apartment,' says Tannery. 'We dusted the pages for prints.'

'And?' says Coats.

'Nothing. The original document was in his computer.'

The judge would not have touched any of this, an open homicide investigation, suicide or not, except that the matter now threatens to wind up in the middle of a murder trial over which he is presiding.

'You haven't shown this to Mr. Madriani, I take it?'

Tannery shakes his head.

'I think he should see it, don't you?'

'I would question its admissibility,' says Tannery. 'It's not signed.'

'That may go more to the weight of the evidence,' says the judge.

'Your Honor . . .' Tannery is not happy.

'Is there a legal reason we should not share this with counsel for the defense?' asks Coats.

'No,' says Tannery.

The judge hands me the document. Harry reads over my shoulder. For two days it has been rumored that there was a suicide note. Until now, we had not seen it. It is dated the second. I look at the calendar on the judge's desk; the previous Wednesday, the day Epperson died.

It is neatly typed, a few misspelled words. I quickly flip to the second page without reading all of it. Harry reaches over as if he isn't finished. I want to check for a signature. Tannery is right. It is unsigned, but Epperson's name is typed neatly in the center of the next page.

I flip back to the first page, and there in the center, two graphs down, is the bombshell, almost buried in the middle of a sentence, a confession by

Epperson that he could no longer live with himself after having killed Kalista Jordan.

'Shit.' Harry says it out loud. The judge doesn't bother to chastise him; I suspect because he is thinking the same thing.

'It's a little too neat, Your Honor. The night before he's to testify he hangs himself. It should not be allowed in.'

'What do you mean by "too neat"?' I ask.

'What he means is a tensioning tool, and cable ties, just like the ones in evidence, were found on the table by the computer in Epperson's apartment.' The answer doesn't come from Tannery, but from behind us. Jimmy de Angelo, the homicide dick in Kalista Jordan's case, is seated on the judge's tufted leather sofa, squeaking every time he moves.

Harry's eyes get big as saucers. He turns to look at de Angelo. 'Really?'

'Yeah, really. Defense lawyer's wet dream,' says de Angelo. 'Somebody went to a lot of trouble. There was just a little too much at the scene,' he says.

'That may be your argument,' says Harry.

'Where were you last night?' de Angelo asks him.

'I was busy with my partner working.'

'I'll bet.'

'Enough,' says Coats.

'I would ask Mr. Madriani whether his client knows anything about this. But I don't think there's a need seeing as he would be aware of the requirement that he disclose it. There is no attorney-client privilege for a felony in progress.'

He would ask, but he won't, since he just has.

'Your Honor, my client knows nothing.'

'Yes, and if he did he wouldn't tell you,' says de Angelo.

'It's possible Mr. Epperson didn't want any questions about the authenticity of the note,' I tell the judge. 'So he left physical evidence along with it.' I'm referring to the cable ties and the tensioning tool.

'Then why didn't he sign the note?' asks Tannery. 'That would have been pretty good authentication. Could it be that whoever killed him couldn't get him to cooperate?'

'You have evidence that it was murder?' I ask.

Tannery doesn't respond.

'You say the note was still in the printer?'

De Angelo nods.

'There's your answer.'

'Why didn't he take it out?' asks de Angelo.

'We can debate why he did or didn't do a lot of things,' says Harry. 'A man about to string himself up is not always rational.'

'What about fingerprints?' I ask. 'Did you find anybody else's on the computer?'

'No.' De Angelo says it flatly, grudging response.

'But anybody could have known about the tensioning tool. It's in evidence. Been in all the papers, along with the cable ties.'

'Then Mr. Tannery can argue it to the jury,' I tell him. 'The fact remains that without some perpetrator, a face and a name to hang on it, and somebody to tie that person to my client, Dr. Crone is going to walk and the state knows it. He was conveniently in jail at the time of Mr. Epperson's death. Unless they can tie Epperson's death to my client, that suicide note cries *reasonable doubt.*'

'What about the physical evidence at the scene?' asks the judge. 'The area around the cross?'

'We found some tire marks that didn't match the victim's van,' says de Angelo. 'We're still trying to make a match. Checking them against tire impressions from some suspects.'

'What suspects?' asks Harry.

'Persons of interest' is all de Angelo will say. My guess is they are checking out anybody and everybody who's had contact with Crone in the last months, jail inmates who have been released who rubbed shoulders with him inside, and people from the Genetics Center. The cops will be spending their nights wheeling every vehicle they can find through plaster of paris trying to make a match they can somehow tie to Crone.

'Have you checked the gardeners, the

groundskeepers at the museum?' I ask.

De Angelo looks at me, not certain what I'm talking about.

'They probably drive the service roads in the park all the time. Have you checked their tires?'

'Not yet,' he says. 'I'll make a note.' He doesn't write it down.

Coats wants to know if they have another witness for their offer of proof, somebody to verify Tanya Jordan's testimony.

Tannery tells him he doesn't.

Coats can give them a day, maybe two. My guess is Epperson was their case. Without a witness to verify the racial evidence, they have no motive for the killing. They have already given up on the twisted-romance theory, and now they are faced with a suicide note-cum-confession from Epperson.

'Your Honor.' De Angelo wades in. 'This is screwy,' he says. 'That this man would take his life like this.'

'Maybe he was afraid he couldn't hold up under questioning,' I tell Coats. 'He had an appointment in court, day of reckoning. Nothing strange about that.'

Coats considers his options. A long sigh.

'We have a problem,' he says. 'I don't like it, but if you can't come up with another witness, evidence to corroborate, I'll have to strike the woman's testimony.'

Tannery starts to say something, but the judge holds up his hand. 'No other choice,' he says. 'It's all hearsay. And I'm not sure it makes a lot of difference at this point.'

'What do you mean?' asks Tannery.

'I mean you're holding a confession there. Unless you have some basis to show that it's not what it purports to be, I can't keep it out.' By this time Epperson's suicide note has made the rounds back into Tannery's hands. He holds it like some burning ember.

'I want a copy of that,' I tell him. 'And I would like an order from the court that the state keep us informed of their investigation as it progresses. I'd like to know what other evidence they found at the scene. For example, fingerprints on the van? I saw them dusting it at the scene.'

The judge looks at de Angelo.

'We found the victim's prints, and two other employees' from the center where he worked. We're checking them out,' he says.

'Names?' I pull out a pen, holding a yellow legal pad.

De Angelo doesn't want to give them up, but the judge tells him to disclose. He pulls out a little notebook from his inside coat pocket, then flips a few pages.

'A Cynthia Gamin, and Harold Michaels. Said

they used the van last week. It checks out, but we're checking their personal vehicles anyway,' he says, 'to see if the extra tire impressions at the scene match up.'

'And you *will* keep us informed?' I say.

De Angelo gives me a pain-in-the-ass look. It's nice when you have the cops working for you.

'Your Honor, you're telling me the note is coming in, is that right?' Tannery had expected it, but he wants to make sure there's no chance of turning Coats around on this before he leaves. 'I'm going to have to take it up the line.' He's talking about his boss, D.A. Jim Tate, and his number two, Edelstein, who is about to retire, and whose job Tannery is in line to take.

'You take it where you have to,' says Coats. 'That's what I'm telling you. You can argue all the fine points. That it wasn't signed. You can argue the physical evidence found in the apartment and at the scene, so long as you disclose it to opposing counsel in advance. I'll give you all the latitude I can on that,' he says. 'But unless you have something more than what I've heard here today, there's more than a good chance that statement is going to come in. I can't keep the jury out of the box much longer. You've got two days.' He looks at his calendar. 'We meet back here eight o'clock Wednesday morning. I'll expect a full report on everything you have on the Epperson thing at that time. Do you understand?'

Tannery nods, but he's not happy about it.

The judge starts to hand the manila evidence envelope back to the prosecutor. 'I know,' he says. 'These things happen. It's a tough way to lose a case.

'And you, Mr. Madriani. I hope for your client's sake when we get back together there's no evidence that he was involved in this thing.'

# CHAPTER SIXTEEN

Every shred of evidence they have found so far is consistent with a suicide, including the bruise on the back of Epperson's neck that formed a deep Y. This we have learned from the coroner's report, a copy of which was given to us this morning.

'What a rope does with the force of gravity,' says Harry. 'But he didn't die painlessly. Spinal cord wasn't snapped. The coroner confirms that he strangled, probably hung from the rope for several minutes before he went unconscious.'

'Tannery is not going to be able to do much with that,' I tell him. 'It would defy the norm if Epperson snapped his neck on the first try. A good hanging is an art form. Most suicide victims strangle themselves walking on air having second thoughts and trying to get back to where they started.'

'Either that or they jump from such heights that they lose their heads,' says Harry. He's talking about decapitation. 'Any way you take it, it's a messy way to go,' he says. 'All in all, pills are much better.'

He flips through the final few pages of the report, which I have already read. 'I agree,' he says. 'There isn't much in here that's gonna help the prosecution.'

'Let's hope they didn't find anything more at the scene, or in Epperson's apartment,' I say.

'You really think he did himself?'

'You don't?'

'I don't know. Could be somebody suicided him.'

I look at Harry, waiting for his list of candidates. It is short.

'Tash. Who else? He's close to Crone. The two are joined at the hip on this project. And it keeps comin' back to that,' says Harry. 'Maybe it had to do with the racial thing. Maybe it had to do with something else. But if you want my opinion, somebody wanted to shut Epperson up.'

'So you think Tannery has the better argument?'

'I didn't say that. It's one thing to think Crone may have had a hand in it. Trying to prove it is another. On the Kalista Jordan thing, I think we may have been delivered by the gods. We should consider ourselves fortunate,' says Harry. 'Cut our losses and keep our distance.'

'What do you mean by that?'

'I mean we shouldn't be giving Crone blank checks on further defense commitments. There's no statute of limitations, and no double jeopardy on Epperson.

We rub Tannery's nose in it on Jordan, force him to dismiss, and one thing is certain, he's not likely to stop turning over rocks trying to put it to Crone on Epperson. And maybe, just maybe, he can make a case.'

'So you think Crone did it?'

'I don't think we should be blind to the possibility,' says Harry. 'Think about it. What were he and Tash doing with all those numbers? The meetings at the jail?'

'Genetic codes,' I tell him.

'I agree they were codes. Maybe genetic, maybe not. Were you able to understand them?'

I shake my head.

'That makes two of us. The guard outside the door makes three. Can you think of a better way to pass messages?' he says.

I don't answer him, because the thought has crossed my mind and Harry knows it.

'Bet you dollars to doughnuts those papers with all their numbers got shredded as soon as Tash got back to his office and deciphered them.'

I don't say anything.

He glances at me over the top of his coffee mug, shod feet propped up against the edge of my desk as he sits huddled in one of the client chairs across from me.

'Maybe we should ask Tash for a copy of one of

those papers,' he says. 'Probably wouldn't do any good,' he says. 'We know what Crone and Tash would say. It's confidential. Trade secrets.' Harry gives me one of those squinting sideways looks, planting the seeds. He can sense he has set off the little neurons in my brain. He has me thinking in his direction.

'How else could Crone talk to him? He had to tell him that it was getting dicey. That Epperson was about to spill his guts about what was going on, the racial stuff.'

'Let's assume just for purposes of argument that this happened. Communication by numbers,' I tell him. 'You've seen Tash. Soaking wet maybe he weighs a hundred and fifty pounds. Even if Epperson had a heart problem, he was more than a match for Tash.'

This slows Harry down for a second or two. 'You meet a lot of people in jail,' says Harry. 'And Crone's made a lot of friends. Maybe one of them got out. Crone tells Tash to get in touch. You know the cost of a killing these days. One of the few things not touched by inflation,' says Harry. 'Some four-time loser might do it for a few coins and a smile from the professor.'

'What does it say about time of death?' I change the subject, point to the coroner's report on Epperson. Harry, juggling the coffee in one hand the report in the other, starts to read.

'Sometime after seven. The best they can figure. Based on questioning one of the gardeners. He pulled out about that time and locked up.'

'Did you see a gate?' I ask.

'I talked to one of the cops about that, at the scene. There was a gate down bottom, near the parking lot. But you could come in up above on the service road. There's a bollard, but anybody could drive around it. Kids did it all the time, according to the cops, when they wanted to park.

'And one other thing,' says Harry. 'Whoever killed Epperson smashed all the lights before he climbed up the cross to string him up.'

'There were lights?'

Harry nods. 'Big floods pointed up from the ground toward the cross. Cops found broken glass all over the place.'

'Epperson could have done that,' I say.

'It's possible,' says Harry. 'But why bother if you're gonna hang yourself?'

For this I don't have an answer. We sit in silence for a few seconds until the phone fills the void, the receptionist out front ringing through.

I answer it, punch the com line. 'Who is it?'

'It's the district attorney's office, Mr. Tate. His secretary on the line.'

I put my hand over the mouthpiece, look down at line one, which is blinking.

'Something's up. Tate on the line,' I tell Harry.

'I'll take it.' I punch the line. 'Paul Madriani here.'

'Just a moment for Mr. Tate.' A soft, feline voice on the other end. A little elevator music while she puts me on hold. A few seconds later, the line comes to life.

'Mr. Madriani, Jim Tate here.' Avuncular, confident, man in command. 'I don't think we've met.'

I start to confirm this, but he doesn't care, steps on my response. 'I have Evan Tannery here in my office. It's the Crone thing. I think it would be a good idea if we got together,' he says. 'Maybe this afternoon in my office.'

'I'll have to check, see if I'm free,' I tell him. I know I am, but his attitude is enough to piss me off. I put him on hold and look at Harry.

'It's Tannery's boss. He wants to talk.'

'What about?'

'Their teat being in a wringer,' I tell him. 'But I doubt that he's going to admit it over the phone.'

'Could be good news. Could be bad. Maybe they found something on Epperson.'

I consider the possibilities. 'We may as well find out.' I punch line one again.

'How about two o'clock?' I tell Tate.

'Can we make it three? I have an earlier engagement.'

'Fine.'

'Just have security call up when you arrive. I'll have one of my people come down and collect you.' He says it as if Harry and I are lost pieces to a game set.

'Right.'

Harry has some papers to file downtown, the lingering gun liability case, manufacturer's nightmare. So we decide to leave the office, head across the Coronado Bridge and take a late lunch at a little spot, a hole-in-the-wall across from the courthouse and the D.A.'s office, one of Harry's haunts.

We stew over lunch, Harry taking bets that any suicide finding will not be blessed until the coroner holds an inquest.

'Tate's gonna be looking for cover,' he says. 'There's too much profile in this thing. If we roll him over in the courtroom, he goes belly-up and Crone goes back to the university, Tate's not gonna be able to show his face at all those fashionable charity events. You want my guess,' he says, 'he'll angle to get the judge to order a mistrial to buy himself time.'

'On what grounds?'

Harry shrugs. 'What if he admits they failed to disclose some evidence? Oversight,' he says. 'Oops.'

'That might get him a week's continuance, to

bring us up to speed. But if I know my man on the bench, Coats isn't going to order a mistrial. Not unless they're withholding film. Some other perpetrator chopping up Jordan,' I tell him.

'So what do you think?' asks Harry.

'Better possibility, Tate tries to get Tannery to force the judge's hand on a dismissal on technical grounds, something the voters won't understand, then blame it on the judge. I'll bet they're up there now burning the oil over the transcript trying to find some way to bury this thing, even if they have to take a lump or two in the process. It's easier than going down on a verdict in a case that's been in the headlines for six weeks.'

'I'll take it,' says Harry. 'Jeopardy attaches. Our man goes free. The D.A. can say the court did it; fingers pointing all around, and the taxpayers get handed a bill for a trial that never ended. Sounds like justice to me.'

Harry is talking with his mouth full of pastrami on rye, mustard running out of the corner and down his chin. He wipes it with a napkin. His elbows are on the table, the knot on his tie is halfway to his stomach. It is vintage Harry.

'I talked with some of the guys in the courthouse pressroom. Conventional wisdom is Tate's running for reelection next year. From what I hear, he has nothing else to do. They take his office away, he's gonna have to hang out at the senior center. Take up cribbage,' says Harry.

'Let's hope he's motivated to deal,' I say.

The place is emptying out. I look at my watch. It's a little after two. Harry and I finish up and play musical receipts with the tab. Harry has to hit the bathroom, so I end up with it. I stand at the register, peel off a twenty to pay the bill. Take a five and put it on the table for a tip.

I look through the front window of the empty diner; there are people passing by on the sidewalk, a bus at the stop takes on its cargo, then blows brown smoke and like a tornado pulls away from the curb.

Suddenly I can see across four lanes of traffic to the courthouse on the other side. I kill time waiting for Harry, gaze at the far corner west of the courthouse. It is the physique that catches the eye. Stopped at the light talking to some guy is Aaron Tash, all six feet four inches and skinny. There's no missing him, a walking streetlamp, human equivalent of a praying mantis.

I wonder what he is doing downtown. He knows the trial has been dark for days. Even if it weren't he wouldn't be allowed in. He's on the witness list.

Then it hits me. He's probably on his way to see Crone. Anger begins to set in, wondering how long this has been going on. I continue to watch them, Tash doing most of the listening. The other guy hands him a piece of paper, something from his pocket. Tash takes it, but doesn't look at it. Instead he slips it into the briefcase under his arm, the same thin leather case he's carried to the jail to meet with Crone each time we've gone.

Harry comes out of the bathroom, waltzes up behind me.

'You get the bill?'

'Yeah.'

'Let's go,' he says.

'Hold on.'

'What are you looking at?'

'Over there, on the corner.'

Harry zones in, picks it up quickly. By now Tash has finished his conversation. He heads up the street in front of the courthouse.

'What's he doing down here?'

'What I was wondering.' I expect him to keep going past the courthouse steps to the corner and down the street toward the entrance to the jail, but he doesn't. Instead he turns and climbs the stairs, then disappears into the shadows under the courthouse door.

Harry looks at me, thinking the same thing. Tash is headed to the D.A.'s office.

'You think Tate is sweating him?' asks Harry.

'I don't know.' Suddenly there is the smell of danger in the air.

'You missed the other half,' I tell him.

'What's that?'

'The guy he was talking to at the corner. Tall, all bulked up, a long blond ponytail, his arms all inked up. The last time I saw him was in the bucket talking to Crone down in the dayroom.'

'You sure?'

I nod. It was the felon fodder joshing with Crone that morning, the first time we took Tash to the jail – the blond Viking.

# CHAPTER SEVENTEEN

Tate's inner sanctum is a monument to longevity in office. The walls are covered with plaques of platitude: brass tablets and framed scrolls celebrating his high ethics, all presented by groups seeking to curry his favor.

There are framed pictures showing a man who only vaguely resembles Tate, darker hair and more of it, without the jowls that are now his most prominent feature.

Harry and I wander around the room, checking these trophies as Tate finishes a meeting down the hall in the library.

There are photos of the man shaking hands with baseball players, and movie stars, other politicians: confirmation of his orbit in the celebtocracy in case he should forget. Some of these shots date him badly, figures in them have held horizontal residence at Forest Lawn for the better part of two decades. Time moving on, catching up.

Harry's looking over my shoulder with an appraising eye at a shot of Marilyn Monroe showing some thigh, seated on the edge of a desk with Tate's name placard on it. Tate is seated behind the desk looking very much younger, an eager and rising deputy.

'When he retires, they're gonna have to take an oral history or lose touch with the ancient world,' says Harry.

'Who says he's going to retire?'

The clutter of memorabilia is a flea market dream. What purports to be the first Padre baseball thrown out in one of the league play-offs sits on the second-base bag from that same game. A three-hundred-pound block of granite, a tombstone, with the engraving

DEATH PENALTY APPEAL
RIP

stands in a corner of the office, proof of Tate's credentials in the cop community and the brotherhood of prosecutors. I am told he drapes this with a black lace handkerchief when closeted with deputies deciding whether to seek the death penalty in capital cases, and has scratched notches in the edges of the stone whenever the penalty was exacted in one of their cases. He is no squeamish liberal when it comes to retribution, and plays his politics the same way.

Before I can move to check the edges of the tombstone closer, the door behind me opens.

'Sorry to keep you gentlemen waiting.' Tate sweeps into the office like an autumn wind. Being sucked along in the vacuum of his wake is Tannery.

'Did Charlotte offer you some coffee?'

I wave him off, but he ignores me, plops himself into the chair behind his desk and picks up the receiver on the phone, hitting the com line.

'Charlotte, bring in some coffee, will ya? Four cups. You guys want cream and sugar?'

Before we can answer: 'Sure, bring it all on a tray. And see if you got some of those little cookies. The ones with the mint.'

He sets the phone on its cradle and he's back out of his chair before Harry and I can say a word, hanging his coat up on a hanger that dangles from the coat tree in the corner.

'You must be Madriani.' He reaches over on his way back to the desk, shakes my hand in an almost absent fashion as he passes by.

'Harry Hinds, my partner,' I tell him.

He has to backtrack to catch Harry's hand. 'Good to meet you. Have a seat. Sit down.' He directs us to the two client chairs. Tannery pulls up a ladder-back chair from the small conference table across the room and joins us.

'Heard good things about you both,' says Tate. This is very much his meeting, in control.

'Seems we have some mutual friends up in Capital City.' He mentions some names, fixtures in the local bar and on the bench.

'You represented Armando Acosta,' he says.

I nod.

'That was a big case. Got headlines all over. Not every day you get a state court judge charged with murder. Especially,' he says, 'where there's a little nookie involved.' He pulls on his right earlobe, smiles as if perhaps he can entice me to share some confidences from the past. Tate is referring to charges that the judge had been snared in an undercover vice sting by a pretty decoy sent out by the cops to nail him. She was later found dead, and Acosta was charged with her murder.

'Those charges were never proven,' I tell him.

'Of course not,' he says. 'You won the case. Judge Acosta is eternally in your debt, from what I understand. Your biggest cheerleader. That was not always the case.'

'I haven't been able to try a case before him since the trial. Judge Acosta is scrupulous in disqualifying himself in any matter in which I am involved.'

'Funny how that works. Do somebody a favor and it comes back to bite you in the ass.'

'The law is not politics,' I tell him. 'That is, if it works right.'

He smiles. 'Of course not. Which brings us to the reason for today's meeting. Some pretty fortuitous events,' he says, 'the death of a witness on the eve of testimony. I'll bet that hasn't happened in one of your cases before?'

'Not that I can recall,' I tell him.

'Obviously it's thrown a glitch into the people's case.'

'We noticed,' says Harry. Harry's getting tired listening to the bullshit. He wants to cut to the chase. 'Why did you call us in here?'

'We still think we have a solid case against your man. Don't get me wrong,' says Tate.

'Is that why you called? To tell us you have a solid case?' I ask.

He looks at Tannery, smiles. 'No. I called you here to discuss a possible resolution. As it stands, your client can't be sure he's gonna beat the wrap. Don't misunderstand; the Epperson thing throws up some dust. It may not be quite as clear as it was before, but there's still the question of the cable ties in his pocket, the tension tool in his garage, the fact that he and the victim were not on good terms. The medical evidence points to a skilled hand dismembering the body. There's plenty there for a jury to chew on,' he says.

'And given this . . . mountain that we have to climb, what are you prepared to offer?'

'A solution that provides your client with a more certain result,' he says.

'What? You gonna pump the poison directly into his heart instead of his arm?' says Harry.

'What if the result avoids the death penalty?' says Tate. 'Perhaps a life sentence without possibility of parole.'

'Not a chance,' I tell him.

Tate looks over at Tannery once more. The expressions that are exchanged between the two lead me to conclude that this was not Tannery's idea. He knows he doesn't have the leverage, but you can't blame Tate for trying.

'Okay. Second degree,' he says. 'We drop all the special circumstances, he gets fifteen to life, with good behavior he could be out in ten. That's as good as it gets,' he says.

I look at him, say nothing, Mona Lisa smile on me.

'Fine, we'll sweeten it a little.' Tate doesn't know when to stop talking. 'Your guy pleads out, we agree not to bring any charges regarding the Epperson thing as to him, if he cooperates with us.'

'Cooperates how?' I ask.

'Tells us what happened.'

'No problem. Mr. Epperson committed suicide,' I say.

'And you believe that?' he says.

'The last time I looked, there was nothing in the Evidence Code giving rise to presumptions based on what I believe. But I think if you look at the facts they might bear it out. Do you have evidence that Epperson didn't commit suicide?'

Tate doesn't have good lawyer's eyes; perhaps that is why he left the courtroom and became a politician. His big brown ones say, *No*.

He swallows, clears his throat, looks over at Tannery. 'Evan, maybe you should get involved here.'

Tannery edges over. 'It's a good deal,' he tells me. The devil in front of me, and the devil in my ear.

'I'll take it to my client,' I say.

'Will you recommend it?' says Tannery.

'No.'

'Why not?'

'Because your case is in a ditch. I'd have to be incompetent to recommend a deal like that.'

Tannery looks at me; his eyes get wide.

'All the testimony regarding my client's alleged motive to kill Kalista Jordan, the supposed racial genetics studies intended to inflame the jury, that's all out. Everything Tanya Jordan testified to is hearsay without Epperson, so all you have are some nylon cable ties and a tensioning tool found in the defendant's garage, that and some bad blood between Crone and Jordan. At worst, this can be characterized as a severe case of professional differences. What's more,' I tell them, 'did you know that Epperson asked her to marry him? That she turned him down just a few days before she disappeared?'

I can tell by the look on their faces this is news.

'Who told you that?'

'You want to find out, we'll do it in court,' I tell them. 'On the other side of the slate you now have a suicide note and a confession typed on Epperson's computer admitting that he killed her.'

'Unsigned,' says Tate.

'Did you find anybody else's fingerprints on Epperson's computer keyboard?'

Dead silence.

'I didn't think so. You have the physical evidence at the scene, which is consistent with suicide. You have cable ties and a tensioning tool found at Epperson's.'

'Very convenient circumstances,' says Tate.

'Convenient or not, the jury is more than likely to find reasonable doubt in those circumstances.'

I wait a beat to see if they want to contradict this. They don't.

'I will assume silence as assent,' I tell them. 'And

we have an order by the trial judge compelling you to deliver whatever other evidence is in your possession regarding Epperson's death to us by tomorrow morning. I'd say we're in pretty good shape. I think we'll wait.'

Tate's eyes get beady, little slits of meanness. 'We won't give up on Epperson's murder,' he says.

'That's going to be a problem for you.'

'Why?'

'Because first you're going to have to prove it was murder, and then you're going to have to find a witness willing to commit perjury.'

'What are you talking about?' he says.

'I'm talking about a witness willing to connect my client to Epperson's murder. Dr. Crone was in jail.' I watch Tate's eyes. If he has something, he isn't showing it. My guess is, they had Aaron Tash stashed somewhere, in the library or another office, while Harry and I cooled our heels. They either didn't pump enough fear into him, or he doesn't know anything, though after seeing him on the street I have my doubts on the latter score.

They may still have him tucked away, hoping we will give them an opening, something they can carry back down the hall and use to sweat him, tell him that Crone has agreed to cut a deal, that he, Tash, may be left to swing on his own for Epperson.

'So you're not willing to deal?' asks Tate.

'Not on those terms,' I tell him.

He settles back in his chair, sucks some air and lightly scratches his cheek with the back of the fingernails of one hand, à la *Godfather*. All the moves are well practiced.

'You know, even if your man beats the wrap on Jordan, there's no double jeopardy on Epperson and no statute of limitations.' Eye to eye, and he just blinked, admitting they can't win on Jordan's murder.

'He'll have to discuss that with his next lawyer,' I tell him.

Tate smiles, shakes his head. 'There's been a lot of press interest on this one,' he says. I can almost hear the sparks jumping the synapses in the brain, sinuous threads of smoke as they overload.

'That press can only get worse if he's acquitted,' I tell him. 'You take it to a jury, given the evidence, and the press is going to wonder why, and so is my client who is likely to lose his job at the university. A lifetime of tenure.'

'We're talking about a woman who lost her life,' says Tate.

'No, we're talking about evidence you don't have.'

Tate has survived this long by knowing when to cut his losses. If he presses, in light of the new evidence, and he loses, the county could be facing an eight-figure lawsuit for malicious prosecution or abuse of process.

At this moment, Tate is the picture of a prosecutor in a box, and he knows it. It's why he called us in. If he agrees to a motion for dismissal, he may be haunted by that decision if evidence later develops that Crone was in fact involved in Epperson's death. Any good defense attorney would look Tate's deputy prosecutor in the eye in a courtroom and, on closing argument, ask the jury why the prosecutor's office agreed to dismiss murder charges against the defendant in an earlier case. Their answer might be *That was a different case*. Still if Crone was such a bad actor, why did they let him go? Conviction or not, it won't make the office look good, and Tate is the office.

'I have to think about it,' he says.

'I wouldn't think too long. Tomorrow morning we get the evidence, whatever you have in Epperson's death. After that, my client is not going to be willing to deal. Unless you've got some solid evidence, you're going to have to dismiss or face the wall if he's acquitted. The county board of supervisors is not going to be happy raising taxes to pay for a zillion-dollar lawsuit.'

He tries to argue prosecutorial discretion, sovereign immunity. Harry and I take up seats at the other side of the room on the couch pretending not to listen as Tate huddles with Tannery, who brings him current, that these protections have been eroded by recent court decisions. Prosecutors who abuse their discretion, based on the evidence, can get nailed big-time. The look on Tate's face says it all. He settles back in his chair, wags a finger for us to join him again. Harry and I cross the room and sit down again.

'So what are you gonna do for us if we agree to some kind of a deal?'

'You'll join in a motion for dismissal?'

'We won't join in the motion,' says Tate. 'But we won't oppose it, based on evidence as we know it at this time, and in the interests of justice.'

'Of course.' I consider my options. We have to throw them some kind of a bone. 'Subject of course to my client's consent, he will waive his right to bring any civil action against the county for his arrest or trial to this point.'

I study Tate's eyes. He doesn't even blink. 'Good.' He's up out of the chair, shakes my hand, all smiles.

I realize what has gone down is a show, something for our benefit. This was all Tate was looking for from the moment he walked through the door, civil immunity. What in the hell is going on?

The following morning, we craft the details of settlement. Harry and I camp with Crone at the jail. He is elated with his good fortune, but wants me to talk to the university about reinstatement. I caution him not to get the cart before the horse. He is more than willing to waive any rights to sue, but we counsel him anyway. Clients in this situation are always jumping to give up everything, assuming their lives will click right back into place. That is almost never the case.

'What if they don't take you back?' I ask.

'What do you mean?'

'The university.'

'Why wouldn't they?'

'There's the question of the sexual harassment complaint filed by Jordan.'

'But you said that died with her.'

'Yes, but now they're on notice.'

'I don't understand.'

'Think of it like a dog bite case,' says Harry. 'It's a question of dangerous propensities. You have a pet, a little dog. The dog has never attacked or bitten anybody. Then one day a neighbor's kid comes in your yard. The dog attacks and bites him. Who knows why; maybe the kid tormented him. The parents go to court. That one bite may not cost you much. But now you have a problem. You know your dog has bitten once. That puts you on notice that he has dangerous propensities. The next time he bites and someone sues, you may lose your house.'

'You're saying I'm like the dog?'

'We're saying the university may see it that way.

They may decide they're better off not to take the chance. If they take you back and some other employee later files on you, sexual harassment or discrimination, the damages for the employer can be excessive. They're the deep pocket.'

'Can they do that? I mean, I have tenure.'

'They can do whatever they want; the question is whether the courts will grant relief to you after they do, and whether you can afford that relief if it drags out.'

He thinks about this. 'How long would it take?'

'It could take years,' I tell him. 'Between administrative hearings, writs in court and appeals. And it could cost a considerable fortune.'

'The money's no problem,' he says. 'But the time. Is it possible I could work, at the center, at my old job, while this was going on?'

'Doubtful,' I tell him. 'It would depend on the university's position, what the courts might order.'

'We don't know whether they'll take me back,' he says.

'No, we don't, but the prosecutors want an answer this afternoon as to their offer.'

'What should I do?'

'There's only one thing to do,' says Harry, 'and that's to take it. We're telling you because if you lose your job, you wouldn't be able to go back and sue the county for bringing the criminal charges.'

'Damn it,' he says. 'I don't care about the money.'

'That's fine. Then you have nothing to lose,' says Harry.

Crone slumps noticeably in his chair. 'I have my position to lose, my reputation.'

Neither Harry nor I have an answer for this.

# CHAPTER EIGHTEEN

'What do you mean he was undercover?' I ask.

'He was working special gangs unit in the jail.' Tannery is showing the stress of the last several days. He is not looking well. He has a kind of whipped-dog demeanor as he stands stoop-shouldered in front of the judge's desk. Tate may not have expected this, but Tannery is now taking a beating for acts that I suspect are not his doing.

Harry and I, Tannery and de Angelo are in the judge's chambers. Coats is behind his desk, his eyes boring holes through the prosecutor.

I'm all over Tannery, in his face. 'Your Honor, we were given no notice. They had an undercover officer in the jail talking to my client, gathering evidence to use against him without notice to counsel.'

'What are you complaining about?' says Tannery. 'We're about to dismiss against your client based on information obtained by that agent. We are satisfied that your client was not involved in Dr. Epperson's death. As for the other' – he's talking about Jordan's murder – 'it does seem that we've run into a wall.'

Harry and I have dragged Tannery in here over his objections. Before we would put the final touches on the deal to dismiss in open court, we wanted to know what the cops were holding in Epperson's death. The court agreed that this was material to our client's knowing waiver of his right to seek legal redress should they rearrest him on that charge later.

Confronted with this demand, there was no way Tannery could avoid letting it be known that the cops had engaged in some serious misconduct.

The blond Viking, it turns out, is an undercover cop. He had been planted in the jail to penetrate the gangs that thrive there. It is the reason Tate was so willing to deal. His man had penetrated more than the Aryan Brotherhood.

Harry and I had good cause to worry about Crone's lack of discretion. It seems he used the Viking to pass information to Tash, a list of numbers similar to those they had exchanged in front of Harry and me.

Tate had the same thought we did, except that he acted on it. He copied the numbers and sent them to military encryption experts. He made a profound discovery. The list represented genetic codes.

Before he got this information back, he had a

brief meeting with Tash at his office the day we were there. The fact is Aaron Tash turned tits up in the conference room. One suggestion that he might be indicted for conspiracy to commit murder, and all the trade secrets in the world went out the window. Tash gave Tate chapter and verse of everything they were working on.

It became apparent to Tate that there was nothing passing between the two men but work. This was the reason Tate was so willing to trade everything for civil immunity. He knew he couldn't get a conviction on Jordan, and from all indications, neither Crone nor Tash knew anything about Epperson's death.

'You do understand the problem?' asks Coats. He's looking at Tannery.

'I didn't know myself, Your Honor, not until this morning.'

'You're telling me that Mr. Tate didn't inform you?'

Tannery doesn't want to name names, especially his boss's. 'It was known only at the highest levels.' He's talking about the undercover agent in the jail. 'On a need-to-know basis. Otherwise, the man's life wouldn't have been worth salt.'

'Nonetheless, he was an agent of the police talking to my client, gathering information from Dr. Crone out of my presence when the cops knew he was represented by counsel. A clear violation of his right to counsel. This was not some jailhouse snitch,' I tell Coats. 'This was a sworn peace officer.'

'It was a futile act, Mr. Tannery. What was your office hoping to accomplish?'

Tannery has no answer for the judge's question.

'If you'd found something, you couldn't have used it,' he says. 'I would have had to suppress it. Or maybe you weren't going to tell me?'

It's always the problem with evidence obtained illegally. If the cops don't mention it, and they can find some independent source, even if that source is tainted by their illegal conduct, you may never know.

'Your office had an obligation to disclose it.'

'I'm well aware, Mr. Madriani.' Coats is steaming. 'You can't erect a Chinese wall inside your office, and claim you didn't know,' says the judge. 'I'll tell you one thing, we're not gonna be doing this deal. If Dr. Crone wants to sue your office, I'm gonna make sure he has every opportunity. If you want to dismiss, you do it with no stipulations,' says Coats.

'I don't have the authority,' says Tannery.

'Then you better call your office and get authority.'

They stare each other down across the desk.

Harry's eyes are beginning to get misty, little

sparkles, tiny dollar signs if you look closely – another civil case in the offing.

'What else did they find at the scene?' asks the judge.

'If you don't mind, I'm gonna let Lieutenant de Angelo cover that,' says Tannery. He's afraid he may say something rash to Coats and get himself thrown in the can for contempt.

Tannery heads toward the door to use the phone in the clerk's office to call Tate. I'd love to be a fly on the wall.

'You tell him if he has any questions to come on over and talk with me about it. I'll be happy to discuss it with him,' says Coats.

'I don't think that'll be necessary.'

'Let's hope not,' says the judge. 'Now to you.' He looks at de Angelo, who by this time is chastened.

'They didn't find much, Your Honor. An impression in some mud. Appears to be a work boot. Large sole in the soft ground around one of the sprinkler heads in the park not too far from the cross. They haven't been able to match it up yet. Probably belongs to one of the gardeners,' he says. 'We're not sure.'

He checks his notes. 'That's it. Everything else you got,' he says.

In the early afternoon a contingent of jail guards

escorts Crone through a tunnel under the street and into the criminal-courts building. Because the jury will not be in the box, our client wears orange jail overalls and is shackled with leg chains, hands cuffed to a chain around his waist. These are removed, and he is directed to the chair between Harry and me at the counsel table.

From the look on his face I can tell that he senses something has happened, but is not certain what.

The press is back in the front row. This has been reserved for them. A few of the reporters, because of over-crowding, have had to take seats in the back rows. One of the journalists tries to worm his way into the jury box, which is empty, but the bailiff won't allow it.

There are the usual courthouse groupies, gadflies, most of them retired, with nothing better to do than to follow the doings in the courthouse. It's the best show in town.

There are people here from the university. I recognize one of the vice chancellors, the woman in charge of legal affairs. She has been a regular. Each time she has maintained her distance from Crone, never talking to him, taking notes, no doubt for briefings with her superiors back at the U.

There are a couple of new faces in the front row, reporters from the police beat who are now picking up on the story of Crone's trial as a sidebar to Epperson's death. As Harry and I guessed, Tate is now calling for a coroner's inquest, trying to spread accountability. If the coroner blesses suicide, Tate and his office are off the hook.

'All rise.' Coats sweeps out from the hallway leading to his chambers and takes the bench. He sits, adjusts his glasses and opens the file handed to him by his clerk.

'I understand we have an arrangement in this matter. Are all counsel present?'

Tannery stands and states his appearance for the record. I rise for the defense.

'It's my understanding that you want to make a motion, Mr. Tannery.' Coats looking at him over the top of his glasses.

The prosecutor glances over at me as if perhaps I will save him. This was not part of the deal, but that has all changed.

'Your Honor,' says Tannery, 'the people would like to move that the charges, all charges against the defendant in this case be dismissed, in the interest of justice.'

'So ordered,' says Coats. 'The defendant is discharged. He is free to go.'

The outcry of voices behind us almost drowns out the judge's order. Suddenly, just like that, two months of trial come to an end, no answers, no one convicted in Kalista Jordan's murder, and David Crone is a free man.

The press swarm around the bar railing. Several of them head for the cameras outside. Tannery still standing at his counsel table is engulfed by pencil-wielding reporters.

'There will be a statement from the district attorney's office. I have nothing further to say at this time.' I can see him as they press in around him, Tannery trying to get his papers into his briefcase, using it like a shield trying to push his way out of the courtroom.

When I turn to look up, the bench is empty. Coats has already disappeared.

Crone seems dazed, perhaps not certain what he has just heard. Several people from the audience come forward, leaning over the railing to pat him on the back, offer their congratulations. He turns, doesn't recognize any of them, but smiles. He looks over at me.

'That's it?'

I nod.

'It's over?'

'Yes.'

One of the sheriff's deputies comes up behind us and taps Crone on the shoulder. 'If you'll come this way, we'll get your clothes, your personal possessions.'

When he stands, I'm afraid for a moment that he is going to collapse. He steadies himself with both hands on the edge of the table. Two of the other guards surround him and try to keep the press away. They still pummel him with questions.

'How does it feel?'

'Good,' he says. 'Good.'

'What are you going to do now?'

Crone looks at them. He doesn't have a clue.

'Will you be going back to the university?'

'I hope so.'

'Do you have anything to say to the police who arrested you, or the D.A.'s office?'

Crone just shakes his head.

Before they can ask any more questions, the deputies escort him toward the door leading to the jury room, where they disappear. From there they will take him back to the jail another way, not past the holding cells.

We are the last participants left, and the press descends on Harry and me. 'Do you consider this a victory?'

'My client is free. I consider that a good result.'

'Do you have anything to say to Tanya Jordan, the victim's mother?'

'What can I say? She has suffered the violent death of her only child. Of course she has our sympathies.'

I do not say this lightly, and in my mind's eye, at that moment, I have visions of Sarah.

'I cannot imagine what it must be like for a parent to lose a child in that way, even a child who is an adult. We hope and pray that the law will find the individual or individuals responsible for this, and deal with them accordingly.'

Harry puts the lid back on our last box of documents and sets it on the floor for the kid with the cart. One of the deputies will keep an eye on these until they are transported back to our office.

We fend off questions all the way to the door, make our way through the reporters, out into the hallway. On the stairs outside we are confronted with microphones and cameras. One of the reporters asks for a statement.

'It is my belief that my client has been vindicated,' I tell them.

'Would you have rather had a verdict from the jury?'

'I am satisfied with the result. Any day your client goes home a free man is a good day.'

'Will Dr. Crone be returning to the university?'

'I'm assuming that he will, if he wishes to do so.'

'Will they take him back?'

'I see no reason why they wouldn't.' I opt for diplomacy rather than candor.

One of the reporters from a local station has me

repeat a couple of the sound bites so that her camera, which was not functioning at the time, can pick this up, recorded for posterity.

Harry and I finally work our way clear.

'A fair day's work,' he says. 'How did you know about the agent in the jail?'

'I didn't. But I sensed that Tate had something, or he wouldn't have given in that easily.'

'What about the civil claim?'

'I think we should take it slow and easy. Give Crone time to put things back together. Who knows, maybe the university will take him back. If so, any economic claim would be limited. Besides, I don't think he would have much of a case. They did find physical evidence in his house. There was evidence that he and Jordan had argued. There was certainly probable cause to arrest.'

'His attorneys' fees alone are approaching seven figures,' says Harry. 'You heard Coats in chambers.'

'An angry judge. Ask him to evaluate the case tomorrow; you'll get a different answer. Besides, somehow I can't see Crone suing. I think he's had his fill of courtrooms for a while.'

Harry looks tired. 'You want to grab a drink?' he says.

'I'd love to, but I have to pick up Sarah. I'll give you a call at home tonight.'

He turns, heads toward his car, swinging his

briefcase as he walks. From behind looking at him in the fading light of day, Harry is the vision of a kindergarten kid on his way home from school.

# CHAPTER NINETEEN

I pick up Sarah at school, and we have dinner at the mall. She has plans to go to a friend's house for an overnight birthday party, so we do some shopping for a present, and head home. She gathers up her things, showers and changes while I hone my skills as a gift wrapper.

By seven-thirty I drop her off at her friend's house and head for the office. I have learned to use downtime, when Sarah is away with others, to get work done so that I can maximize my time with her. My daughter is growing up in front of my eyes. There is not much time left. One day I will look and she will not be there, off at college or married.

I decide to straighten up the office, get a little work done so that I will be free to do something with her on Saturday.

The bright lights on Orange Avenue emit an ethereal glow in the evening mist that drifts in off the Pacific. Heavy traffic is backed up, Friday night, a constant stream of cars pulling into the parking lot across the street at the Del Coronado. Its wedding-cake roof, gingerbread and twinkling lights studded by palm trees, their palmettos swaying on ocean currents, exude an aura of fantasy; spiderweb to the flies of tourists.

On the other side of the street, the quiet side, the blue neon sign for Miguel's Cocina flickers and buzzes as I walk under the adobe archway and through the garden leading to the office.

Harry and I are miles from lawyers' row here. Instead we have taken a small cabaña in the courtyard amidst a number of other businesses. We peddle no image. If clients want to pay for such luxuries, they can do it across the bridge in the large high-rise firms of the city.

Outside our office, the overhead light on the little cabaña porch is on. There are the strains of music from the bar at Miguel's, and the flicker of candlelight coming through the windows of the Brigantine as patrons settle in for dinner.

I climb the two steps to the wooden porch and work my key in the lock. I feel for the light switch in the dark and flip it. The overhead fluorescents flicker on, bathing the outer reception area in bright light.

The kid with the dolly has done his job. Six transfer boxes of documents are stacked against the wall, delivered from the courthouse. The lid is off the one on top. It is lying on the receptionist's desk along with a bunch of papers strewn out next to it. Harry must have come back to the office after all, gotten tired and left. I'm wondering if he's at Miguel's or the bar at the Brigantine. If so, he'll be back.

We have had to rent a large storage shed a few miles away to archive documents, and we are already running out of space. Monday the secretaries will go through these boxes with Harry, thin out the essentials, trash the rest and have the kid with his truck pack them away in storage. One of the secretaries will code the boxes with numbers and enter a description of the contents into a computer file so that if we have to go looking we can find what we need. We will save these for at least six years. The friendliest client on the planet can sue you for malpractice. Lawyers on appeal in criminal cases will tell you that you have an obligation to admit to being incompetent counsel if that will help your client get out of the joint. I have never succumbed to this philosophy, though I will turn my records over to them without hesitation if they wish to look.

I leave the boxes and head for the disaster that is my office. I open the door, swinging it wide, turn on the light, stand and stare. For weeks I have been stacking up correspondence, putting things off until after Crone's trial. The surface of my desk looks like the floor of a pulp mill. There is paper everywhere.

It's always the problem, where to start? I hang my coat up, roll up my sleeves and start with the in-basket. I grab a stack of papers, incoming letters. The secretary has opened each of these envelopes, the contents taken out and unfolded then stapled together in the upper left-hand corner along with the envelope in case a postmark date is critical. The basket is overloaded and separate stacks of unanswered letters lie in piles next to the wooden tray.

I work with the correspondence in one hand, a small portable dictating device in the other. The device is missing its mini-cassette. I check the drawer of my desk. I'm out.

I head out to the reception area and start rummaging through drawers for an empty cassette. That's when I hear it. The sound of a metal filing drawer sliding closed, then clicking shut. It comes from Harry's office down the hall. He's slipped in, and I didn't see him.

I head toward the office, open the door; Harry is silhouetted, for some reason standing in the dark behind his desk.

'Why don't you turn the light on?'

He doesn't answer. I stand there smiling, Harry in the dark, some kind of a weird fucking thing on his head. The thought that enters my mind – latest Harry toy, shooting a bright beam of light onto his desk. His head comes up, and the beam catches me square in the eyes. I shield them with one hand. Then I realize it isn't Harry. The figure is too big, boxy shoulders, the rest of him lost in shadows. All I can see is an outline cast against the light coming in through the window from Miguel's behind him.

For a fleeting instant we are frozen, time and space, standing there looking, adrenaline beginning to kick in, fight or flight, chemistry acting.

He makes his decision, heads for the open window behind him, knee on the credenza. In an instant half of his body is through the open window, agile and quick for a man so large.

'Who the hell . . . ?' Careless bravado, I'm around the desk. I step on something large and soft. I trip, lash out with one hand at the intruder's upper body before he can clear the window. I catch him by one hand just above the wrist. The stupid things we do. I lose my grip, but my fingers latch onto something in his gloved hand, a file, papers. Bare skin against cloth, I win, the file comes free.

Before I realize what is happening, I feel the shock. With the other fist clenched he hits me dead center in the chest. The impact is like a freight train moving through. I sail back against the desk, hitting it with my butt, landing flat on my back on the top.

The pressure in my sternum makes me think he's broken something. The last thing I see is the bright light on his head as it focuses on me, eyes blinded, blackness beneath the light. Then he is gone.

It takes an instant or two to gather myself, adrenaline doping the body, killing the pain. I stumble back to my feet, lean out the window. There is a fleeting beam of light bobbing through the bushes, and then it too is gone.

I stumble around the other side of the desk toward the front door, my forearms crossed, holding my chest, wheezing to catch my breath, fighting off the pain. I get to the door, open it; one foot in front of the other, I stagger out onto the porch. Bracing myself against the railing, I look in the direction of the arched gate, out toward the street. There is nothing. Music and voices of merriment are still coming from Miguel's. Whoever it was is gone.

It takes me a couple of minutes sitting in the outer office, my knees shaking, before I am certain nothing is broken. I remove my shirt and check my chest in the mirror of the bathroom. There is already a lump forming in the center. There is a sharp pain when I touch it, like a separation. By tomorrow I will have a bruise the size of Connecticut. There's a contusion on my back near the kidneys that I didn't feel until now, where something sharp from the top of the desk caught me when I fell.

I walk slowly down the hall toward Harry's office to survey the damage. I steady myself by holding on to the walls, reach around the corner of the door for the light switch and turn it on.

Inside, the place is a mess. There are papers and files on the floor behind Harry's desk, part of the contents of one of the filing cabinets dumped there. Books from the credenza have been knocked to the floor and a desk lamp lies next to them, its bulb shattered.

It's not until I enter the room with the lights on that I see him. There on the floor on the other side of the desk is Harry's crumpled body.

# CHAPTER TWENTY

I move around the desk, stepping on papers as I go, and kneel down behind Harry's body on the floor. He is curled in a fetal position, motionless. My first instinct is to look for the rising signs of respiration. Is there movement? I glance at the wrinkles in his shirt. I can't be sure, vacuous hope, what the brain wants the eyes to see.

I lean over him, roll him onto his back. His eyes are closed. I lift one lid gently with my thumb. The eyeball has rolled back into his head. I cannot get a fix on his pupils.

The eyeball rotates down, like the tumbler of a slot machine clicking into place. Harry stirs, a hand comes up reflexively to shield his eyes from the brightness of the lights overhead. He groans.

I brace his back, sitting him up. 'Easy. Don't try to get up.'

'What the hell hit me?' he asks.

I feel around the base of his neck. He flinches when I touch it. 'Jeez. Careful.'

Harry has a lump at the base of his skull the size of an orange.

'Something hard,' I tell him. 'Did you get a look at his face?'

'Uh-uh.' He reaches for the back of his head, touches it gingerly, then checks his fingers for blood. There isn't any.

'Last thing I remember,' he says, 'I came through the front door, out there. I think I was turning on the lights. Then nothing.'

The man clubbed Harry as he came through the door in the office, then dragged his unconscious body back here to get him out of the way.

'Did he take anything?'

'I don't know.'

'What about you?' Harry is looking at my shirtless body.

'I had a little more warning,' I tell him. 'Not that it did me much good.'

'Did you see him?'

'Only shadows,' I tell him. 'And his fist. It was real big, and hard. How are you feeling?'

'I won't know 'til I try to get up,' he says. Harry is propped against the wall, behind the desk. He brings his knees up to brace himself. I help him to his feet.

Harry groans. I settle him into the desk chair. He

lowers his head. The blood rushes in. 'Feels like a building fell on me.'

'You're not going to be feeling great for a couple of days. Maybe we should go to emergency.'

'No.'

'You could have a concussion.'

'Ever seen that place on a Friday night? We'd sit there 'til morning. They'd send me home and tell me to take two aspirin.'

He stretches his neck, turning it from side to side, making sure it still works. 'All I need is a new head,' he says.

With some pain I manage to get the window behind his desk closed and latched. I can see scratches at the top of the double-hung lower wooden frame where it has been jimmied.

We could call the cops and have them dust it for prints, but it would be a waste of time. The man was wearing gloves. I could feel them on one hand as I grabbed him, just before the other fist nailed me.

I step over the mess, back to the front of the desk, looking down at a manila folder, not legal, but letter sized. Its contents are still fastened inside with an Acco clip, punched through the top of the folder and taped. It's the file I ripped from the intruder's hand when he hit me.

With some pain, I reach down and pick this up. The folder has no label; instead, the words 'Grant

Application' are penciled on the tab in a familiar hand – my own.

I open it and begin to flip pages. Ninety seconds later, eleven pages in, the pieces suddenly begin to fit into place.

I take the file out into the other room. There on the receptionist's desk next to the lid for the open box are some of the financial documents for Crone's work, the annual financial reports. These were in our evidence boxes. I look at the file in my hand and the most recent annual statement.

Given what they knew, the innocent genetic information passing between Tash and Crone from jail, Tate and his prosecutors concluded that William Epperson killed himself. It may be the biggest mistake Tate has made in years.

Harry is still doubled over in the chair in his office, trying to get the buzz out of his head, as I come back into his office. I reach for the phone, call information. I look at my watch; it is now almost nine. The automated voice comes on at the other end. 'What city?'

I take a guess, 'La Jolla.'

'What name?'

'Aaron Tash.' What I really want is his home address.

'Just a moment please.'

A couple of seconds pass with dead air on the line.

'Who are you calling?' asks Harry.

Before I can respond, a voice comes on the phone. 'Sorry, we have no listing for that name.'

'Try San Diego.'

'Just a moment.' She checks.

'Sorry. Nothing.'

He could live in Escondido, or up in Carlsbad, anywhere. There are a dozen different directories.

'Thanks.' I hang up; think for a moment. I pick up the phone again, dial another number. In my mind I am trying to consider what I will say if anyone answers. It rings five times. No one picks up. I let it ring seven, then nine times. There's nobody home. I consider the dark possibilities. I don't want to think about it.

'Who are you calling?'

'Do we have a home number or an address for Aaron Tash?'

'I don't know. Probably,' says Harry. 'Process server would have gotten it for service.'

'Do you think you could find it?'

'It's probably in one of the boxes outside.' Harry stumbles to his feet. I steady him. Together we work our way to the outer office.

I put my shirt on while Harry rummages through the boxes. It takes him a while. He has to sit to get his bearings, legs like rubber. Several minutes later he finds what he's looking for, a return of service on a subpoena we had served on Tash in case we needed him as a witness.

He turns the form over and puts it on the reception desk in front of me. Tash's home address is listed. I was right. He lives in La Jolla. His phone number must be unlisted.

'How are you feeling?'

'Better,' he says.

'Are you up to a ride?'

'If you drive.'

Ten minutes later Harry and I are headed up I-5, cutting in and out of traffic in Harry's Toyota.

'You should be careful,' he says. 'Unless you wanna get clocked by a cop. And I'd rather not flash all over my own front seat.'

'Sorry. But we don't have much time.' I get into the fast lane and try to smooth it out, just staying ahead of the flow of traffic. 'I can't be sure, not certain enough to call the cops, but unless I miss my bet our visitor has one more stop to make.'

'What the hell's going on?' Harry looks a little green, head in his hands.

'The information was in front of us all the time. Jordan and Epperson were competing for money on different portions of the research project. They'd filed competing grant applications, drawing on funds Crone had set aside. I didn't realize it until I went looking back through the papers tonight. Up until a month before Kalista Jordan was murdered, there was a surplus of funds. Not a huge one, but enough. A hundred and eight thousand and change, according to the figures. That's what the argument between Jordan and Crone was all about.'

'Money?' asks Harry.

I nod. 'I've got no hard evidence. No proof. But I think I know what happened. Crone had carved the surplus out of funds originally earmarked for their budgets. Jordan found out. She went to him, and they argued. Crone refused to rescind his action, so she took some papers from his office. My guess is they were funding documents, probably conditions for the grant from Cybergenomics. As far as Jordan was concerned, she was entitled to the money and she was going to get it. She tried to turn the screws on Crone, but he wouldn't budge. She was angry. It became a blood feud. She ended up filing the sexual harassment complaint. He probably was harassing her, but it had nothing to do with sex. He wanted the papers back. She wouldn't give them to him, and he wouldn't back away on the funding issue. As far as Crone was concerned, it was his project. He was calling the shots.

'So she went to Epperson, and the two of them

filed supplemental applications to get the money back. They probably went around Crone to the university. Jordan did a little lobbying. Crone wasn't well loved in high places, and she ended up getting the funds restored for their research. Suddenly the surplus disappeared.'

'I don't get it,' says Harry. 'Why was Crone holding back funds?'

'Because I asked him to.'

'What?'

'It was Penny Boyd: the children's research project. Crone had come up with the funding by cutting into Jordan's part of the pie. She got it back, and the children's project died.'

Harry is looking at me, the details beginning to seep in even as the lump on the back of his head throbs.

'There were three signatures on the final forms,' I tell him. 'Jordan and Epperson signed the supplemental applications to get the money back. But Crone must have refused to consent to it, because even after the university ordered the funds to be restored, he didn't sign the form authorizing it. He had Tash do it.'

Harry looks at me, a question mark.

'What he didn't realize,' I tell him, 'is that Tash was signing his death warrant.'

Suddenly it registers on Harry.

'I didn't realize until I put it all together. That and the conversation I had with Frank Boyd. He was round the bend, but I didn't realize how far.'

'It was Boyd,' says Harry.

I nod. 'I didn't realize it until tonight. He must have gone out of his mind when the project for Penny was killed. He was convinced it would save her life. I tried to tell him it was a long shot at best, but he wouldn't listen. I should have realized when he came to me talking about divorce.'

'He murdered Jordan because he held her responsible for killing the project,' says Harry.

'And Epperson, and anybody else whose fingers might have touched the thing. I suspect he came to the office tonight because he thought we'd figured it out.'

'Why did he think that?'

'Because you retrieved the file from Doris, the one she gave you, the one I left at their house after I did the original workup with Crone. That file had everything in it, the project application for the kids' portion of the Huntington study, along with the copies of the supplemental applications for funding from Jordan and Epperson. I'd let Doris keep them because they had nothing to do with the firm. They weren't legal files. She and Frank clearly had a larger stake than I did. All the while Frank was watching the money dry up in front of his eyes.

'My guess is he didn't know you'd come by to pick up the file until he went looking for it. He probably asked Doris. She would have told him where it was.'

'It's a wonder he didn't kill me,' says Harry.

'He was interrupted.'

Harry looks at me wide-eyed.

'He was gathering information. Probably figured he had one last chance to get anybody who was involved before we turned him in and the cops got him.

'When I got there tonight the lid was off one of the boxes out in the reception area. You didn't do it. He nailed you before you got the lights on. So it was Frank. He saw the same papers I did. The stuff you got from the university. The ones with Tash's signature on them restoring the money and killing the project. They were open on the desk. Those weren't in the file I gave to Doris. The twisted mind,' I say. 'He probably figures Tash was in it with them from the beginning.'

# CHAPTER TWENTY-ONE

Tash lives in a condo development out on the rocky shoals a few miles below the village, just south of a place known to surfers and locals as Wipeout Beach.

It takes Harry and me twenty minutes to find the area, stopping twice for directions. When we finally locate the street, we are confronted with another maze. Every unit in the massive complex looks like every other one, with numbers on the clustered mailboxes out front.

We find the address for Tash's unit and park in front.

'He's probably out with Crone celebrating,' says Harry.

'Let's hope.'

I reach for the door.

'Let's think about this,' says Harry. 'We could call the cops.'

'And tell them what? Tate and Tannery aren't

exactly in a mood to accept my theories on the case at the moment. They're not likely to put out an APB on Boyd based on a few documents. But then they didn't have the conversation I did with Frank about schemes for divorce to avoid medical bills. The guy was desperate.'

It's the problem any prosecutor would have at this point. After holding Crone in jail for months and trying him on capital charges, it's tough to go before the public and tell them, 'Oh, by the way, we found another perpetrator.' They are not likely to do it, even if it's the right perpetrator.

'So what are you gonna tell Tash when you find him?'

'For starters, I'll tell him to get a hotel room for the night. He and Crone both. I don't know exactly what Frank has in mind. But I'd rather not find out. Tomorrow I'll try to get hold of Tate. It's Saturday, the offices are closed, but somebody should be able to reach him. Maybe I can convince him to bring Boyd in, at least for some questioning.'

'If you're right, he's a nut case,' says Harry.

'I'm banking on it. I'll warn the cops every way I can.' I am thinking if they approach him, Frank may go berserk. If they can get him into custody safely, that would cause them to take a hard look.

'What about the family, Doris and the kids?' says Harry.

'I thought about that. I tried calling Frank's house earlier. There was no answer.'

'You think he's done something to them?'

'I don't know. I'm hoping maybe Doris took the kids and went somewhere. At the moment, Frank seems to be on a flat trajectory, single-minded. I think his sights right now are fixed on Tash. In his mind, he's racing against time. I'll check on Doris as soon as we're done here.'

'That could be dicey,' says Harry.

'I know. I can drop you somewhere before I go over there.'

'Fat chance,' says Harry. 'Just so long as you understand I'm not blocking any bullets for you.'

I smile at him. 'Let's see if we can find Tash.'

As Harry and I open the doors to the car we can hear the crash of surf on the other side of the development. The condos back up on the cliffs overlooking the beach. We check the numbers on the mailboxes. They are clustered in groups, by address, with unit numbers assigned to each box.

We find Tash's mailbox, unit 312.

'Third floor. Up top,' says Harry. We head up the walkway toward the door. When we get there, it's locked.

'We could wait until somebody comes out,' says Harry.

On the wall next to the door is a speaker for an

intercom system, with buttons lining the wall, names penciled on placards next to them.

I press one of the numbers on the second floor and wait a moment. Nobody answers. I try another. A voice comes over the intercom.

'Yeah.'

I look at another name, this time from the first floor, hoping they won't know each other. 'This is Mr. Symington in one-oh-eight. I left my key in the lock to my apartment. I wonder, could you let me in?'

Whoever it is doesn't respond, but a second later there is a quick buzz and the lock snaps open on the front door. Harry yanks on it, and we're in. We move quickly up the stairs before the guy on two can check to see who came in.

By the time we get to the top floor, both Harry and I are sucking wind. He's holding the back of his head like it's going to come apart. I'm feeling like some NFL linebacker tattooed me in the chest with his helmet. We lean against the wall, catching our breath.

'You all right?'

'Yeah. Gotta start jogging again,' he says.

'When did you ever jog?'

'When I was a kid,' he says. Harry winks at me.

I look at the number on the door across from the top of the stairs. Tash's unit is to the right. We work our way down the hall, trying not to make it squeak as we walk. We pass four doors, two on each side of the hall, until we come to 312. Tash's place is on the back side, an ocean view.

There's a peephole in the center of the door at about eye height. I lean in and take a look. Shielding the light from around the lens, I try to peer through it backwards. All I can make out is light and dark, what appears to be an absence of any movement inside. A couple of points, specks of brightness, bleed rays of light. These, I assume, are lamps that have been left on.

'See anything?'

I shake my head. I put an ear next to the door and listen. Nothing.

'We could just knock,' Harry whispers.

I hold my hand up, shake my head.

Farther to the right there are two more apartment doors. Beyond that the hallway widens and forms a T. Quietly I move toward the intersection in the hall. On one side, in the intersecting hallway toward the front of the building, are two elevator doors. In the other direction, toward the ocean, is a sliding door leading out onto a veranda.

I head toward the sliding door. Harry follows. I flip the catch lock on the door's handle, slide it open and step out onto the balcony. There is a brisk breeze off the Pacific, rising as it hits the cliffs below us. I slide the door closed, and Harry and I can talk.

'What do we do?' he says.

I'm looking toward the balcony outside Tash's unit. It's about thirty feet away. I can see from here that the sliding door to the unit is partway open.

'I want to take a look inside that condo.'

'How?'

I look toward the balcony next to the one Harry and I are standing on. There's a span of about six feet between metal railings, a three-story drop and jagged cliffs below that, white surf crashing on the rocks. I would have to negotiate two of these spans to make it to Tash's balcony. It's not a long reach. It's just the fall if you miss.

'You're crazy,' he says.

'Do you know any other way to get in there?'

'We could ring the buzzer. Knock on the door.'

'And what if Boyd is in there? He'll kill Tash in an instant. Cut his throat and throw him off the balcony.' As I'm talking to Harry, I'm sliding the belt out of the loops in my pants. Leather, about an inch and a half wide.

'Give me your belt,' I tell him.

'I'm not going over there.'

'No, you're not. I'm going alone.'

'As long as we have that settled.' Harry whips his belt out of the loops of his suit pants and hands it to me. I string the two belts together, putting the tip of one belt through the buckle of the other, the tongue through the first hole, and pull on them, making sure they will support my weight. Then I loop the belt over the steel railing and buckle the ends together. I adjust it for length, and look at Harry.

'Wish me luck.' I ease myself over the railing, my feet through the wrought iron spindles so that my toes are supported by the concrete deck of the veranda. Harry has me by one arm looking at me like I'm crazy. He is no doubt right.

I slip my right foot into the loop made by the belts and use it to swing out just a little at first, testing it. I can feel the pain in my chest pulling where Boyd nailed me.

Then, with my foot in the belt supporting my weight, one hand on the railing near Harry, I swing out once, come back; swing out twice. On the third try I catch the far railing, plant my foot through the spindles and in less than two seconds I'm over the railing.

I signal to Harry to uncouple the belts, and carefully he tosses them to me. I set up the arrangement on the far railing nearest to Tash's apartment. I avoid looking down, though it's hard to ignore the sound of the crashing surf below me.

I swing out. This time I catch the railing on the second try, put my free foot through the spindles and ease myself over the railing. Now the belts are behind me, left on the other balcony. The only way out is through the door in Tash's apartment.

The slider is open about four inches. The vertical blinds are pitched so that I can see everything in one direction, the right side of the room. To the left, visibility is more obscured by the canted blinds that dance and clatter in the breeze from the open door.

There is no other movement in the living room. Two lamps are on. I slip my shoes off and step to the other side of the balcony. From here I can see slivers of the kitchen, visible through the openings as the blinds waft back and forth. Though I can't see it all, there are no shadows being cast, and the kitchen lights are all on. If there was an energy crisis, you wouldn't know it from Tash's condo.

There's a smaller window a few feet over from the sliding door. This looks into the bedroom. While the lights are off in this room I have no difficulty seeing in, reflected light streaming down the hallway. The bed is neatly made. I can see the door to the master bath. There's no one home.

I signal to Harry, shaking my head. He hangs by the railing, watching. I motion that I'm going in. He nods.

I pick up my shoes, and quietly slide open the door, stepping through the vertical blinds.

I am focused to the front, the hallway off to my

right, the kitchen to the left, sock toes buried in the deep pile of Tash's carpeted living room, wondering what I'm doing breaking and entering, stealing across some stranger's living room with my shoes in my hand.

'Hi, Paul.'

When I turn, he's behind me. Frank Boyd is seated in a tall wing-back chair in the corner, his back against the wall at the far left of the sliding door: the one blind spot in the room. In his lap is a short double-barreled shotgun, the muzzle pointed lazily in my direction. His finger is outside the trigger guard, but close enough that I'm not going to argue with him.

'I was hoping you wouldn't come,' he says. Frank's face is etched with deep lines, a countenance that is tired, worn, showing no emotion, a lifeless mask. His hair that hasn't seen a barber in months is hanging ragged halfway down his ears. There is a kind of wild look in his eye, the glassy gaze of some jungle cat on the prowl.

'I hope I didn't hurt you,' he says.

I smile. 'Oh, no. Not at all.' I touch my chest. 'Just a little bruise.'

'That's good. Why are you carrying your shoes?'

I look at them, a sick smile. I give him a face, shrug my shoulders. 'I don't know.'

'Maybe you should put them on,' he says.

'May I sit?'

He nods. 'Sure.'

I back into a chair across the room from him, a tufted sofa back.

'When did you figure it out?' he asks.

'Figure what out?'

'Don't play games,' he says.

'Oh, you mean . . .'

'Yeah.'

I take a deep breath. 'Tonight.'

If he's surprised, his expression doesn't convey it. 'When I put all the papers together and looked at them,' I tell him.

'You mean if I hadn't come by your office, you wouldn't have . . .'

I shake my head.

His eyes look away, a quizzical grin, wonder on the level of a galactic riddle. 'Goes to show you,' he says. 'I thought sure that when you picked up the file from the house you were on to me. *Huh*.' A vacant stare, like how can he go back in time?

'I heard Crone got off,' he says. 'It was on the radio.'

'Earlier today,' I tell him.

'That's good. I always felt bad that he was being blamed for something he didn't do. I had to take care of it,' he said. 'Did pretty good, don't you think?'

'You mean the suicide note?'

He nods. 'Never was any good at typing. It took me a while. One finger at a time. But then he wasn't going anywhere. He was a tall one, a long drink of water. I didn't think the ladder was gonna be high enough. The note – I had to play with it to get it right. Wrote it out longhand at home first. Took it with me. The printing was a bitch,' he says. 'I almost called Doris to ask her if she could help me over the phone. That woulda been a mistake.'

'Doris doesn't know?'

'She has no idea.'

'Why did you do all of this, Frank?'

'What do you mean?' He says it as if killing two people and lying in wait for a third is a normal evening's work.

'I mean Kalista Jordan.'

'She ended the program. Penny's program. What do you think I was gonna do, just sit there?'

I don't argue the point. His finger slides toward the trigger. I try a different subject.

'How is Doris?'

'What?'

'Doris and the kids?'

'Oh. They're fine. Fine.'

'Where were they tonight? I tried to call.'

'Doris is out of town. Took the kids with her.'

'Where did they go?'

'Took a few days off. She needed to get away.

They went to her mother's up in Fremont. We had an argument.'

I don't know whether to believe him or not.

'Did she leave tonight?'

He looks at me as if he can't quite figure this out. 'What day is it?' he asks.

'It's Friday night.'

'Oh.' He thinks for a second. 'I guess she left a couple of days ago.'

'What did you argue about?'

'The file,' he says.

'The file from Penny's project?'

He nods. I can see him flinch with the mention of his daughter's name. It's as if something has rubbed this point raw on his soul.

'When do you think he's gonna be home?'

'Who?'

'Aaron Tash,' he says. 'Man whose house this is.'

'I don't know. Maybe he went away for the week-end.'

Frank looks at me as if this is not a pleasant thought.

'He's not a good person, Paul. He ended the project for Penny. He wanted the money.'

'He didn't,' I tell him. I watch his eyes for signs of anger. He looks at me warily.

'He signed some papers, but he didn't know what he was signing.'

'You're just telling me that because you want to save him.'

'No. I'm telling you because it's the truth.'

'I don't want to hear it,' he says.

'Dr. Crone was trying to keep Penny's project together. Other people ordered him to end the funding,' I tell him.

'Who?'

'I don't know. They didn't know what they were doing either.'

'I don't believe you,' he says.

'Do you think Dr. Crone was trying to hurt Penny?'

'No.'

'Do you think I was trying to hurt Penny?'

'No,' he says. 'That's crazy.'

'Then you can believe that Aaron Tash wasn't trying to hurt her either.'

'Then why is she dead?'

I sigh. 'There are no simple answers,' I tell him.

'I don't want to talk about it.' The muzzle of the gun is going up and down, tapping against his knee in frenetic movement, a kind of weird half-light in his eyes, what I can imagine Kalista Jordan might have seen as she took her last breath.

'We can't wait much longer.' He says it as if Tash has stiffed the two of us on a scheduled meeting.

'Why don't you go home? Get some sleep. You'll probably feel a lot better.'

'I can't sleep. I tried. Besides, you think I'm stupid? Why didn't you call the cops?'

'Why would I want to do that?'

He looks at me, not sure how to answer, as if I've asked him to solve one of the deep mysteries of the cosmos.

'I was hired to represent Dr. Crone. I did my job. Now that's over.'

He nods as if this makes perfect sense. Then stops his head in midmotion. 'Then why did you come here?'

'I was looking for Dr. Crone.'

A dense look. What would Crone be doing at Tash's house?

'How did you get outside? Out there?' He points with the barrel of the shotgun toward the sliding door and the balcony.

'I was out there all the time.'

'You mean when I came in?'

I nod. At this point, I'll try anything. 'I didn't hear you come in,' I tell him.

'Yeah. Used some tools,' he says.

'Why don't you put that down?' I gesture toward the shotgun.

He looks at it, looks at me; the expression tells me he's not sure how the two go together. Man on the edge.

'You're not going to shoot me, are you?'

'Oh, no,' he says. 'I wouldn't do that.'

'I didn't think so. You got scared tonight, didn't you? At the office.'

He smiles, nods, his head canted off just a little to one side. 'Yeah. You surprised me when you came through the door.'

'*I* surprised *you*?'

The smile turns to a broad grin; he laughs, middle-aged kid. I look at Frank and wonder what dark and twisted thing got ahold of his mind. Whatever incarnation of the devil it is, we are still struggling. Frank hasn't put the gun down.

I take a quick glance at my watch. It's after ten. If Tash comes through that door, the place is going to turn into a shooting gallery.

'Frank, you can't go on like this.'

'I know.'

'What are you going to do?'

'I don't know.'

'Let me help you.'

'How? How can anybody help me?'

'We can start by ending the violence,' I tell him. 'Do you think Penny would want you to do this?'

The look in his eye tells me he's never asked himself this question before. What little life is left leaves his face.

'Why don't you put the gun down? Let me make some phone calls?'

Eyes darting. He wants to say yes, but he doesn't know how.

'Please.'

Slowly the muzzle of the gun goes toward the floor. His grip loosens. He looks up at me. Gently he lays it on the floor next to his feet.

I'm afraid to make a play for it, especially now that he's going in the right direction. I might set him off.

'Can we call Doris? Maybe you could talk to her?'

'That would be good,' he says.

'Do you have the number, up in Fremont?'

'Somewhere,' he says. He's reaching around, patting his pockets, the front of his shirt, seat of his pants. He stands up and pulls his wallet from his back pocket. He opens it and from the inside he pulls out a slip of paper and steps over the shotgun toward me.

There are penned notes, some names, probably jobs Frank has worked on, and some penciled numbers. He points to one of these, an area code and number. He wants me to place the call, as if killing Tash is all right, but using his phone would be a social violation.

I take the slip of paper and walk toward the phone in the kitchen. I dial the number and wait. A tired voice, half asleep, answers.

'Is Doris Boyd there?'

'Just a moment. I'll get her.'

The sigh of relief that rifles through my body in this moment causes my knees to go slack.

Doris comes on the line. 'Hello.'

'Doris. It's Paul Madriani.'

'What is it?'

'Can you hold just a moment?'

'Sure.'

I step back out into the living room.

'Frank, she's on the line.'

Something's wrong. The wind from the ocean is filling the room, blinds rattling. The first thing I notice is that the shotgun is gone.

I look toward the balcony, and from the corner of my eye all I see is a flash of pant leg and two boots as Frank Boyd sails over the railing and into the darkness.

# EPILOGUE

Eight days later, a couple walking along a lonely stretch of beach nearly four miles north of Tash's apartment stumbled on Frank's remains, washed up, battered by the rocks, almost unrecognizable.

Harry and I knew there was no way Frank could have survived the plunge from the balcony. We talked for several minutes, considered the options, and in the end I wiped the phone and a few other surfaces for fingerprints, and we left as quietly as we'd arrived. The only evidence that we had ever been there were the two dangling belts left on the balcony between the apartments. No doubt some tenant would find them and wonder where they came from. They would never know.

We looked for Frank's floating body from the rocks below the complex for almost an hour and decided there was nothing we could do. It was fruitless to call the police. It would only open new wounds for

Doris and the kids, and could accomplish nothing for either Epperson or Kalista Jordan.

Harry had been right; Tash and Crone were out celebrating. They never knew we were at the apartment that night. To this day, we have kept our silence.

Seven months have now passed, and after a coroner's inquest, Frank's death has been ruled an accident. Only the insurance company fought this finding. The million-dollar policy Frank's parents purchased years before contained a double-indemnity clause paying two million dollars on accidental death. Even a suicide guaranteed the face amount of one million since Frank had held the policy long enough to establish that it hadn't been purchased in contemplation of his killing himself. For the carrier it was not a happy scenario, a desperate family in financial need pitted against a Goliath insurance company with its offices in some skyscraper in another city.

Doris wanted me to represent her at the inquest. I told her I could not, but I didn't tell her why. My only advice was that she not volunteer information to anyone regarding my telephone call to her that night. It was better that way. She could testify truthfully about what she didn't know. And no one ever asked. To this day, Doris doesn't know why I called or how I got the telephone number to her mother's house. When I went back to the phone that night, after Frank had disappeared over the balcony, I told Doris I was looking for him. It was the best I could do under the circumstances. She didn't know where he was.

On the stand they asked her several pointed questions. Yes, her husband was despondent over the death of his daughter. No, he never threatened to take his own life. No, she never found or saw a suicide note. What they don't know, and could never guess, is that the only suicide note Frank ever wrote was for someone else.

If the hearing officer at the inquest was in doubt, he came down on the side of the angels. After all, there was no solid evidence of suicide. Even I could not testify with certainty, should some psychic have called me to the stand, whether Frank jumped or fell that night, though the details of what I do know would have caused much pain. I have no difficulty sleeping with my secret, though the visage of Frank's tortured soul visits me from time to time in my dreams.

When it was over David Crone, then back at the center, tested the two surviving Boyd children, Jennifer and Donald, for Huntington's chorea. They were both negative. Frank would be happy to know, and perhaps he does, that his family has finally found peace.

# Critical Mass

## Steve Martini

Joss Cole, a burned-out public defender from LA, has opted for a quieter life in Washington State. Then into her office walks Dean Belden in search of a lawyer to help him set up a business. Within days Belden appears before a federal grand jury and, just minutes before testifying, he is killed.

Meanwhile, Gideon van Ry, a nuclear fission expert in California, is troubled by the failure to account for two nuclear devices missing from the former Soviet Union. Under a false bill of lading, they were shipped to a company called Belden Electronics, and Gideon's only lead is the lawyer who incorporated Belden Electronics – Joss Cole . . .

'The best debut, in my opinion, is *Compelling Evidence*'
John Grisham

'A hard-punching climax' *The Times*

'Thoroughly absorbing' *Literary Review*

'Sensationally good' *Los Angeles Times*

0 7472 6062 1

# The List

## Steve Martini

Can a man kill an author, steal her novel and ride the crest of literary fame – without being caught?

Gable Cooper has penned a novel worth six million dollars. But he doesn't exist. Abby Chandlis is a lawyer-turned-novelist and is the creator of Gable Cooper. She is looking for a charismatic man to pose as the author of her knock-dead thriller.

When Jack Germaine enters her life, Abby is convinced that his charm and good looks will clinch success for her novel, so they make a deal. But as her book rockets to the top of the bestseller list and Jack is propelled into stardom, Abby senses peril. A series of deadly accidents persuades her that her life is in danger and, with Jack in pursuit, she races to the one person who can put an end to the nightmare that was once her dream . . .

Praise for Steve Martini:

'Absolutely irresistible' *Kirkus Reviews*

'Thoroughly absorbing' *Literary Review*

'Compelling indeed' *Sunday Telegraph*

'The best debut, in my opinion, is *Compelling Evidence*' John Grisham

0 7472 4996 2